To Max,

Happy Reading!

SPELLBODA

J C Clarke

The Book Guild Ltd

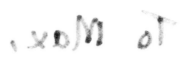

First published in Great Britain in 2021 by
The Book Guild Ltd
9 Priory Business Park
Wistow Road, Kibworth
Leicestershire, LE8 0RX
Freephone: 0800 999 2982
www.bookguild.co.uk
Email: info@bookguild.co.uk
Twitter: @bookguild

Typeset in 12pt Minion Pro

Printed and bound by CPI Group (UK) Ltd, Croydon, CR0 4YY

ISBN 978 1913913 410

British Library Cataloguing in Publication Data.
A catalogue record for this book is available from the British Library.

MIX
Paper from
responsible sources
FSC
www.fsc.org
FSC® C013604

The Hunt

She flew over the crag-ridden landscape, hugging the contours of the Derbyshire peaks and valleys, in search of a thermal, the warm current that would suddenly propel her on high. Revelling in swift and unpredictable wind currents she jinked this way and that, adjusting deck and primary feathers, as she streaked through the Dale of Goyt, over the ruins of Errwood, skimming age-old crags and waterfalls swelled with recent rainfall, which sang to her as she passed.

She cried out as she searched, alive with joy. Her high-pitched call cut through the wind and echoed across the reservoir as it lazed and twinkled in the heart of the valley. Wind-beaten walkers lifted their heads at the sound, and grouse shrank, frozen, within clumps of heather when she flashed past them as, calling still, she levelled to the horizon of the peaks, and began to climb.

Lifted up in her dance with the wind, the warmth

suffused her as sun broke through the scudding clouds and dappled the peaks with light. Then at last, as she rose over Shining Tor, she found it. The thermal. She spread her wings and tail wide with unconscious instinct of long and vast experience as it wrenched her up with breathtaking, jolting, delicious speed.

Effortlessly she soared now, rising up and up as she circled in the ever-lifting warmth. The countryside below transformed into patchwork as she climbed, her wings buoyed on the current. Fighter jets on manoeuvres roared by, and still she rose.

Now only a keen earth eye would pick her out, amongst clouds, through wind and sun, but still she could scan every blade of grass, every tiny movement of the valley in minute detail. Focused, the hunt began, as she soared, her head statue-stiff as the rest of her body tilted and turned, accommodating the ever-changing current. And finally there it was! The movement she'd been waiting for.

Almost imperceptible, down in a remote valley. There was nothing around it except a few houses nestled on the slopes, and that risk was acceptable. She coasted a moment longer, confirming her target. Happy, she checked her flight pattern one last time, turned on her tail, and her ill-fated stoop to the ground began.

Folding her wings tight to her body, bullet-like, she dropped out of the sky. The wind screamed past as her speed grew to terminal velocity. Closer by the second, she could see her target now with ease. A pigeon, injured, and her hopes grew for an easy, straightforward kill. The bird took off drunkenly as she bore down upon it. She closed her third eyelid to protect herself from the wind force and imminent impact as she drew out her talons ready to strike. The pigeon had no time to realise what was happening as she hit it with the force of a juggernaut and ran her rear talon up its neck, binding her to her prey. The pigeon was engulfed in an explosion of noise and loose flying feathers. Instant death at such a speed of impact is the only outcome.

She caught her breath, delighted with her quarry. Bushes rustled nearby. Most likely a marauding fox, hoping to cash in on the spoils, so she roused swiftly and made to take off.

But what was this? Fine lines wrapped around her, constricting her, and fear spread like an epidemic as she realised she was grounded. The more she flapped, the more entangled she became. Fear exploded to terror as the rustling grew closer. Dark shadows fell. It was man, not fox, who was the marauder here. Would she be lucky? Could they be The Gifted? She cried out, but her heart chilled and cracked to ice when the darkness grew and her calls made no difference.

Bound and powerless, she sprawled and panted on the ground as two figures, blurred by the lines and wires of their trap, towered over her. Their hands grew larger as they stretched out towards her, changing her life forever.

"Well, this is a right result, that's for sure! Peregrine, and female! I told yer this bait would work. Come on, let's have a look at her."

"Get that hood on her, Dad, if you can, it'll calm her down. Mind her beak there. Them talons too. Razor sharp, they are."

"Easy, birdie, there we go. Good catch this one is, Ron. Good size, too."

"Top job. Mature, all blue and grey. Just what we need to go with male in't shed."

"Let's get the net lines and the pigeon off her."

"Careful, Dad, don't damage the goods. He said peregrine babies'll fetch hundreds each – let's hope her and that male hit it off."

"Ay! We'll be laughing then. Here's the sack. Get her in."

"Wait, look! There's some folk over there, look! Sort it in a minute, QUICK, get down!"

The men crouched, clutching the stricken peregrine between them as two figures, a vast bear of a man and a skinny boy trudging behind him, walked a path further down the slope.

The man was lost in anger; his voice boomed on the wind, and his words blew upwards, straight to the ears of the two men.

"I'm done. You know what? You can't do anything, Trevor… you're an irritation. All this, it's pathetic. You're pathetic. Just read the compass! I should've known it would be pointless making an effort. Shouldn't have bothered wasting my time, again. Why bother speaking to me? Nothing useful ever comes out. You're a loser!"

The thieves crouched, barely breathing. The boy's head was fixed towards the ground, his collar turned up against the wind. He said nothing as the man ranted. The peregrine struggled, and the shoddy leather hood slipped, uncovering her eyes. She saw the boy. Wild hope filled her when she saw the glow around him, and she wrestled to escape, frantically trying to flap her wings, but the thieves tightened their grip. She called out as the boy moved further away, desperate, but he didn't hear her. It was too soon. He wasn't ready.

"Come on, Ron, me lad! Let's get out of here before someone sees us. Ha! What a day!"

The men bundled their prey into the sack and jumped up like weasels, rushing back down the track to the car park. The engine spat into life, and the sack of peregrine bounced on the back seat as the car sped away.

One Year Later

1

Moonlight spilled through the window into pools on the floorboards, casting a cold, pale light over Trevor's tear-streaked face. He sank to his knees and hunched over his rucksack, jamming clothes inside with shaking hands.

He sniffed as he fought to control the pain hammering his chest. The noise of the film still playing in the lounge, with haunting echoes of Ariel singing 'Part of Your World', floated upstairs, a stark contrast with his dad's shouts.

"Stay up there! Out of my sight!"

Fine. You'll be lucky if you ever see me again, '*Dad*'. Trevor wanted to shout the words out, but then his dad would win. He sat up, his mind grasping for answers as he switched on his lamp. He couldn't do this. He'd kept out of the way all day, knowing he'd be in trouble after school yesterday. Five minutes ago all he'd done was walk across the hallway with a ham sandwich on a plate. His father, red-faced, grizzly, with his wild dark hair and beard streaming everywhere, was sprawled in his armchair in the lounge. He was watching *The Little Mermaid* again with a bottle of red wine, his totally freaky Saturday-night habit, and for once, the door was open. He saw Trevor and exploded. Wrong place, wrong time.

Dad kicking off wasn't weird, but tonight was like someone had plugged him in and amplified him. Trevor was used to dodging the sting of words, but this time Dad had gone too far. Trevor ducked when the apple core flew across the room, and lost his balance. When his head met the corner of the sideboard his so-called *dad* hadn't even noticed. The bump under his hair throbbed with a heartbeat all its own.

Trevor scanned his possessions strewn across the floor. All he had to show for thirteen years. Bert, his tired old cloth badger, frayed and patched. The book on birds of prey, her gift to him. Inside the book, the photograph of her, his only one. The most treasured thing in the world. He'd found it behind his chest of drawers; it must have fallen and been missed in the big clear-out.

His hand shook again as he picked it up. She was perfect, her hair shining like an angel's, framing her smiling face. She had one arm around him, and in the other she cradled her cat, the mackerel tabby who rarely left her side. Trevor and the cat both stared up at her with adoring eyes. Trevor turned the picture over. Even her writing on the back was precious, beautiful. 'My Trevor, Mrs Bingo & Me – Part of my world!' He was twelve when it was taken, and they looked so alike; matching noses, blue eyes and blond hair. Then she was gone. Just like that. It came out of nowhere… and changed everything.

Trevor frowned. The TV noise had stopped, replaced by staccato sounds of Dad stomping and slamming doors. He'd be thumping upstairs next to slide into one of his snore-infested sleeps. Saturday nights were always worst. Trevor slipped the photograph between the pages of his bird book and added all his treasures except Bert to the rucksack. He pushed it under his bed, and the rough jute snagged on splinters as it scraped over the floor. He leapt under the covers fully clothed, clutching Bert, and pulled the ancient blanket around his neck as the stairs creaked. Home was crap, school was crap, life was crap. And no way was he going to get hurt like that again. That was it. He'd wait till the snores started. Then he'd go, just disappear. He'd find a way to get by.

Footsteps stopped just outside his door.

"Be ready. Eight o'clock. I'll take you, then you'll be out of my way. But if you pull that stuff at school again it's the only time you'll go. Trust me."

After a pause the voice slurred again, muffled through the wooden door. "I need your help too, boy. Just say something. Anything. Thank you would be a start."

Trevor bit his lip as his father walked away. Seriously? Helping, speaking… saying thank you? He'd got to be joking. Since that rubbish day in Goyt Valley, when his father properly lost it for the first time, Trevor had decided to stop talking… to anyone. Except Mrs Bingo-Wings. He looked at her, curled up and purring on the shabby wicker chair by the window. His memories were stacked full of the three of them together. In the kitchen, Mrs B winding herself round Mum's legs, tail curling and uncurling, always purring. Finding the closest places to sleep, always on Mum's lap whenever she sat still. Mum spoke to Mrs B all the time, like she was a person, so since Mum had gone he did the same. Mrs B was his shadow now, his symbol of happy days.

"Oi, Mrs B," Trevor whispered, sitting up on his elbows. "Shall I run away tonight? Or hold off, and go to the bird of prey centre tomorrow?"

Mrs B's purrs paused and her ears twitched as she stretched, all four legs rigid.

"I didn't think he was going to take me," said Trevor. "Honestly... I was excited about going. I thought I'd blown it. School must have said it's still OK."

He studied the slender cut curling across his palm like a crisp new moon. At least he knew now that metal could be sharp if the chair had a nail in it and you gripped it hard before you threw it.

"Maybe they went on at him again, after the meeting. Mr Mac's not scared of him..."

Mrs B drew one mackerel-striped leg up and started her ritual of cleaning; slow deliberate licks punctuated by snuffly old-cat grunts. Her eyes flicked to Trevor, then back to her paws.

Trevor let the blanket go loose and watched Mrs B's silver ears switch left to right. His first volunteer day... it could be amazing. To see those birds, maybe even meet the legendary Adam Shotlander in person. He sighed. No matter how he felt, it was reason enough to stick around.

"I should stay, Mrs B, right?" he said. "Tomorrow could be one good day. I could go to the centre, then run away after."

Mrs B paused and held Trevor's gaze for a moment, her tongue stuck out of her mouth in a familiar frozen pose. She looked so gormless, it was hard not to smile.

"Even if it's a letdown, I wouldn't be home all day. So… I'd only have to put up with him for a few more hours tomorrow night, and then I could—"

A door slammed suddenly, so hard it made the window shudder. Mrs B leapt up in the kind of startled shock only a cat can manage. Trevor jumped with her. If only his father would just go to sleep. Calm after the storm would be helpful, seeing as things were never calm before one in this house. Some days it felt like a charge was building, a steady rise of pressure and static before a lightning strike. The bump on Trevor's head pulsed again, and sudden white-hot anger flared. If his father wanted him to talk then he damn well would… in his way. He flung back the blanket, reached over to his bedside table and flicked on the lamp. Mrs B padded across the wooden floor and jumped on the bed. She pressed her head against his other hand, purring and insistent.

"Not now, Mrs B."

Trevor grabbed his notepad, and a red felt tip from the pot on his table.

"I'll give him something to think about tomorrow night. When I'm gone and he's all alone."

Mr Sykes,
    Well, I can't call you Dad, can I? You aren't one. You'll be happy I've gone. In case it needs saying, don't bother looking for me. I won't be back. You're

7

the loser, not me, shouting and being a pig. Why should I talk? You're the reason I stopped. Ever since Mum went you never helped me. Why do you hate me? Everything's your fault.

A scratching noise made him stop and look up. Mrs B stopped purring. It was coming from the window, but when he looked over there was nothing there. A mouse? No, outside, maybe. Mrs B's jade eyes were fixed on Trevor, and she gave a single plaintive 'meow'.

Trevor gnawed the end of his felt tip, waves of fury still building. He should say it. Why not?

Anyway, I hate you. Why are you so horrible? Why couldn't you just be my dad, like you used to be? It's not my fault she went. You don't love me. If Mum was here she'd

He couldn't do it. The wave broke, tears welled and spilled, fat drops mingling grief and anger, splashing off the notepad, bouncing off Mrs B's coarse white whiskers as she stood up and pushed her head against his neck. He brushed the tears away with a swipe of his hand. If only. If Mum was still here, Dad would be happy, and everything would be OK. Why had life worked out like this?

Teardrops smudged his writing, blending words and letters to blood as they trickled down the page. It was easier to keep it all in, screw the hurt into a ball, shove it deep inside and carry on saying nothing to anyone, ever.

Trevor ripped out the page and crumpled it tight in his fist, gripping the little ball until his palm hurt. He leaned out of bed, arched underneath and fumbled for the strap of his rucksack, hauling it over the floor. He rammed the paper ball deep inside and, with a vicious shove, sent it all back into the shadows.

*

It was the darkest part of the night, just before dawn. Mrs B had long left the room to curl up downstairs by the remnants of the fire. Trevor slept fitfully, roused from his sleep by random night sounds. Scratching sounded outside his window again, and he turned, murmuring, half-opening his eyes before drifting back into unsettled dreams.

The little owl on the windowsill ruffled his silver-grey feathers and turned, snapping crossly.

"Watch what you're doing!"

"Sorry," muttered the tawny owl, looking down. "I bodge the landings sometimes. It happens when you're a bigger bird."

"Stop showing off," retorted the little owl, and it turned back to watch Trevor. "It's getting really bright now, his glow, isn't it? I saw him from over the street. The room's full of light. Someone needs to tell Garnell."

"Give him a chance. Plenty of time for that." The tawny owl bobbed his head as he looked through the window. "But you're right, it's unmistakable. Any doubt I had is gone. Do you think the boy knows himself yet?"

"If he doesn't, he will soon," said the little owl. "Any day now." He turned his head to look at his companion. "And when he does, his whole life is going to change."

2

"Not speaking... yet again? Come *on*, it's boring. Snap out of it!"

As his father's rust-bucket car groaned and coughed its way up the dust-gravel track, Trevor opened his eyes and kept his face blank, squashing any look of hope for the day to come. Dad had been silent for the ten-minute journey, so up to now he seemed to be in a decent mood. He didn't want to set him off. The car jolted as it hit a pothole, and Trevor's head smarted again when it banged back on his seat.

"Dammit. Tyres don't need that. Can't see the point you doing this. If you carry on saying nothing they'll all think you're stupid."

Trevor studied the fence posts as they passed them. He didn't want to call him Dad, or even Father. Sykes, that's who he would be from now on. Just his name and nothing more. His eyes widened as he caught sight of the back end of a weasel, bouncing off into the hedgerow, and he held his breath. It felt good knowing his rucksack was ready, full of everything he needed to run away. And a big bit of him really did want today to happen. It was surprisingly easy to pack his pain away for later. All day he would be free.

The car juddered to a stop beside the entrance. Sykes looked straight ahead, his dark hair flopping in a mess over his face.

"What are you waiting for?"

Clutching his jacket and rucksack, Trevor scrambled out, trying to ignore the insistent ding of pain from the lump on his head. He didn't pause for a friendly goodbye. He couldn't remember the last time Sykes had smiled. Since Trevor turned thirteen, Sykes had got much worse. He used to make some sort of effort, occasionally, like going hiking or the odd kick-around with a football. But it always ended badly... Sykes getting fed up, frustrated, and shouting. Hurt and anger were piled up deep down, desperate to ooze out of Trevor, but no-one knew. There was no point, it didn't change anything. Silence was his wall of protection, his safety zone.

The car leapt forward with a scrunch of rubber on gravel, little stones spitting rudely from its tyres as it conjured up another dust cloud. The window slid down and Sykes leaned out.

"I'll be back at five. On the dot. Don't muck it up. If you're late you can find your own way home."

Trevor held his breath again until Sykes had driven away, then let it go in a hissing rush as he kicked the nearest tree trunk. Sykes wouldn't spoil this. After tonight he wouldn't spoil anything. He opened the entrance gate and went through.

Trevor had been to the centre once before on a school trip, but this was different. He hoisted his rucksack over his shoulder, pulled his beanie hat down around his face and walked down the path that wound through a wildflower meadow. He kept his eyes fixed to the ground, vacant, but his mind was alive, buzzing for the day ahead. He was barely aware of the warmth of the sun on his hands as an unfamiliar feeling began to bubble up. He got closer to the first enclosures, stopped walking and looked up. He pinched himself on the wrist, just to make sure it wasn't a dream.

He really was here.

The rays of the new summer day beamed through the trees as he carried on, going under the wooden pergola where the sign saying 'Flights of Fancy Conservation Centre' stretched out above him. The sky was deep blue, fresh and bright like it had been freshly washed. Cobwebs shimmered across the grass, trimmed with diamonds of dew. More droplets hung pendulously from the chicken wire covering the bird housing, garlanded with grain-encrusted feathers. Trevor stopped again and peeped through the wire. Pungent air filled his nose, cloyed and musty from the damp sand. Birds stood in a neat line; hunched, peaceful, heads tucked under wings with one leg drawn up, their feathers ruffled by the light breeze. Trevor smiled. He recognised so many of them from his book. A tremor of excitement ran through him.

The closest bird, a chocolate-brown harris hawk, jerked

up its head, suddenly alert, and stared straight at him… really hard. So intent it was unnerving. The hawk opened its beak and a strident, duck-like, squawking cry pierced the calm. Trevor flinched. Within seconds, all the other birds down the row looked up, saw him and joined in.

The noise built swiftly to a cacophony of squawks and screeches. Trevor put his hands over his ears, bewildered. What had he done wrong this time?

A door slammed and someone ran over the grass towards him as the wall of noise began to die away. Trevor let his hands fall to his sides. It was a girl, well, not quite, but she didn't look that old, maybe about twenty or something. She was short, with long dark hair scraped tightly into a ponytail. And she was frowning.

"What's going on? What did you do?"

Typical. But Trevor ignored her, screwing his eyes shut as aches of fresh pain began. His throat was throbbing too, not just the bump on his head.

"Hey! Can you hear me?"

It wasn't the girl. This voice was high-pitched and strange, like wind through reeds. It came from across the grass. Trevor spun around, squinting through sunbeams. Great. He was turning into a proper freak now. The lawn was empty. There was no-one there.

"Are you OK? What's going on?" The girl was staring at him.

The pain ebbed away. Maybe he was getting a cold… Trevor glanced at the girl as she nodded.

"Ah… I know who you are. Did you do something to make them call like that? They don't normally make a fuss when someone comes in, unless they've seen a dog or something…" The girl stopped and rubbed her nose, no doubt thinking he was useless. "Oh, look, don't worry about it. You're Trevor, aren't you? You sure you're OK?"

Trevor inclined his head in a tiny nod. His eyes flicked up to her face for a second before returning to the ground. He knew he looked weird, with his ankle-swinging jeans, grubby trainers and frayed beanie. Typical that she thought he was to blame too. But he wouldn't answer. No way. School must have told her anyway.

"You *are* Trevor, the new volunteer, right?" She was trying again, after the uncomfortable pause, like they all did. "My name's Elise. Did your dad not come in with you?"

Trevor stared at the grass tufts sprouting at the edge of the path and picked at the dried splatters on his muddy coat sleeves. The silence became more awkward.

"OK. Your teacher gave me your forms and stuff. Look, come with me while I do the morning check round the aviaries, and I'll show you the birds. You can help us with the cleaning-out, after I've gone through the safety stuff with you."

She turned to go without waiting for an answer. Trevor looked back to where he'd heard the voice. Then he hurried after Elise. She was heading towards some aviaries: more bird houses of wood, wire and netting, flanked by a copse of woodland. She glanced over her shoulder as she walked.

"Come on. First off you need to get used to where everything is." She indicated the set of housing to their left with a wave.

"This block is called the mews. It's home to hawks, falcons and eagles who've been trained to fly in demonstrations to show visitors, and each bird has his own cubicle. They're tethered on their perches when they're not flying."

Trevor gazed at the row of birds. His eyes widened as he spotted more hawks, falcons, and the huge one at the end of the mews was definitely an eagle. Trevor stopped, arrested by the eagle's haughty stare and huge yellow talons gripping his perch. Those tiny golden flecks at the tips of his burnt coffee-colour feathers, unfurling like a fan as he stretched out his wings... awesome. The pictures in his book were nothing next to the real thing.

"Keep up, Trevor," said Elise, but he barely registered her talking.

The eagle was staring at him, just like the hawk. And the longer he looked back, the more he felt like he was disapproved of, in trouble. Trevor fidgeted and rubbed his neck, a flush of heat rising as the eagle narrowed its eyes and leaned forwards. Was he really such a loser that he could offend an eagle just by looking at him? He had to get a grip and stop overreacting. But the eagle didn't look away.

The silence grew heavy, and he stiffened. Elise was watching him too.

"Look, Trevor, I'm going to be up front about this. It's best. You're volunteering here, to work with the birds and learn what we do – right? And from the look of you now, it might be what you want?"

Trevor managed a second nod.

"Let's be clear then. I'm the falconer in charge, so I'm responsible for you. School's already told me you don't talk... no, sorry, you've chosen not to talk. And I don't expect you to decide to start just because I want you to. But I do need you to communicate and be helpful. And not get moody or stroppy."

They'd told her that too? Trevor looked her full in the face and Elise raised her eyebrows.

"So yes, please do look at me. Seriously. Whatever stuff you have going on, you leave it at the gate when you come here. It's for your own safety. I need to know you've heard me, and that you're calm, sensible and that you know what you're doing. So let's agree. Obvious nods, head shakes and notes at least, OK? If you can't do that it's not going to work out for you to be here. Not even for the rest of today."

Trevor frowned. Not a good start. If he let a bad mood show she'd just be another one who thought the worst of him. It normally took a while to size someone up before he decided if they warranted his version of 'advanced communication'. But there was no way he could muck up this chance to be near the birds. He couldn't stop looking at them.

"Have you got a note book?" Elise carried on. "I was told you use one at school."

Decision made. Trevor reached in the front of his rucksack and pulled out his tatty school pad, littered with torn remnants of missing pages. Comments and questions from various lessons were scattered over the lined paper. He didn't write notes for many teachers, just the ones he liked, and only when he had to. Elise nodded.

"Fab. Nice hand-writing! So do me a favour and use it. You can't learn to handle and train birds of prey if you don't." Suddenly Elise grinned. "And something else. I know the stuff about school and I still wanted you to come here. So try to crack a smile sometime, won't you? I need to know you like it here, and that I made the right decision."

He was going to handle the birds? And she wasn't going to judge him. Trevor pulled out his pen and scribbled as a warm feeling grew.

OK, agreed.

"Great!" Elise nodded. "Deal. Come on then. We've got different sheds and the office that way – and the flying arena is behind all that. You'll see it all later. This is the start of the aviaries, where breeding birds and owls live. Soon you get to see your favourite bird." She smiled. "Told you I know loads! Peregrine falcon, isn't it? Cue your nod, Trevor!"

Trevor couldn't help smiling back. It was so cool – every bird was breathtaking. And Elise was actually alright. He couldn't trust her, of course, but his shoulders relaxed a little as he nodded.

"There you go – progress! These three aviaries start our falcon conservation breeding zone. They're more nervous than other birds – they need peace and quiet."

Elise tilted her head towards the nearest enclosures as they walked on.

"These two have merlins and hobby falcons in them. When they're breeding we put up screens to give them privacy. So, aviary three. Don't get too close. The pair of peregrine falcons in here are wild birds. The female was caught last year, not far from here. You might have heard about it, it was a big story. But what you won't know is the female laid eggs and we now have babies."

Trevor had heard. The stolen peregrines was his topic when they'd done journalism in English. The picture of the bedraggled falcon had stood out from the newspaper cuttings, and the story made him so mad. Those peregrines were actually here? He stopped walking and lifted up his pad. This was so worth the effort. He poked an itch away from his chin with the biro and wrinkled his nose as he wrote.

I know the story. Babies! What happened?
Peregrines are totally epic.

Elise smiled.

"They are. You know the men who stole them got caught? Father and son, a couple of right charmers."

Elise leaned her elbows on the wooden barrier rail running alongside the path and her ponytail slipped over her shoulder as she shook her head.

"You should have seen the state of the birds when we went to pick them up. Disgusting doesn't even cover it. The men were sent to prison, for cruelty as well as stealing from the wild. Just not for long enough!"

A deep hoot sounded from the other side of the peregrines and Elise laughed.

"That's Wol. He's next door and wants to say hello… he can hear us. Let's walk round. It's better not to hang around near this aviary, we could spook the parents and disrupt them raising the babies."

Trevor drew her a quick smiley face and followed. There hadn't been anything in the news about what happened to the birds after. It was brilliant to know they were safe, and… eggs, babies… his head throbbed. The owl hooted again, and again, three times; each hoot got louder. Shrill calls rang out from other aviaries as the pounding in his head deepened. The harsh call of a crow rang out from a tree and Trevor's throat tightened as pain kicked in there again too. What was going on? The last thing he wanted was for Elise to think he was soft, especially when she already thought he was weird. He swallowed the pain away as he fumbled the pad and pen back into his rucksack, ignoring the set of crazy purple spots beginning to pop and explode in his vision as he followed her. He winced as the bird calls got louder. He had to concentrate. Come on, it was just a stupid cold.

"I don't get why they're so noisy this morning, it's so unlike them! Anyway, here's our oldest owl, Wol. He's a European – oh no!"

On the other side of the peregrine enclosure a tear in the side screening flapped in two pieces. The aviary wire behind it was visible, and it was split too, near the ground. Something had hollowed out a shallow tunnel underneath and bent the wire up on itself, pushing it into the aviary to get through. A single feather lay just outside.

"Oh, please, not the peregrines!" Elise cried out, eyes wide and her face blanching. She turned and ran, calling over her shoulder, "Trevor, stay there! I need keys."

Elise shot across the grass, her dark ponytail streaking

out behind her. The crow shrieked again from the trees overhead. Trevor stared at the damaged wire, his mouth open.

"Hey! You've got to come here. Right now!"

Who was that? It was coming from the aviary, but who would—

Without warning the pain blindsided him, erupting to a whole new level. It was an iron hand, squeezing him, snatching away voice, breath, vision. His throat was tight, thick, and his eyes shone, bulging in surprise as the air he took for granted was suddenly scarce in his lungs. It spread to Trevor's ears, stabbing them like knives. He stumbled forward and fell to his knees in front of the aviary, paralysed in panic and pain. What the hell was going on? Was he having a fit... *dying?* Just as it became unbearable and he began to crumble, the pain vanished. Trevor looked around, shaking, seeking disaster. But all was still, just like before. As if nothing had happened.

The crow called again and Trevor scrambled to his feet, heart pounding, skin clammy. He moved closer to the peregrine aviary and grasped the wooden rail for support. What should he do? He tried to stamp down the urge to run as the crow called a fourth time, deep and guttural.

The voice came from the aviary again, now a clear, pure sound, settling deep inside Trevor with a tremor, resonating like no sound ever had before.

"Yes, alright, Crispin, I can see him now."

Trevor froze.

"That's your light, isn't it? Your glow? You're really, really bright. Look... I'm trapped. You've got to help me."

3

"Quick! I have to get in!"

Elise's shouts echoed across the centre as she raced back towards him, a set of keys jingling from her hand. Trevor leaned against the rail and made himself look normal. At least the pain had vanished.

"Elise – calm down! We've got visiting public due in any minute and you're screeching worse than a bloody barn owl! What's going on?"

Trevor recognised the man striding into view, and momentarily forgot everything else. Adam Shotlander. Local celebrity, presenter of bird demonstrations and the person who should have been his dad. He'd watched Adam give talks in town, mostly by squeezing his face through gaps in the open windows of halls, or through hedges before being chased away, as he didn't have money to buy a ticket. Eyes wide, Trevor absorbed everything, close up for the first time. Adam was tall, with dark hair shaved close to his head and stubble across his face. His chest and arm muscles bulged, making him look like he'd stepped off the set of an action movie. The only part of him that didn't live up to superhero was his massive conker of a nose, which loomed up on Trevor before the rest of his body did. Adam strode past Trevor as if he was invisible, following Elise into the aviary. Trevor edged closer, past the barrier railing. He peered through a gap in the screen between aviary panels, careful not to get noticed.

Elise was crouched in the middle of a mess of broken branches and loose leaves, her head in her hands. She looked up.

"They're all gone, Adam. Parents and babies! No trackers on them, so we haven't got a hope of finding them, even if they are alive. I can't believe this. I said that mesh needed sorting!"

Trevor's heart sank as Adam shook his head.

"Damn shame. I'll do what needs to be done. Looks like a fox, doesn't it? So unlucky."

"Unlucky?" Elise stood up, her voice cracked. "Adam, if we'd fixed that mesh. I know it was only a little break, but look how much worse—"

"Come on, Elise." Adam frowned. "We have to make hard decisions sometimes. You're upset, but think about it. You know if I'd gone in to mend it they would've panicked and hurt the fledglings. They could have died and then we'd have no chance of releasing them at all. Maybe the fox got spooked after getting in and then they just got out... it is possible. The babies are fledging now so they could fly. When you've worked with birds as long as I have, you'll think all the options through. It's just a damn shame."

Elise bit her lip and looked away.

"I can't believe it's happened."

Adam rubbed his hand over the top of his head. "I know. Me too. Gutted."

Adam turned and walked towards the aviary door, calling back over his shoulder.

"Best thing to do is keep busy. I'll call Harry. You sort this mess out, before the public come in. Get the lad there to help you. Just get on as normal."

Elise nodded. "OK, you're right. Thanks, Adam."

Trevor turned away from the aviary and pretended to study the fencing as Adam emerged. This time Adam glanced his way as he strode past.

"Morning, lad, and welcome. Get in there and help her out, will you please?"

Really? This was insane. First the peregrines, now Adam had actually spoken to him. If it wasn't for the pain thing, and this niggling feeling that strange voices no-one else could hear were the first sign of madness, the morning would have been panning out to be the best he'd had for years. He felt alright now, kind of normal, so he pushed the voices to the back of his mind. If he really was going loopy it was definitely better not to know.

Trevor walked past the barrier and into the aviary. It was like a storm had hit. Feathers littered the sandy floor, and foliage and broken branches were strewn everywhere. Elise's eyes were glittering. She tried to smile.

"Sorry about this, not ideal for a first day. You look like I feel… and a bit pale. You OK?"

Trevor nodded as she cleared her throat.

"It's a shock, I know. But we need to clean up." Elise walked over to the door. "Starting with the leaves and branches. Underneath there's going to be a stink-pile of poo and pellets. We can't clean them out when they've got babies, so it all builds up. You wait here. I'll tell the other falconers what's going on and get stuff from the cleaning shed."

She managed a small smile. "That was Adam, by the way. He's in charge, but he's a softie. Addicted to *Twilight* films, but I haven't told you that! Just hold on, OK? I'll be back with gloves, buckets, rakes… and hopefully a calmer state of mind."

Trevor nodded as she left. A whole family of peregrine falcons getting attacked by a fox was awful. He hoped Adam was right… that they might have got away. But there were other questions refusing to be squashed. He couldn't ignore the voice. What if it was real? If it was someone calling for help? Had some kid lost their mum? But that was nuts, the centre wasn't even open.

Trevor shook his head. Adam was right. Thinking wasn't helping. Best to keep busy. Plus Elise would be pleased that he'd got on with something; it might earn him an anti-weirdness brownie point or two. He bent down, emptied a green water bath swimming with grit and broken twigs, and stood it up against the wooden aviary wall. Next he moved on to branches and foliage, stacking them in clusters beside the water bath. Elise was right about the poo: there were mounds of it, and if he disturbed them with his foot a sudden sharp rancid smell of ammonia rose up and made his eyes water.

A soft ripple of wind floated through the aviary, diluting the bitter smell and coaxing stray downy feathers into the air. Trevor watched their path as they drifted through the cord netting that stretched over the aviary roof, beyond its limits. Clouds were piling into each other in some sort of race across the sky, high and free in the wind. Trevor smiled. There was a way he could shut his head up. His old, favourite way. He closed his eyes and let his imagination run free, following the feathers.

He drifted into the blue and ranged out over the valley. Leaning this way and that, he was buffeted by breezes until warm air lifted him up and the view spread out beneath him. He drew in a deep breath. It felt so real. He could do what he wanted, go where he wanted, be happy and free and... OW! His ears exploded anew with exquisite, sheer pain. His throat burned, on fire. In an instant, the blue sky turned black and his legs crumbled beneath him.

★

Trevor turned his head slowly, fighting the fuzzy feeling and an acrid smell. With a start he opened his eyes to find himself nose-deep in crusty bird mute. He sat up, rubbing his eyes and wincing. Something was different. He looked at his fingers and saw every line and crease of his skin in more detail than he ever had before. Noises were loud, too loud. He winced again as the owl next door hooted. What was wrong with him?

There was a rustling noise in the corner of the aviary. Trevor stiffened. Someone was there. Or something. He wasn't alone.

Rustle. Crack. Filled with stomach-clenching fear, Trevor scrambled to his feet and backed away. Was it the fox? Was it about to leap out and grab him in a panic to escape? Animals could be dangerous and unpredictable when cornered. What if it got him by the neck or something? Trevor glanced over his shoulder to check his escape route was clear. Time to make a run for it.

"I see you. Your glow is so bright. You are one of the gifted. And you're ready now. Please help me."

Trevor stopped. The voice was coming from the same corner. The part of the aviary with the biggest mess of sticks and shrubbery. The owner of the voice must be underneath. He fidgeted on the spot. Whoever they were, and whatever glowing stuff they were going on about, they were in trouble. He looked back to the door, but there was no sign of Elise. What was taking so long?

"Look, I'm stuck. I need you to get me out."

Trevor walked to the corner. He lifted broken boughs with shaking hands, trying to copy what he'd seen on the news, when rescue teams were looking for people trapped in fallen buildings. A piece at a time, nice and slow, to make sure he wouldn't hurt them more. He gritted his teeth. As he uncovered the first level of stuff, it looked like some of the perching branches had toppled together underneath, making a kind of wigwam; a makeshift shelter. He lifted one of the larger leafy branches, and the voice came again.

"Keep going!"

So there was someone there for sure, someone small. His shoulders tense, Trevor shifted branches with increased urgency. The last step was to make a gap to get into the wigwam. He hesitated. Would whoever it was be alright? Safe? He stared at the wigwam, trying to see inside. They had to be, right? Plus they were small, so if they turned out to be violent he could deal with it.

He bit his lip, put out his hand and lifted a group of branches away.

Two bright round eyes stared up at him, dark and sparkling, trimmed with the palest yellow lids. His mouth hanging open, Trevor stared back at the fluffed-up bundle of feathers attached to them. He took in the sharp curved beak and the out-of-proportion yellow feet tipped with slim, smoke-grey talons. Frozen, bird and boy stared at each other as time stood still. The bird opened its beak and Trevor stiffened, bracing himself for an ear-splitting call of fear. But no call came.

"At last! This is so weird, and I'm aching. I need to stretch… and get out of this mess. Where is everyone? What in the sky is going on?"

Trevor jumped back. Who *was* that? There couldn't be a person there too, there just wasn't enough room. So that would mean… his legs gave way and he sank back to the ground. Fear bubbled like a pot boiling over, and the urge to leg it swept over him like a wave. But the bird's piercing gaze didn't leave his face. It tilted its head to one side, like it was trying get a better view, and opened its silver beak again.

"What are you even doing? I wouldn't sit on that floor. It's not comfortable, take it from me. Plus you need to be higher up. It's safer. Why are you looking at me like that? You can't glow and expect me to ignore you. I'm not that young, and I'm not stupid. I heard the other birds earlier. I know what you are."

With a huge gasp Trevor realised the incredible truth. The bird was talking to him… the bird was talking to him!

And he could understand every word it said.

4

The clatter of a bucket and rake bashing against the aviary heralded Elise's return.

"Ow, I hate these narrow doorways, I'm always covered in bruises. Wow," she said, "thanks for making a start. Let's get the muck in the buckets, then we can rake." She frowned. "You OK?"

Trevor just stared at her, his eyes wide and shocked, like a stricken rabbit pinned in a car's headlights.

"What's wrong?" There was a tremor in Elise's voice as she let the rakes fall. She moved closer and gasped.

"Oh Lord, it's one of the fledglings!" Her hands flew to her mouth and she sank to the ground beside Trevor.

"Did you just find him? Was he stuck? What happened? We've still got one! Oh, it would help so much if you'd talk. You will write it all down, right?"

Trevor nodded. Was this all a dream? Elise would have to have an edited version. He couldn't possibly write down what really happened. True or not, he'd be off to the funny farm faster than a mad cow.

Still squatting, Elise began to shuffle towards the wigwam. "Look, we need to make him safe. Hospital shed first, to check him over. If he flies off now he won't live. His muscles aren't ready and he hasn't got a clue how to hunt for himself." She looked at Trevor. "There's no time. You've got to help. Move over there, block the space between the bird and the door."

Trevor scrambled to his feet and did exactly as she asked. He was sticking to that bird like glue. Wherever it was going, he was going too.

Elise took off her jacket. "Move towards him as quietly as you can. If he panics, he'll try to fly, and I need to get this over him before he does." She shook the jacket out in front of her. Trevor frowned, and her eyes flickered to his face.

"It's OK, it's called casting." She re-focused on the peregrine. "Wrapping a bird up to keep him calm. Just move when I do, and keep that area blocked. Put your arms out, and distract him from looking at me. He won't try to fly if we're in his way."

Trevor fixed his eyes on the falcon, and held his hands out, slowly moving his arms up and down. Hopefully enough to be ready for any take-off attempts. Elise crept forwards. Trevor copied. The bird looked from one to the other. Elise raised the jacket in front of her as she drew closer and the peregrine suddenly bent its legs, crouching low to the ground.

"He's gonna take off!" squealed Elise. She half leapt, half threw her jacket over the bird as he let out a series of high-pitched calls. "Yes! Got him!"

Petrified, his arms sticking out from his sides like an awkward scarecrow, Trevor could only stare as Elise drew her jacket around the fidgeting bird. The calls were loud and clear.

"Don't stress," the falcon called as its head bobbed up from the folds of the jacket. "I get it, really. I'm not going to take off. But this cloth thing is heavy. Can't you tell her I don't need it? Or at least make it looser?"

Elise was oblivious. With both hands closed firmly around the jacket, she lifted the bundle up and held it close to her, letting out a sigh of relief as she gazed at the peregrine.

"You feel safe now, don't you, little guy?" She glanced at Trevor. "Look, this is hectic, but can you catch me up? I've got to get him to the shed so I can check him."

Elise walked slowly, cradling the jacket of bird. Trevor's face felt hot, rising up from his chin, as his shock began to defrost. The bird's voice rang out again.

"Glowing boy, we need to talk. Soon!"

With a hiss of breath, Trevor took a beat. Was this even possible? Who was going to believe any of it? Had he actually, truly gone mental? Why could he hear the bird? And glowing… gifted, what was all that? He wrenched up his sleeves and checked his arms. No strange light there. He shook his head. All too, too weird.

In the end Trevor stood up and forced his legs to work, one foot in front of the other. That bird had answers and he'd left it too long already. He scrambled out of the trashed aviary and re-traced his steps, heading for the sheds to find the hospital.

Elise was just outside the mews, talking to two guys. Tall and lanky, their long legs looked out of proportion to their spindly bodies. They were wearing falconry gloves and green jackets like Elise's, emblazoned with the centre's emblem of a proud eagle. Elise looked round and put her hand on the arm of the older-looking one. He stopped talking.

"Hey, Trevor," she said. "You still look gobsmacked! This is Lennox and Rash, our other two falconers. They're brothers. Lennox is next most experienced after me. You'll learn loads from him."

"Alright, Trev," said Lennox. Strands of dark hair caught on the stubble over his chin as he grinned. "Bit of a morning, right? Bet you're wishing you hadn't come in!"

Trevor shook his head as he grabbed his pad and pen.

☺ Elise, please can I see the falcon?

Elise hesitated, then nodded, glancing at Lennox. "OK, but just for a minute. He's fine, no damage, but he needs to be calm. Hospital shed is that one just there." She indicated with a slant of her head. "Don't get too close, right? It'll upset him."

Trevor shut the hospital door behind him and took a deep breath. Epic… there was the falcon, perched in a small metal enclosure against the opposite wall. Trevor took a step forward, then stopped as the sound of Elise's voice filtered through the open window. He looked out to where she and Lennox were walking across the grass, and suddenly realised he could hear them.

"…so I got stressed. But Adam's right, we couldn't have gone in and disturbed them."

Lennox nodded. "Never a good move."

"It's gutting, though." Elise sighed. "Is everything OK in the mews? No sign of fox damage?"

"Nope, nothing." Lennox paused. "Elise, you know this newbie…"

Trevor leaned closer to the window.

"Trevor?"

"Yeah. Do you think he's OK? He seems a bit… odd. Are you sure he's OK to be here?"

Elise laughed.

"He's fine! Look, he's going to be a bit challenging, with his notepad and stuff, but it's not like we haven't helped people before. What about Callie last year?"

"I spose, but she was older, wasn't she?"

"And you thought she was pretty!" Elise laughed again. "Don't stress on it, he seems like a good lad. Just try your best with him."

Trevor tried not to feel anything as they walked away. It was always the same. Weird, difficult, not wanted. At least Elise wasn't completely against him, but Lennox was firmly on his don't bother list.

A gentle buzz, a vibration, pulled him out of his head and back in the room. The bird was shaking himself. It was a rouse, something he'd read about, happening for real, and he froze, fascinated. Every chocolate and cream feather was alive with movement and trembled softly as the peregrine aligned them into position. The shiver spread across his body and culminated in a sharp shake of his golden-brown tail feathers. Close up he was stunning. Nearly fully grown, most of his plasticky feather casings were splitting where his flight feathers were growing through, and his speckled chest feathers were overlapping and smothering his downy grey baby fluff.

The bird watched him with the same unwavering, piercing gaze as before. Trevor waited, trembling, taking swift, shallow breaths, still hardly daring to move. His heart hammered.

Speak. Please.

One minute passed, then two. Nothing. With a familiar sinking feeling, Trevor accepted the inevitable. He was losing the plot. It was all just in his head. Would he slowly descend into insanity, or did it happen quickly? Come to that, though, if you really were turning stark raving mad, were you able to tell? Would you even want to know?

A third minute trawled by. Still the bird didn't move.

With a heavy heart, Trevor let the dream end. Everyone was right about him. There was nothing special going on and never would be. He was just plain weird. It was time to go.

He walked to the door.

"Hey!"

Trevor's heart leapt and he wheeled round. The bird hadn't moved, except for its head, tilted to one side.

"I knew you could hear me. You had to, glowing like fire. Quick, come here."

His head alive with wild, weird hope, Trevor crossed the room. The falcon's beady eyes bored into his.

"The more I look at humans, the more confusing it is.

You're such a clumsy shape. What happened to your wings? Anyway, no time. I'm Midge. Who are you?"

Trevor opened his mouth. He wanted to answer. But silence was his wall. If he dropped the barrier he'd get hurt. He couldn't. He grabbed his pad and pen, quickly scribbled his name and held it out to the falcon. Midge tilted his head and blinked.

"No offence, but do you honestly expect me to read your scratchmarks? Have you noticed I'm a bird? And don't you realise what you are? Mum told me if I ever met someone like you, I could trust them. I heard them out there, saying you don't talk. *But you're a spellboda.* And you're glowing again, right now. Plus you can hear me. Which means you're mine. So you've got to talk – to me."

Midge lowered his head for a moment and nibbled a feather casing, sending motes of dust billowing out from his chest, dancing in the sunlight that streamed through the hospital window.

He looked straight at Trevor again, pinning him with his fathomless dark eyes.

"And if you didn't know till now, if you haven't realised what you are, wouldn't you like to know? And see if I can understand you too?"

Trevor broke eye contact and studied his peeling trainers. He needed a butterfly net to catch up the swarm of thoughts fluttering round his head, all bashing into each other. The bird was talking a mixture of sense and crazy, and there was something amazing and unbelievable going on. Even magical. Something worth taking a risk for.

But it was such a big step for him to speak…

"Are you OK in there?" He jumped as Elise's voice came through the open window. "Why's the peregrine making a noise? Don't get too close, will you?"

"Look at me!" Midge urged. "Quick, before she comes. Trust me, please. I need to work out what's going on. My family's in trouble and I know you can help!"

Footsteps crunched over gravel outside. Trevor's heart raced faster. How was Midge in trouble? What if he could stop it? Could he live with himself if he did nothing? And what the hell was a spellboda?

"Come *on*," said Midge, "just say your name."

The footsteps were right outside. Trevor took a breath, opened his mouth and changed his life forever.

"It's Trevor," he whispered. "I'm Trevor."

5

Elise and Trevor raked their way methodically through the sand in the mews, scraping mounds of poo into dustpans, while Lennox and Rash carried hawks, falcons and eagles on gloved hands over to the display lawn. By the time visitors arrived, birds were sunning themselves, wings outstretched to soak up the heat, and their enclosures were fresh and gleaming. Trevor made himself look calm and peaceful, but he was a duck on a lake. On the water he was gliding across a smooth surface, while his brain was paddling like fury, whirring along underneath where no-one could see. Why had he heard Midge speak? Midge had said, "Hello Trevor," as Elise walked in. So they could understand each other. Clearly no-one else could talk to Midge. They'd have said something. Either that or they were all brilliant liars. Trevor returned rakes and buckets to the cleaning shed and realised he couldn't last another minute. There was no way he could tell Elise, but he had to do something before his brain exploded. He whipped out his pad and started writing.

"Nice work, Trevor," said Elise as she emerged from the mews and closed off the barrier that separated visitors from the no-go area. "You've picked up cleaning well. We'll do a couple of owl aviaries later on."

Lennox and Rash walked over to join them and she held out a brown suede falconry glove, with two tassels swinging from the edge. "First piece of kit for you, Trevor. You guys weigh the birds as normal. Take Trevor with you so he learns about flying weights, and he can get used to where everything is. And do an extra check everywhere for any other signs of damage or disturbance, just in case, OK?"

Lennox nodded. "No worries. I'll let you know if we find anything. Can I grab your keys, though? I've left mine in my car."

"Sure," said Elise, pulling the keys out of her pocket as Trevor shoved his pad under her nose.

Can I clean out the hospital?

Elise smiled. "At some point, yes. But for now it's better to leave the peregrine calm and quiet. I'm well impressed you're into cleaning, even if it is an excuse to see your favourite bird! Stick with these two for a bit, watch what they do, you'll learn loads. See you later."

Elise walked back to the empty peregrine aviary as frustration lodged itself in Trevor's throat like a half-chewed piece of food.

"Right, Trev. First we pick up a bird." Lennox walked

onto the lawn and crouched down beside a buzzard. "Watch how the knot works. You slip this bit out…"

At any other moment in his life, being told he was going to learn about handling birds of prey would have been epic, even if it was with Lennox. But Midge was priority. Impatience bubbled up, a churning urgency. He had to grab the first moment he could to get back.

"…and then we make sure they're safe on the glove, like this."

Gripping his notepad, Trevor forced himself to concentrate. Lennox talked on, as the buzzard perched calmly on his gloved hand. The bird's hooked beak ruffled along its wing, tidying dark flight feathers.

"Rash, show him again. Pick up Brock. Slowly, so Trev can see, right? Rash crouches down so he isn't above the bird. He puts his gloved hand out and the bird steps on. See? Now he holds the leash that ties the bird to the perch. Before he undoes the falconer's knot, he slips the jesses under his thumb. Then, one pull on that leash, it's quick release, right? And it's undone. He loops the leash through his fingers and stands up."

Trevor managed to listen, and consider the moment when he could put on a glove and pick up a bird himself, but the diversion was short. Brock called out as Rash stood up and Trevor froze, half-excited, half-terrified to see if he could understand him. But it was just the normal call of a hawk.

"Alright, Trev? Next we take them to the prep room," said Rash. "Come on."

Both buzzard and hawk perched on the gloves as

comfortably as if they'd been in the branches of a tree. Trevor followed the brothers as they stepped over the display barrier. Even with their uniforms they couldn't be described as smart, more like they'd made just about enough effort to get away with it. Lennox's curly hair had managed to escape its ponytail almost completely and Rash's trousers were ripped in three places.

"Shut the gate behind you, Trev," said Lennox as they went through the gate with the 'Falconers Only' sign. "We don't want the public following."

Rash snorted. "Following? Yes we do, I need to build up my Insta numbers. Going to be an influencer, me. *@therenegademasterfalconer*, Trev, look me up."

"Why is it all you ever talk about is your flaming profile?" said Lennox, as Trevor hid a smile. "You've got to up your mental age, bro. Concentrate on the job. You're sixteen now. Adam and Elise won't have it, you know."

"Well, I'll stay quiet then," Rash replied. "But I can't help my growing fame, can I?"

"Or you can set an example to Trev," said Lennox.

"Yeah, I can," said Rash. "And it'll be an example of how to have an awesome sense of humour, get hundreds of followers and not be boring like you, with your twenty-six. *And* they're all family."

"Great, thanks, mate," said Lennox. "Do me a favour and at least stay quiet from bragging round Adam. It's down to me you got this apprenticeship and I'm not getting the blame if you muck it up. Sorry, Trev, my *little* bro hasn't pulled himself out of his social media obsession yet."

He opened the door to the prep room with his bird-free

hand as Rash pulled a face behind him. "Come in, mate, shut the door. And stand over in that corner."

Trevor walked up the three steps leading into the prep room, liking Rash more by the second. The room was tidy, with rows of equipment hanging from hooks on the wall. There were intricately stitched falcon hoods, and lures, brown pads of leather which he recognised from his book. A whiteboard on the other wall had names and numbers scrawled over it. In the opposite corner stood two sets of old-fashioned sweetie scales, one large, one small. Short perches were sticking out from them, and Trevor worked out what would happen next as the brothers walked over to them.

"So we weigh them," Lennox said, "then we record the weights." The buzzard hopped from his glove to the perch attached to the scales, lifting up one yellow-taloned foot after the other on the spot, as it got used to the new surface. "All the stuff we use to fly them is in here… lures to chase, gloves, bags and so on."

He paused to study the scales, as the buzzard stopped fidgeting and the dial settled.

"One pound two ounces," he said, as he picked the bird back up. "We still work on old weights. Falconers are dinosaurs." He walked over to the whiteboard and wrote the weight under a column headed 'Skye', as Rash, a sulky look on his face, went through the same process on the other scales with Brock.

"What is he, mate?"

"One pound one ounce," came the brusque reply.

"So we write the weights in, Trev." Lennox ignored his brother as the marker pen squeaked its way across Brock's section. "Then we know if a bird's on weight or not. These two are about right, so they'll have a good fly today."

"Yeah, and you'll see." Rash grinned again. "They always poop, just before they take off for the first time."

"Geez. Are you going to give it a rest today?" Lennox shook his head.

Trevor couldn't stop his smile, then raised his eyebrows as a brilliant idea popped into his head. He scribbled on his pad and showed it to Lennox, hopping from one leg to another.

"Alright, mate," said Lennox. "You look desperate. You know where they are yet? Follow the signs. We'll put these back, get some more birds and meet you back here when you're done."

"You'd better hurry up, judging by the weird look on your face," Rash sniggered. Lennox shot him a look.

"Ignore him, Trev. He just thinks he's funny. Come on, laughing boy, we'll weigh the caracaras next, they'll go well with your mood."

Trevor followed them outside, then went in the opposite direction towards the toilets. As soon as Lennox and Rash were out of sight he doubled back and skulked along the path to the hospital. Having access to the no-visitors area was like being backstage. He left the path and crept round the other side of the hospital, out of view, but as he got to the edge near the door, he stopped. Voices. Holding his breath, he crouched and peered round the hospital wall with one eye. His heart hammered.

Adam was leaning out of the office further down the path, holding the door open in his hand. Elise was walking backwards, away from Adam, smiling.

"What do you think you're doing?" Adam pinned her with a stare.

"I, er…"

"Well? Come on!"

"Sorry, Adam, I was just about to knock when you moved and I saw your screen was on. I didn't mean to interrupt. I was only going to mention—"

"I never said you were interrupting."

"But…" Elise began to giggle. "Look, it's really not an issue, Adam, everyone I know loves the Cullen family too."

Trevor was transfixed as Adam's face flickered through a host of colours, from pink, to red and a deep shade of beetroot, like a cuttlefish.

"I am *not* watching *Twilight*. I was opening my address book to get the wildlife officer's number to talk about the falcons."

"Ah, right. Actually, that's what I wanted to ask," replied Elise, "so it's all good. Have you told him about—"

"Yes. Yes, I have. So you can get on with whatever else needs doing now, can't you? Talk to me later. And stop saying that stuff about *Twilight*."

Elise put her hands up. "OK! But how many times have you tweeted Stephanie Meyer now?"

"Oh, just shut up and get on with your work!"

Elise grinned. "Of course, Adam. Sorry, couldn't resist. You make it too easy."

Trevor watched as Elise walked away. The slam of the office door silencing Adam's chuckle signalled the all-clear. He waited a moment, then slipped into the hospital with a huge sigh. At last. Time for answers.

6

Trevor closed the door as the peregrine popped out his head from under a wing. His dark eyes sparkled.

"Yes, Trevor! Now we can get somewhere. First, do you get what's going on?"

Trevor swallowed. This was so direct. It felt weird, forming words in his mouth, using breath to speak to anyone except Mrs B. His tongue felt too big, almost as big as the choice he was making.

"No, well... um, sort of."

"What does that mean?" said Midge. "Umsortof?" He lifted a talon to his chest and scratched.

Trevor shifted his weight from one leg to another. "I don't know what I mean. Some things I get. Like, I know I can understand you." This was difficult. Midge stopped scratching.

"Look... Trevor. I don't know loads, but there's some stuff I've been told. Just ask and I'll try to help. Then you can help me."

Trevor nodded, organising his brain and forcing questions into order. "Right... OK. I need to know... what's a spellboda?"

Midge bobbed his head, the rest of his body staying still. "Trevor. I know this one. It's only one of the most awesomest things I've ever heard of, that's all. You're one of The Gifted. You didn't know?"

Trevor shook his head.

"Not a clue. What does it mean? Is it why... why I can talk to you?"

"Yes," said Midge, "and it might not be just you and me. Some spellbodas can talk to loads of different animals. Four legs, two legs, sometimes even stuff in the rivers and sea. It depends on the spellboda. Us animals have been able to understand humans all along, but none of your lot are supposed to know. Stupid dogs, though, they nearly give it away all the time."

Midge stopped moving and stared at Trevor.

"You're special. Only a handful of your kind are spellbodas. Gifted ones. You're one of the first things we learn about, almost straight from when we hatch. After catching dinner, of course."

A swell of something new rose from Trevor's stomach as he took hold of what Midge was saying. Hard to describe. Disbelief, then hope; a threat of happiness, and a feeling he could be worth something. He bit his lip as he considered. Suddenly, talking out loud didn't feel so weird.

"I can't hear any other birds or animals. Only you. This morning was the first time it happened. Why hasn't it happened before?"

Midge bobbed up and down again. "Not sure. But Mum told me you don't do it from when you're born, only from when you're ready, when the time's right, when you're needed by one of us. Mum said when the gift starts, you glow, a lot, and it hurts. Does that make sense?"

"Yes, yes!" exclaimed Trevor. "It was my neck, and my ears, I was—"

"Exactly," Midge cut in. "So you've just started. It's why you shone so bright. Things were changing so you could understand me... us. Ears and voice are used the most, but Mum told me all the, what are they called?" He looked up, then back at Trevor. "Yes! Senses. You could start to smell things better, see and hear more too. Mum said it's slow, though. With the talking, it starts with one of us, then the more gifted you are, the more animals you hear. And you can control it. Like when you want to hear, you can make it happen. But it all happens when the time's right."

"So that's why I could hear Elise and Lennox so well." Trevor frowned. "Will it hurt again?"

"Not that I was told," said Midge. "Maybe that's only when it kicks in."

"Why do you keep going on about glowing?" said Trevor. "I can't see it."

"We can see it, even before your gift starts working," said Midge. "Remember when all the birds called out this morning? That's why I shouted you. They were all yelling about you, saw exactly what you are. It's how we know."

"So I will see it too, the glowing? Like I'll end up talking to more animals?"

"I don't know," said Midge. "Mum didn't tell me that.

But she said people like you are here for a reason."

The trickle of relief gathered momentum. A spellboda. Gifted. Trevor sighed. He wasn't mad. He wasn't ill. He wasn't dying. Could he really be something special?

"My turn for questions." Midge fidgeted on his perch. "How come you're here? And why don't you talk to the other humans?"

Trevor stiffened. He bit his lip again. "Um, well… I'm here… because… er—"

"Trevor, not being rude, but we haven't got long for you to fire your voice up. I'm a bird, right? We don't muck about, don't have time. Think about it. It's not my nature. I mean, look at the way we falcons hunt. I'm a get in there and get on with it predator. It's in us from the moment we hatch – in our blood, see? I can't help it. So not being funny but could you get a move on? You're talking to me, right? Not a human!"

Trevor had to smile. He leaned against the wall and tried again.

"Fair enough. I'm here because, well, I love birds of prey… my teacher sorted it for me to be a volunteer. And I don't talk to people because… because… it's to do with Sykes."

"Who's Sykes?"

"He's my dad. But he's not really a dad at all."

"What do you mean?" said Midge. "When is a dad not a dad?"

"When he's a git, and he's miserable and angry. And when he never speaks to you except to tell you how useless you are," Trevor replied softly, staring at his trainers. "When he's shouting, banging things around. When he makes you feel like you're an idiot, and you wish you'd never been born."

"That's rough." Midge fidgeted on his perch. "My dad was a bit full-on, but he was decent enough. Mum said I'm a bit like him. What does your mum think?"

"I wouldn't know," said Trevor. He looked up at Midge as a door in his mind opened; all the dross backed up against the other side had got too heavy not to tumble through.

"She died. Sykes won't talk about her. To anyone. And I only know that because some nosy, interfering woman at school thought finding that out would help me talk again." He scowled. "As if I'd feel sorry for him! Anyway, now you know. She's gone, and I'm stuck with Sykes. I won't call him Dad now. Ever. And I don't talk to anyone cos I don't want to."

"Until now."

Trevor rubbed his forehead and nodded. "Until now." He smiled suddenly. "But you're not anyone, you're anybird. So why is it you? Why can't I hear the others?"

"I reckon it's because I'm in trouble," Midge said. "Remember? You hear us when something's wrong. And you can help me, see? Like you can find out who took my family."

Trevor felt hot. There was no kind way to do this. But Midge said he liked things direct, so…

"I'm really sorry, Midge, but they're gone. They think a fox got in, but—"

"Fox, shmox," said Midge, feathers bristling. "They've got it wrong. I was there! I know it wasn't a fox. It was a man. Two of them, actually. They took everyone except me. I stayed really still, and they didn't see me."

Trevor's eyes widened. "Seriously? But how did they get through that hole? I thought it was too small for a person."

"They used the door, of course," said Midge. "Like all humans. Then they made the hole after. They said it would fool them."

Trevor crouched down. "This is crazy! Elise had to run for the keys."

"Not crazy to lock the door after if you want to make it look like a fox." Midge bent down and nibbled off a stray feather casing. "So who are they? Where have they taken them?"

Trevor frowned. "This is bad. How can I tell Elise? She'll never believe me." He looked up. "Two men. Did they say more? Did you see them, their faces or anything?"

"They didn't say much else," said Midge. "One did call the other one Dad. I got a look at them through the branches. They had those light things… torches?"

Trevor's brain whirred. "Were they, like, weird-looking? And hair? Long, or short?"

Midge tilted his head. "They both had really, really short hair. Maybe even not there. As for weird… I'm not sure about your human ideas, but they both had ears that stuck out even more than yours, and I saw one had big red spots on his face when the light flashed on it."

"Yes!" Trevor shot a look out of the window and lowered his voice. "I think I know who they are. I saw their pictures in the paper. Bald, big ears, spots, boom! It's the same guys.

Has to be. The ones who stole peregrines from the wild. That was your mum and dad, wasn't it?"

"I don't know, but maybe," said Midge. "It makes sense. They said they were caught from the wild. We were supposed to go free again, as a family. So you think the people who stole them before have stolen them back?"

Trevor nodded so hard his neck ached. "It must be them. Total idiots. Maybe they're still planning to sell the babies." He grinned. "I know! I'll write something to Elise. Like I've thought of it. Get her thinking."

Midge flapped his wings. "Do it!" Then he suddenly stopped. "If the balds work out they've left me, that I'm here on my own, then I'm in trouble, right? They'll come back and get me, won't they?"

They stared at each other. Trevor's chest tightened as the falcon's body trembled. He looked like a baby bird for the first time.

"Please do it fast."

Trevor grabbed his pad and pen from his pocket. "I'm on it."

He was about to write when a voice shouted outside. The pad slipped out of his hands and hit the floor with a loud slap. The voice was extra loud too. Midge was right: his senses were definitely getting sharper.

"Trev? Trev! You alright? You having colonic irrigation, mate?"

Trevor grabbed the pad and shoved it in his rucksack. He smiled at Midge.

"Got to go," he whispered. "I've got this. You'll be safe, and soon you'll be back together!"

7

It wasn't until late afternoon, when all the day's jobs were done, that Trevor finally got the chance to get a note to Elise, just as he was on the edge of dying of frustration. He couldn't write it until the afternoon flying demonstration, when no-one needed him to do anything. He nodded as he finished it… he hadn't been sure what to put until he started writing, but then it came easy to him and it had turned out just right. As soon as they'd finished putting birds back in their spaces and giving them dinner, he reached in his pocket and gave Elise the piece of paper. She leaned against the wooden barrier beside the mews.

"Seriously?" Elise frowned. "You sure about this, Trevor?"

Lennox loped over from the weathering ground. "What's up?"

Elise glanced up at Lennox, then back at the paper.

"Trevor thinks the falcons going might not be a fox."

"What? Why?" Lennox looked at Trevor. "No offence, mate, but it's your first day here. How are you going to know something like that?"

Trevor got his pad out of his pocket as Elise looked at the note again.

"He heard something. Listen... *I've been thinking about the peregrines and maybe it wasn't a fox. Someone should check the men who took the falcons last year. There was someone at school last week talking about them. They said they knew they were stealing birds again. They could have taken them.*"

Elise looked up again. "Trevor, are you sure that's what you heard? Just a few days ago?"

Trevor nodded as Lennox shook his head. "I don't get it. They couldn't have got in and out under the wire. It's too small."

"Well..." Elise tilted her head. "You say that, but it would have been possible to bend it up more. Then put it back down a bit." She looked at Trevor. "Could one of us talk to this person?"

Trevor had already thought of this. He wrote fast.

He's one of their family, so I don't think so. Plus he doesn't know I heard. So I'd be in massive trouble if he found out.

"You could be in massive trouble for accusing people if they haven't done anything wrong too," said Lennox. He turned to Elise, while Trevor stared at him and imagined punching him. "What are you going to do?"

"I've got to tell Adam," said Elise. "Just so it gets followed up. I'm sure it can be done quietly."

Lennox shook his head. "Bit dodgy, though... assuming."

"Maybe... but I can't leave it. If there was a chance to get them back and I didn't do anything, I wouldn't forgive myself."

That's what Trevor was counting on. He wrote *thank you* on his pad, while Lennox nodded.

"I get you. Adam will be able to sort it. Maybe part of police enquiries. They always say that, don't they?" He looked at his phone. "Blinking heck, have you seen the time?"

5.04pm. Oh no.

Trevor gasped, waved wildly in Elise's face and raced across the grass. Elise and Lennox's goodbyes floated in the air behind him as he sprinted to the car park. Sykes's car was reversing out of a space as he reached the gravel. Trevor ran over, smacked the boot and the car bumped to a halt. Trevor opened the passenger door.

"Don't keep me waiting! And don't touch my car!" Sykes glared at Trevor, his dark eyes flashing and his brow carved into trenches. "I told you not to muck me about. You're not coming back. I'm done with driving you around."

Six minutes late. Trevor kept his face expressionless as he got in the car.

"You can't even write sorry on your bloody stupid pad. I won't even get that, will I? Idiot."

Trevor followed his routine. Weather the storm, don't wind him up, dodge the lightning. Sykes slammed gears in place and jerked the car forward. Trevor kept his head still but rolled his eyes to the right, sneaking a look at the man he was supposed to love. Sykes stared straight ahead, looking wild and untidy as ever with thick dark hair sticking out in all directions, and his food-encrusted beard wrapped round his face.

Trevor looked down at the filthy car mat. It was out of the question not to go back. The urge to run from Sykes resurfaced, and he remembered his rucksack and treasures all ready. But he had to help Midge... and he had to work out this gift. Running away would mean he wouldn't see Midge. If he went missing, then turned up at the centre, the falconers would have to tell Sykes as soon as they saw him. So he was stuck – for now. He'd have to put up with things a bit longer and work out how to get back to the centre, if stinking Sykes wasn't going to drive him.

Trevor slid his fingers under his beanie and rubbed around the bump on his head. Options. His old bike had been thrown out. Rusty bits were dropping off it, plus it was too small. The centre wasn't near a station, and buses were hit and miss. Anyway, he didn't have any money. Either he'd have to walk, which would take forever, or he'd have to make Sykes bring him back, and he was more likely to be discovered as the next Justin Bieber than get that to happen. Trevor stopped rubbing and stared out of the window. There had to be a way. He just had to think of it.

As they passed fields full of oil-seed with yellow swathes of colour, a heavy fragrance hung in the air. Happy thoughts that wouldn't stay muffled for long pushed their way back in. It had been the best day. A spellboda. His amazing, precious secret. Wonder washed over him. All this time of keeping everything to himself was really going to come in handy. And he was already making a difference, helping someone. Well, somebird. Now Elise would tell Adam, he'd tell the police and they'd get Midge's family back. He forced back a smile.

With a lurch, the car stopped, and Trevor snapped back to the present. Sykes unclipped the seatbelt that strained across his chest with a recoil and a sharp ping.

"That took too long. Uses too much petrol. Another reason not to go again."

Fists clenched, Trevor followed him up the path across the front garden, with its eclectic mix of weeds, nettles and thorny shrubs of varying height and ferocity. Sykes was not going to dampen his mood. All he had to do was think and plan. He could do this. He was going back.

*

Sunday evening plodded by in relentless slow motion. Trevor holed himself up in his room as usual, where Mrs Bingo-Wings had made a new habit of sitting on his windowsill. He stared at her as his mind wrestled with a way to get back to the centre. If other animals could talk to him, then surely of all of them she would? She could help loads. He tried a mixture of approaches as the evening wore on.

"Mrs B, you won't believe what happened today."

"Hey, Mrs B, guess what? I met a falcon and I'm a spellboda."

"I can talk to animals! You understand me, right?"

"Oi, can you talk to me or what?"

But Mrs B just stared back at him, blinking almond eyes, then returned to cleaning her paws. Either Mrs Bingo-Wings was going deaf or he wasn't one of the super-gifted people. Trevor sighed. At least he could talk to Midge.

Deep sleep eluded him as his dozing mind replayed jumbles of birds, thieves and spellbodas, weird dreams tumbling into each other as he turned in his bed. One dream kept surfacing. Midge was flying in circles above his head and someone was talking. But it wasn't Midge; there were two voices and they were both different. The voices stopped, and he could only hear meows and owl hoots. He looked for them, but then, still in the dream, felt tired, so he sat down and edged into sleep. No. He shook himself. He should be awake. He looked up at Midge flying again and listened as bird calls and meows shifted into words. The first voice had a precise, clipped accent.

"No. Leave him alone. Too much too soon."

"But he's aware… *now*. You know the rules. He needs to—"

"She taught me. No-one knows rules better than me. He can't know what I know, not yet. This can't be rushed. Go away. Go on, go!"

Trevor opened his eyes and the dream slipped away. It had felt so real. He sat bolt upright. Street lamps cast a soft shadow through his curtains. A tap tap tap against his window was rhythmic, matching the gusts of wind. So that was it, disturbing his sleep. The tree outside was bending; he'd heard it before. Twigs at the end of branches brushed against the glass as if they were asking to come in, to be dry and warm, as rain smattered the window, thrown sideways by the wind. Mrs B, her eyes gleaming like small orange lamps, was still crouched on the windowsill. She stood up, and with a thump, and the small grunt of a soft landing, padded over to the bed. Jumping with graceful ease, she settled down against him. Trevor rested his hand on top of her head and sank back into the covers. Her soft purrs were regular as her warmth began to wash over him. He fought the feeling as his eyelids drooped again. He really had to think about making his plan. But sleep wouldn't be overcome. Trevor sighed, determination drifting with him. Leave it. Tomorrow would bring the answer. It had to.

8

Trevor stuck to his morning routine like a robot. He got up, washed and dressed, and was ready to leave for school before Sykes had even stirred from his room. Monday was usually his slowest day, but today he had a reason to get in early. He'd woken up with an idea. He grabbed two bags of crisps for today's breakfast and set out on the ten-minute walk to school, praying today he would know what to do about Midge. Maybe this idea would help him work it out.

St Jude's, the local comprehensive, was an unimposing set of characterless, grey stone buildings, but it suited Trevor. After he'd stopped speaking he'd been pretty much left alone, after the first couple of weeks of heckling to try and rile him. They'd given up in the end, and he was able to do things his way and fade into the background – most of the time.

Trevor fixed his gaze on the steel entrance gates, pulled

back for arrivals, and strode through. Still early, about half an hour before the rush, but that was perfect.

He headed for the library, the sweaty sock-smelling room ruled over by Miss Worley, a skin-and-bone librarian who wore nothing but black and looked like a leftover spectre from a Hallowe'en fancy-dress party. She stood up as soon as he went in, and her reedy voice cut across the room.

"Now then, Trevor, you're only allowed in here if you behave yourself. Don't disturb anyone – or anything. You know what Mr Delaney said last week. Any trouble and I'm calling someone straightaway."

Trevor raised his hands, palms out, and tried to look blank while she lowered herself back into her seat, her eyes never leaving him. God, why did she have to make such a drama? It wasn't like he'd done anything that bad before. He slung his rucksack, now empty of his re-hidden precious possessions, under the table and sat at one of the computers. He googled the word that was constantly in his mind, but after three pages, 'spellboda' still returned nothing except some Anglo-Saxon weirdness about it meaning 'messenger' and 'bringer of intelligence'. The first definition fitted, sort of, but if Midge expected him to be a genius he was going to be disappointed. Trevor closed his eyes and tilted his head back, leaning backwards on his chair as the endlessly irritating drone of Miss Worley whined on as she talked to one of the school brainiacs.

"Where did you see it last, Nick?"

"Can't remember. Not being rude, Miss, but if I knew that I'd probably know where to find it."

"Don't be smart. It's one of our expensive books. I'm not impressed, young man! Have you checked lost property?"

"Not yet, Miss."

"Well, go there now. With any luck it's found its way there."

Trevor mused over the idea of a book having legs and enough intelligence to take itself somewhere that it would be found. Miss Worley had been here too long. Although to be fair, he'd managed to a grab a few second-hand beauties from lost property to replace stuff he'd got too big for, and only last week a pair of trainers, but that was another story... was it?

Trevor opened his eyes and pushed forward on his chair. The front legs hit the ground with a sharp thud of metal on wood. Miss Worley jumped, frowned and opened her mouth, but Trevor was already on his feet. Of course. That was the answer, right there. He grabbed his rucksack and headed out of the library.

The corridor was filling up. Students roamed the halls in packs, and Trevor glanced at the arty group as he walked past them. One of them, a girl with cropped hair, was talking animatedly about some local band she was going to see. She saw Trevor, then rolled her eyes as she looked away, her nose stud twinkling in the light. Trevor looked down at the floor with a twinge. But being the school weirdo came with the no-talking rule. At least now he could be worth something. There was just one big, bearded, wine-drinking obstacle in his way.

He took a left turn, headed for Mr McKinnery's office and knocked.

"Come in." Trevor got his pad out of his rucksack and put his head round the door.

"Trevor! You're in early. Come on, have a seat."

Mr McKinnery was coming across normal, which was impressive seeing as it was the first time Trevor had gone to see his form teacher of his own accord. Trevor looked at him as he sat down, expecting something, but Mr McKinnery smiled and leaned forward in his chair, his elbows on the desk in front of him.

"What can I do for you then?"

Trevor put his pad on the desk and began to write. He thought he'd worked it out already but two tries of the first line ended up in an angry scribble of crossing-out.

"Take your time, mate."

Trevor glanced up. As Head of Science, Trevor had biology lessons with Mr Mac, and to be fair these classes were the least boring on his timetable. Loads of students, especially the girls, seemed to think Mr Mac was the coolest teacher, but all that didn't make this easy. It never was.

Mr Mac studied his fingernails, then ran them through his short blond hair.

"You're all good, Trevor, just put what you need to say."

Trevor looked down at the pad. Focus. They'd been in this situation loads of times before, but this was different, right? He wasn't in here defending himself, or stopping them from interfering or trying to make him open up. And Mr Mac was the one who'd sorted the volunteer stuff at the centre, so he was his best bet right now. He started to write, and this time the words flowed. Like his brain had suddenly caught up and realised he needed this to happen.

He flipped his pad round and pushed it over the desk.

Mr Mac. I loved going to the centre yesterday. I really want to keep going, not just one day a week but more often, like after school.

But my dad isn't feeling well. He doesn't like to talk about it, but he's not OK to drive at the moment.

If I had a bike I could get there. There's one in lost property. Can I borrow it?

Mr Mac's eyes widened.

"There's a *bike* in lost property? Really?"

Trevor nodded and grabbed back the pad.

But it's not lost, it's Miss Campbell's. Broke her leg, didn't she?

Mr Mac shrugged his shoulders.

"Nothing surprises me anymore. I'm pleased you liked it. So being around the birds was good?"

Trevor couldn't keep a smile from lighting up his face as he nodded. Mr Mac smiled back.

"Trevor, it's really encouraging to see you like this. And I want to help. But I need to check this whole bike stuff out. You need permission. You can't just borrow it. And your dad needs to be OK for the bike, and if you want to go after school." He frowned. "If your dad's not well, is there something we can do, to support you? Is he getting help?"

Trevor scribbled.

Tell my dad it's good for me. And tell Miss Campbell I'll look after it.

He shoved the pad across the desk, then grabbed it back before Mr Mac had a chance to read.

But don't tell my dad I told you he's not well. It's not serious but he's private and he'll not be happy if you talk to him. He's doing alright, though, so don't worry, OK?

Mr Mac closed his eyes for a moment.

"So many instructions, Trevor, and no magic word! So my mission, if I choose to accept it, is to pull out a lot of stops for you."

He leaned forward and pushed the pad back to Trevor.

"Let's talk about what you can do in return. If you want to go after school I don't think it's unreasonable to expect a project from you. A biology project on birds of prey. Which includes plenty of detail on their physiology."

Trevor leaned back.

"Don't look at me like that. It will improve your grades and give you a reason to go. Which I can explain to your dad... and Miss Campbell when I talk to her."

Trevor met Mr Mac's eyes and tried to read his expression.

"I also need you to make me a promise about making a change."

Trevor's pen flew across the pad.

Mr Mac raised his hands.

"I know, not that again. But I want you to promise you won't lose your temper again. You have lunchtime detentions all this week now."

He leaned forward again.

"You just can't behave that way, Trevor, no matter what. Actually if you communicated more – yes, I know you don't want to – but even if you wrote more on your pad, you might feel less angry. Especially when someone wants to wind you up like that. Anyway, if you want me to help I need your word."

Trevor put his elbows on the table and rested his chin on one hand. Losing it had felt good, in the moment. But now there was Midge. He reached for his pen with his other hand.

OK, I promise. It was only once, and I know not to listen to Jez now if he starts on me. I'll be calm, and I'll do the project. If I can borrow the bike... PLEASE.

Mr Mac smiled.

"You really want to go, don't you? OK... let me see what I can do."

★

Sykes's deep voice, booming intermittently, drifted out of an open window as Trevor walked up the path. He edged the back door open and crept in to the kitchen.

"Yes, that's OK... what? No... I'm not sure about that. Really? So you think it's a good idea. Whose bike is it?"

There was a pause as Sykes shuffled around in the drawer of the sideboard in the hall. Trevor held his breath, his chest tight with tension.

"Hmm. Well, if you think... could see if it helps. Give me their number again. I've lost it. I'll call them if he loses interest and backs out. After all, he won't tell them himself, will he?"

Trevor's heart was beating fast.

"Yes, got it. OK. As you say, it gives him something to do. You'll sort it? That quick? You got a helmet for him? OK. Right. Bye."

Sykes stomped into the kitchen and flicked the kettle on, grabbing a tea bag from the cracked caddy. His face was littered with angry lines that never went away, and his lips were tight. Waves of dark hair escaped the tangled mass and fell across an eye. Trevor couldn't move. He prayed Mr Mac hadn't mentioned the 'illness'. He'd been so careful about how it was worded. Please, please, don't let Sykes twig.

"Why do they have to keep poking their noses in? Your teacher thinks you have go to this bleeding centre. And they've gone and found a bike for you. Some other teacher, sticking her views in too."

He slopped boiling water into the tea-stained mug and stabbed the tea bag viciously with a spoon, before fishing it out and slinging it over into the sink. Brown drops of tea followed it through the air like a dirty comet tail.

"He says you've been better today, improved. I wouldn't know, though, would I?"

Trevor began to breathe more evenly. He watched Sykes's broad shoulders as he went to the fridge for milk. His thick sausage fingers fumbled to open the little cap.

"If they want you to do it so badly you'll have to go. And you'll do this project. You can keep them all off my back, and yourself out of more trouble."

Sykes headed to his den in the lounge, more tea slopping from the mug as he thumped across the hall. Trevor hoisted his rucksack over his shoulder and retreated upstairs, keeping his face neutral. But when he got to his bedroom a huge smile erupted. He dumped his bag on the floor and flopped on the bed, making Mrs Bingo-Wings jump from her afternoon nap. Trevor tickled her chin with one hand and put the other behind his head, watching her stretch and stare at him as if she was waiting for something. He leaned so close to her ear it tickled his lips when she twitched it.

"I only did it, Mrs B. I had a plan, and I made it work. I'm going back!"

9

Trevor's hands slid on the rubber handlebars as he turned the corner and wobbled his way across the centre's gravel drive. Late afternoon sun bore down like he was under a magnifying glass, and he felt twice his normal size. The light breeze that buffeted him on the way hadn't helped. It was warmer by the day... rain was something that used to happen. He lurched his way to the main entrance, and got off with a sigh of relief, fiddling with the chain and lock Miss Campbell had given him.

"Look after it for me, Trevor, won't you? I'm hoping to be back on it by Christmas!"

Trevor smiled as he stood up and stretched, giving his legs a chance to get over the pedalling. Things could totally go his way, if he stuck his neck out. Not everyone was against him. Like Mr Mac, a total legend. He'd come through, and fast. It was only three days since Trevor had first walked through this gate and met Midge.

School day and sun's heat forgotten, he jogged down the path through the meadow, his rucksack banging against his back. Midge's family should be back now! Would he understand them too? Plus he could find out more about being a spellbo—

"Woo-hoo! Woo-hoo!"

Trevor skidded to a stop just inside the centre as the hoots rang out. They sounded different, like before now his ears had been full of static or something, and they were tuning in to a new soundwave frequency, like finding a radio station. He began to concentrate, hard.

"Oo-hoo! Can I join in?"

A tingle of excitement spread across Trevor's body. That wasn't Midge. And he hadn't heard anyone else – yet. He trembled. Was this it? He shut out everything and just zoned in on the voices.

"No, Wol. Shut up. Samson, logic please. I realise common sense isn't a strong point amongst redtails, but this isn't rocket science!"

"Well, I see what you're saying, sir, I do. It's egg science, isn't it? But I can't think straight. How do *you* manage to think so clearly?"

Trevor turned in the direction of the voices, hardly daring to breathe. One had to be Samson, the redtail hawk he'd seen last week, but the other, harsher voice...

"Think, Samson? I don't think, I *know*! And I'll always know better than you. Just expect I'm going to know best because I *am* the best. This is elementary. As is the answer to your stupid question. You don't get a bird without an egg."

"I do understand your superiority, sir, you're largest, cleverest and most dangerousest. But how do you get an egg without a bird? You see the dilemma?"

Trevor stifled a gasp as he realised where the other voice was coming from.

"Samson! You're not paying attention. These are the facts. I. Am. Right. I am always right, and I will always be right because I am the most powerful and important raptor here." The voice rose to a shout. "So enough! Silence, and know your place in the pecking order!"

Trevor turned as another voice called across the grass, deep and drawling.

"Come on, man! Can't you do this another time? We should be talking about those dudes who took the falcons. And the boy. Or are you going to let the wild ones do all the work? What does this crazy egg thing matter anyway?"

"Of course it matters!" the voice rang out again. "Where would you be if natural leaders like myself didn't consider the big issues? Keep out of this, Austin, and keep out of the falcon business too. We don't need a human interfering. Or the wild ones, sticking their beaks in. And leave off with your stupid accents, faker. Your kind might come from Argentina but we all know you hatched in Scunthorpe."

Trevor pressed both hands to his mouth as the voice called back.

"Well, that's just groovy. Insults as usual. You can't knock me, man. I just hope not all eagles have the same funky manners as you. You'd better hope Garnell feels the same way about you keeping him out of this. Plus everybird knows you can't have an egg without a chicken, you dumbo."

Trevor walked on along the mews path and held his breath as the eagle came into view. Eyes flashing and stiff gold-tipped feathers sticking up on top of his head, the bird looked like he was swelling, about to pop. He threw his head back and with huge wings outstretched, he was oblivious to Trevor.

"How dare you! Have respect, you… you minion! I am king of the bird world, the ultimate power! Never speak to me again! If I get anywhere near you I'll rip your feathers out one by one and crush you with just the edge of my talon! My word is law! I'm telling you it was the egg that came first. In fact, it was a golden eagle egg, and that's the end of it. So shut it! I am the pinnacle of the food chain and I will NOT be challenged!"

The eagle folded his wings in tight to his body and stood tall on his perch, feather hackles up and fierce amber light flashing in his eyes as he lowered his head and stared straight at Trevor. Trevor couldn't move. The eagle snapped his beak and turned one-eighty on his perch to face the back wall of the mews. Trevor tried and failed to breathe evenly as he stared at his back. Why was the eagle so against him? He opened his mouth and got as far as breathing in before his hands went clammy, his tummy clenched hard and his nerve failed. All he managed to get out of his mouth was a strangled 'errr'.

A gate clicked and squeaked open, and Trevor jumped. He turned round. Lennox walked in from the falconers' area with a stack of water baths piled high in his arms. He grinned.

"Alright there, Trev? Sore throat?" He raised his voice. "Elise! Trev's here."

There was an answering shout from the cleaning shed. Lennox looked at Trevor and raised his eyebrows.

"She was well pleased with you from Sunday. Said you've got passion. That counts for a lot."

Trevor's face went warm as he pushed the eagle to the back of his mind. She was pleased with him. He couldn't remember that happening, not since Mum had gone. Maybe Lennox wasn't so bad. He returned his fist bump and smiled at Elise as she strode through the gateway. Rash was right behind her, looking about as cheerful as he had three days ago when Lennox had a pop at him.

"Hey, Trevor," said Elise. "You made it! Just as well. We've still got loads to do. Another aviary to disinfect and scrub and three bird travelling boxes to clean out."

Elise paused, her eyes shining.

"Oh, and a young peregrine falcon to train, but I guess you're not so bothered about that!"

Trevor couldn't control himself. Train Midge? Really? A huge, true smile spread across his face like a cloud drifting away from the sun.

Elise laughed.

"It's official. The wildlife liaison officer confirmed it yesterday. We're sticking to the plan: train him to hunt and then release him back into the wild as soon as he's able to survive on his own. I thought you'd like to help. After all, you're not just here to clean."

Rash snorted and Lennox glared at him. "Not again, bruv. It's only fair. Trev found him, after all."

"And you're going to train the merlin, so you've got nothing to complain about," said Elise. "Can you get on and finish up with filling those water baths? It's hotter than ever. Me and Trevor can do the redtail aviary."

Lennox nodded. "Righto. Then I can sort the black kites' aviary if you like?" He put his hand in his pocket and jangled it. "Remembered my keys from the car today."

"Yes – fab," said Elise. "Thanks, guys."

As Lennox and Rash walked away, Trevor grabbed his pad and pen and scribbled fast.

Who's training the other peregrines?

Elise looked surprised. "We haven't got any other peregrines. Do you mean the lanner falcons? They look the same."

Trevor wrote again.

No, the others, the ones you've got back. From the thieves.

"Oh," said Elise. "Sorry, I get you now. They didn't have them, Trevor. Adam called the police and asked them to check. Hope you don't mind, but I told Adam it was my idea, to make sure he'd take it seriously. They sent officers over, but there were no birds. Even the old aviaries they had are gone, all taken down."

She smiled at Trevor. "Don't be down about it, it was

worth a try. It's one of those things, as my gran says. Your mate must have been showing off. We reckon the wire was just gone. It was old and damaged, easy to bend... and a fox would find that kind of weakness. Honestly, they're too clever, they can be really strong when they need to."

Trevor stared at her as his heart sank and his tummy took its second lurch of the afternoon. What could he say? There was no way she'd believe him... "Oh yes, well, I was chatting to the peregrine and he saw the two men with their big ears." It wasn't going to happen in a million years. His first mission as a spellboda, and he was failing. He wrote quickly.

Can I just go and see the peregrine?

Elise shook her head.

"Not yet, no. We have to finish the cleaning first, that's our rule. Get the duffer jobs out of the way, then we train birds and have fun."

With gritted teeth, Trevor flew through the cleaning, working alongside Elise, raking, poo-scooping and scrubbing. Elise chatted on about birds, telling him funny stories about things going wrong in flying demonstrations. It would have been fun if he wasn't so desperate. The sooner they were done, the sooner he could get to Midge. As they got to the last travelling box, he scrubbed and rinsed at top speed.

"Trevor, where's the fire?" Elise laughed, as she rinsed out the box and stacked it beside the others against the wall.

Trevor fished in his rucksack for his pen, but Elise put her hand on his arm.

"I know what you're going to say. Slow down. Let's just get a drink and cool off for five minutes, then we'll get to the peregrine. It's only half four, we've got plenty of time."

Trevor was a coiled spring. He looked away, hiding the look on his boiling face, and with pad and pen still in his hand, he followed Elise.

The demonstration birds were on their perches on the grass display area, being admired by the last visitors of the day. Lennox was walking across with the golden eagle on his gloved hand. The bird looked at Trevor and his hackle feathers rose again. What was his problem? Lennox perched the eagle right in the middle of the lawn, with the smaller birds set out around him like courtiers in a palace, then he set off towards the kites' aviary. The eagle threw back his head and called, and Trevor stiffened. But it was just a call. No words. Had he tuned out on the frequency again?

"That's weird," he murmured.

Elise stopped and turned.

"What did you say?"

Trevor bit his lip and looked down, cursing himself. He scribbled a note.

I didn't. It was a visitor.

He pointed at a nearby family who were leaning over the aviary barrier, watching Samson and Delilah nest-building.

Elise's eyes narrowed, then she smiled. "Come on. I've got some bottles of water in the fridge." She walked on to

75

the office door, and knocked. Adam's deep voice travelled through the open window.

"Come on in."

"Everything's done," said Elise as she grabbed a couple of bottles from the fridge and threw one over to Trevor as he stood by the door. He caught it, with a fumble. She looked at Adam.

"You want one?"

Adam was sitting at his desk, surrounded by papers that he was arranging into a neat pile. He nodded.

"I'll take one on my way out. Got to meet the county show people about a demo they want next month. You finish up today, OK? I won't be back in time. And while I think about it, make sure you lock this door if you're the last one out. It was open this morning."

Elise nodded and took a huge swig from her bottle.

"Whoops. OK, sorry. I won't do it again."

Trevor couldn't help staring. Adam fascinated him. He looked double hard, flew incredible birds and his job was so cool. Even his secret addiction to *Twilight* was fun, quirky. Why couldn't his dad be less beardy and more Adam-y? Adam glanced over as he got up, grabbing his mobile and car keys from the desk.

"You doing alright then, lad?"

"He's doing good," said Elise. "Working hard and learning fast."

"Well done." Adam nodded. "Keep it up."

Trevor realised too late his mouth was opening and closing like a goldfish as he watched Adam put on his sunglasses and walk out of the office.

Elise laughed.

"You'd better have that drink now, Trevor. Your tonsils are looking a bit dry from here!"

Trevor took a gulp from his bottle as Elise poured water on her hands and rubbed her face.

"That's better. Come on then, I thought you couldn't wait," she teased. "It's peregrine time! Manning, here we come!" She threw her empty bottle in the bin and burped.

"Oops, sorry. Not much of a lady!"

Trevor tried not to laugh as he looked down and wrote. It was getting harder to keep control of emotions here, and keep things hidden. Happiness was in danger of squeezing through.

Manning? That's handling a bird, right?

Elise looked pleased. "Exactly! The first stage of training, the start of the relationship between bird and falconer. It's getting the bird to accept you, and for you to work together as a team."

The bird learns to sit on your glove. The more time you spend with it, the more the bond grows.

"Brilliant, yes," said Elise. "You've been reading up on it..."

Trevor nodded as she carried on.

"...you put some food on the glove: meat, between your fingers and thumb. When the bird stops staring at you, bows its head and eats, then the bond is made."

Trevor added one word to his pad.

Trust

"Trust." Elise looked at Trevor. "One of the most precious things in the world."

She picked up Adam's fancy designer jacket from the back of his chair.

"Just in case he freaks and we need to cast him again. Don't tell Adam! Come on then, expert, let's go for it!"

10

Elise grabbed a couple of gloves, a falcon hood and put a plastic food pouch full of small pieces of raw chicken and rat into her green canvas falconry bag.

"He's still in the hospital," she said. "We'll move him after training today. I wanted to take it slow before putting him in the mews. Lennox's sorting a spot for him by Tiberius, the golden eagle."

Wow. Poor Midge. Having the eagle as a neighbour was going to be one big party.

"We've sorted his equipment so he's ready," Elise continued, as they walked down the path.

Trevor nodded, understanding. All the info from his book was really handy. Outside the hospital shed Elise paused and looked at him.

"Don't expect too much, OK? I'd love you to be involved, but you're going to have to watch me do a lot of this. I'll let you hold him on the glove if it goes well, but you're going to need a lot more experience before you can handle a falcon. They're really temperamental."

Trevor's heart dropped like a stone. How could he talk to Midge if she was always in the way?

He followed Elise into the hospital, shut the door and turned with a start. Midge had changed already. More of his flight feathers had grown down, and his eyes looked different, more clued-up... older altogether. Midge stared straight back at him, a statue on his perch in the middle of the room. He was surrounded by sheets of newspaper spread out over the floor, which he'd littered with small, neat droppings.

"Hi, little guy." Elise spoke softly, as she dropped the jacket by the wall. "Trevor, I'm going take his jesses – you know, the leather straps on his leg – in my free hand when I get close to him, then I can encourage him to step onto my glove. Stay still, so he doesn't get spooked."

Trevor risked a small wave in Midge's direction while Elise was looking the other way. She bent down and crept towards Midge, who lowered his head and let out a series of high-pitched piercing calls. Elise crouched down and undid his leash.

"It's OK, shh, no need to worry, kiddo."

Trevor trembled with a thrill of hope. It was happening again. Elise didn't have a clue. He focused as Midge shouted rapid instructions.

"She thinks she's doing this and not you? That's not happening. I need you, Trevor. There's more going on and you need to know. Put that other glove on, now, while she's turned away from you. I'm going to let her pick me up. But as soon as she's undone my leash, get ready."

Shaking, Trevor slipped on the glove. Midge beat his wings rapidly even though his talons were still gripping the perch. Elise gently coaxed him onto her glove and began to straighten up, the leash attached to the jesses now untied and in her left hand.

"Quick!" called Midge as they turned towards Trevor. "Put your arm up now. Left, not right, the one with the glove on! Then don't move!"

What happened next was like slow motion... Elise standing with the falcon perched on her glove, Midge going mental and managing to avoid Elise's frantic grasping as he shrieked, jumped, beat his wings wildly and launched himself. Then he was airborne, flying across the room, and it was Elise's turn to shriek.

"Get the jacket!"

But a handful of wing-beats later and Midge was sitting on the glove at the end of Trevor's outstretched arm, looking as calm as a canary. Trevor's mouth was hanging open, and Elise's face had turned bright red.

"Trevor, I am so sorry," she stammered. "How awful of me. I've put you and the bird at risk. Thank goodness you had the sense to pick up a glove. Stay still. I'm not going to talk, it might help to make him calm. I'll just come to you, really, really slowly."

Midge called again, less loud now. "Nice one, Trevor. Keep your arm up. I'm going to make a fuss but I won't leave you. And I won't hurt you, you know that."

Trevor knew it. Beyond any doubt – and through the

shock and surprise it was a truth so strong he couldn't remember feeling anything like it before. A feeling of purpose washed over him again, and for a strange moment all he could think of was his mum. An image of her smiling face rose up out of nowhere. What would she look like now? Would he still recognise her? What would she say if she saw all this? She filled his head, and an echo of her voice rang out, like she was there, as a memory flooded in. "Trevor, trust yourself, this is what you were meant to do. Live life in colour!"

He looked away as his eyes prickled with a sudden heat of tears. This was crazy. But he trusted it. He trusted Midge. The falcon called again.

"Keep it together, Trevor. You've got this. We'll show her you can train me. Then we can talk."

Trevor blinked hard as Elise drew closer. The pressure of Midge's feet on his hand through the suede of the glove was an incredible feeling, knowing he trusted Trevor to hold him steady as his talons gripped harder and harder. As Elise lifted her hand towards them, Midge made a huge racket, beating his wings and shrieking. She backed off, looking confused. Midge stopped and went back to sitting peacefully on Trevor's glove. Elise tried again, and again, but got the same result every time. Finally, she stared at them both from a distance and shook her head.

"I don't know what to say. Honestly. I don't know what to do. Nothing like this has happened to me before."

Trevor felt a bit sorry for her. Elise frowned and rubbed her forehead.

"This sounds absolutely potty, but it's like he wants you

to handle him. It makes no sense, but I shouldn't try to force him to trust me when clearly he doesn't want to. Are you up for giving it a go? I'll make sure we're really careful."

With a massive effort, Trevor held back the delight that wanted to spill out over his face, and forced a calm, sensible expression. But as he nodded, he couldn't help the smile.

Midge's plan had worked.

11

With the leash looped and knotted through Trevor's glove, and jesses tucked under his thumb, Midge looked chilled as they walked. The falcon had refused to wear the leather hood that Elise wanted Trevor to slide over his head, so after a few goes she'd given up on that too. Elise stuck close beside them, with a steady flow of instructions as they walked to the flying arena. Trevor kept glancing and nodding at what he hoped were the right moments, but he wasn't really listening. Midge was making soft calls and noises with every step.

"Stay cool, OK, I know what I'm doing. I've seen it. I'll flap my wings and maybe bate a bit – like I'm trying to fly off. But don't stress, I'm not going anywhere, I just want this to look convincing."

Trevor picked his way across the grass with care, scared to blink in case he opened his eyes and found this wasn't really happening.

Midge gripped harder on the glove with his talons again. "Yes, be careful! After all it's taken to get this far, it's going to be harsh if you fall over and squash me!"

Trevor snorted with laughter and tried to cover it up with a cough.

"You OK, Trevor?" said Elise, shooting him a look. "Don't get poorly on me! Go and sit in the arena. It's all about him getting used to you now."

Trevor walked through the open gate and into the large field that was the birds' exercise ground and demonstration arena. He headed for the old wooden bench nestled in shade under the boughs of a spreading oak tree. It was an oasis in a desert. The sun beat down, relentless as a spotlight as he crossed the grass. He sat down carefully, keeping his arm steady for Midge, and sighed with relief as the cooler air settled around him. He rested his arm on his leg, not taking his eyes off the falcon. Midge perched placidly on the glove and busied himself with nibbling a loose scale away from a talon. Elise hovered a few steps away.

"Alright? You're doing really well."

Trevor smiled and nodded.

"Well, he can't go anywhere, that knot won't give," said Elise. "Doesn't look like he wants to anyway." She looked over her shoulder. "I really should pop and see how Lennox and Rash are doing, OK? Won't be long."

She reached into her falconry bag and pulled out a black tin whistle, dangling on the end of a thin green rope. "Just stay there, and if anything, absolutely anything at all goes wrong, or you need me, blow this. I'll be back like before you've finished blowing. You good with that?"

Trevor nodded again as she moved towards the bench and slowly put the whistle on the seat beside him.

"Just sit there," she repeated, as she began to walk. "I wouldn't go if I didn't think you could do this. Man him up, get him used to you."

She paused at the entrance and closed the gate.

"In case visitors get too close!" she called. "Blow that whistle, OK? And don't worry if he keeps on calling, that's normal too."

Trevor grinned. What if she knew? A mix of relief and elation filled him as she walked away. He was handling a peregrine falcon. 'Best day' was the definition of spending time here. Being close to Midge was enough, but to feel his feet through the glove, stare down at him; his intricately marked chest, every tiny detail of his plumage, his hooked silvery beak and huge dark eyes. All epic, but add in his gift, and it went way beyond that. Midge raised his head and looked at him.

"You've heard then?"

Trevor cleared his throat. It was getting easier, but he still needed to make an effort to get started, like vocal jump leads.

"About your family? I'm really sorry, Midge. I don't understand why they weren't there, why the police didn't find them."

"The balds have hidden them somewhere," said Midge. "Stupid we didn't think of it."

"I reckon you're right," said Trevor. He sighed. "Now they know they're suspects, so they'll be even more careful. Do you think they know you're still here?"

"Maybe. It doesn't help you saying that."

"Sorry," said Trevor. "But what are we going to do? I can't tell Elise how I know, she'll think I'm mental."

Midge didn't reply. Trevor sighed again.

"I feel really bad. I wish I could think of a plan…"

Dead ends loomed at every turn. Humans couldn't help, birds wouldn't help, thanks to Tiberius. He stared across the arena, following Midge's tilted head. The blunt tips of newly mown grass smouldered from green to golden brown. Heat had arrived so early. A haze shimmered across the valley that opened out before them, spreading to the distant peaks. Remote houses and cars dotted across the landscape basked, blurred and shifted in the glow of sunlight. Trevor cursed his useless brain, wishing there was something he could come up with. There was no way they'd find the other falcons now.

"The only thing we can do now is get me flying," Midge said at last. "Quickly. At least when I'm free I can look for them, and you can help me. And then, if they do know I'm here, they can't steal me."

"I suppose," said Trevor. He hadn't thought about what would happen when Midge was free. At least Midge was thinking they'd still see each other. His spirits lifted a little.

"You keep listening out for anything strange," Midge continued. "Stay on it."

"Definitely." Trevor racked his brains. There had to be something more. A wild thought jumped into his head.

"I know!" he exclaimed.

Midge started, and flapped his wings.

"Don't – you made me jump! You know what?"

"I could steal you myself! I could wrap you up in my jacket when no-one's looking."

Midge pondered.

"Nice idea, and if I'm ever going to be stolen I'd want it to be by a spellboda, especially you. But if you did, wouldn't someone notice? What would happen?"

Trevor's enthusiasm shrank faster than a popped balloon. He groaned. "I didn't think about Sykes. He'd ruin everything."

"Your dad," said Midge. "Honestly, is he that awful?"

"Worse," said Trevor. "Especially on his film night."

Midge tilted his head.

"What do you mean?"

Trevor looked down as he ground the heels of his trainers into the grass.

"Most weekends he watches a stupid kids' film. Says stupid things. Then every time he sees me he shouts at me and tells me I'm useless."

"Is it just you?" asked Midge. "Have you got brothers or sisters?"

"Nope," said Trevor, "just us. Lucky me." He pressed his lips together.

Midge was quiet for a moment, looking out again over the valley.

"Can you hear what he's saying? When he's watching this film thing?"

Trevor shook his head.

"Not a lot. Sounds like a mixture of 'Why' and 'Please'. But I never get too close. Once he threw something when he saw me. So now I leg it to my room and shut the door."

"Right." Midge ran his beak through his feathers, teasing out some fluff. "I get why. But have you talked to your dad about it, why he's like it?"

"Call him Sykes, he's stopped being my dad now," said Trevor. "And no. And I won't. I'd rather stay as far away from him as I can."

He stopped, trying to control bubbling feelings. "Sometimes it sounds like he's crying. I hope he is."

"Is he unhappy then?" said Midge. "Or angry? Or what? I don't get it. You should try to talk to him. My mum said we should always get it sorted when me and my family had rows, like over food and stuff. And can you stop clenching your fist? You're trapping my talon."

"Sorry," said Trevor, relaxing his fingers. "But that's not going to change anything. I'm not dodging another missile. No way. Anyway, I'd rather talk about you than him."

There was no answer. Trevor looked at Midge. "What you doing? Why do you tilt and go up and down like that?"

"It makes me see even better if I move my head. Look." Midge's head was bobbing as he scanned the valley. He shifted his grip on the glove. "See that?"

"What?"

"Over by the copse. It's Roger."

Trevor strained to look in the same direction, where a small family of pine trees stood proud in a clump of green halfway across the valley.

"You said my eyesight could get better, but I don't think it is. And who the hell is Roger?" A niggle of jealousy jarred. "Have you already got another human friend?"

Midge laughed. "No, not human. That's Roger Ginger – he's my fox."

"What? What do you mean, *your* fox?" Trevor concentrated, really hard, and suddenly he was sure he saw a flash of red between the trees.

"He hangs around the centre," said Midge. "Knows quite a few of the birds. But he likes me best."

"But… wouldn't he eat all of you?" said Trevor. "You make it sound like you're mates!"

"We are, I suppose," Midge replied. "He doesn't bother with us. There's loads of easy rabbits and rats around, they're more tasty for him. And – for a fox – he's totally likeable. He's getting on a bit. And I've never seen him hanging out with another fox. I reckon he likes the company. We had a really long chat yesterday. "

"How did you manage that?" asked Trevor, still niggled. "I mean, you've been shut up in the hospital."

"He came and sat outside the door," said Midge. "The wall's thin, so we talked through it. He says he likes falcons, that we're sharper than other birds."

Midge raised himself up and shouted across the field.

"Roger! Rog! You OK? This is him. Trevor."

Roger's red and white body was unmistakable now, as he emerged from the cover of bushes. A series of clipped, husky barks drifted over the valley. Midge bobbed his head again.

"He's saying it will be a pleasure to meet you, but apologises that he's 'indisposed at the moment'. That means he's going off hunting."

Midge looked at Trevor. "Could you hear him?"

Trevor shook his head, frustrated. "Not a word. But I did hear some of the birds this morning." He looked down. "So I know they don't want to talk to me."

Midge spread his wings out. "It's harsh. But not all their fault."

"Yep," said Trevor. "Anyway, it's stopped again and now I can't hear them, so whatever. But I don't get it."

"Same," said Midge. "I'll ask Roger later, he knows loads about your sort. I bet he'll help you with the others. He'll be a good friend to you too."

Trevor grinned suddenly.

"I'm sitting on a bench in a field, talking to a bird about getting info from a fox. Like it's the most normal thing in the world."

He reached over and picked up the whistle, letting the cord play through his fingers.

"This is all barmy, right? Are you seriously telling me neither you or the fox are freaked out about you and me talking?"

Midge tilted his head, his stare direct. "Nope. Trevor, you need to get this. You're looking at things as a human, but that's not going to help you now. You're stepping out of your world and into mine. We see much more than your lot do. And not just with our eyes. Loads more. Mum said once everyone was like you. But you closed your minds to magic years ago. Now, only a few can cross over. You, and ones like you, are all that's left."

"It would be good to meet someone like me," said Trevor.

"Totally," said Midge. "But it's rare. Getting close to us will hopefully help you find one. Stories are passed down through our families about spellbodas and gifts, so somebird somewhere will be able to help."

Midge shook his tail feathers with a buzz.

"Anyway, enough about you. Put the whistle down and concentrate. I need to fly as soon as, and you need to help."

"Agreed," said Trevor, as he shoved the whistle back on the bench. "Look, why are you so savvy all of a sudden? You're different to Sunday. You were younger. And you've got more feathers now, less fluff."

Midge preened his flight feathers, running his beak down them in tiny, chattering movements as if Trevor had reminded him how new they were.

"We grow really fast. In my world, we're full grown and out flying by my age. We have to be," he said, in between feathers.

"I did read that. It's crazy quick," said Trevor.

"We learn fast, as soon as we hatch, pretty much, and grow up fast too," said Midge. "The sooner we can fly and hunt, the more chance we have of staying alive. It's normal for us, but for you it would be like going from a baby to your age in a few days."

Trevor scratched his nose with his free hand. "I get it. It's like you're on fast forward or something."

"Exactly. My brain works quicker, so I'll be ready to fly soon. So you need to help me," Midge said pointedly.

"Sorry." Trevor grinned. "Noted."

He sat up straight.

"Hey! What about this? Why don't I have a look round the office when I can? For the thieves' address or anything about them, in case it's in bird records... or something?

They must keep files of that kind of stuff. They have to." A memory from his first day clicked into place. "Yes! Elise said they went to pick them up, so it must be written down somewhere! If I find their address I could cycle round and have a look."

"OK…" said Midge, as he stretched his wings. "Actually that could work! You could watch the house. You might see them!"

"Yes! They won't be suspicious of a lad hanging round on a bike," said Trevor. "This is great. I need to do something, so I feel—"

He stopped and looked down as Midge's feet gripped the glove, hard.

"Shh."

Elise appeared round the corner of the cleaning shed, waving.

"You've done amazing!" she called as she opened the gate. "He looks so relaxed. Well done."

As she got closer she slipped her hand into her falconry bag and rummaged inside, then looked up and smiled at Trevor.

"Right then, falconer. Time to see if you can make that bond."

12

Elise crouched a few steps away and brought something out of her bag, hidden in her hand. She glanced at Trevor as she edged closer, then looked at the grass to check her footing.

"It's a rat," she whispered. "I'm off the rule book again with this. He should be wearing a hood, it would keep him calm and make it easier to get the food into the glove. But I want him to see me put it there. It might help him trust me too."

Midge watched her, unmoving, his dark eyes sparkling. Trevor found he couldn't control himself quite so well. His free hand shook, and he held his breath so long he was positive he was turning blue.

Elise was in touching distance now. Leaning beside Trevor, against the bench, she placed the meat on his glove, squeezing it between Trevor's first finger and thumb.

"Keep it there, nice and secure. Game on." Elise sat next

to Trevor. "So far so good. Now we wait. When he trusts, he'll lower his head."

She smiled as Trevor's breath came out in a rush, hissing through his teeth.

"Relax. Sometimes it takes days. In fact this is way too soon. He'll be hungry, but…"

She stopped as Midge looked down at the meat.

"I'll shut up. No distractions."

Elise got her phone out of her pocket. Midge looked up. Then back to the meat. And up again. Trevor willed him to eat. Minutes crawled by. What was he waiting for?

The three of them were silent, Elise scrolling through messages with her thumb, as sounds drifted by. Lennox's voice in the main centre, a tractor chugging a few fields away, wind through leaves as the sun sank lower in the sky. Trevor tried to ignore how tight his chest was. Focus on animal noises instead. There was birdsong in the hedgerow, a dog barking in the distance. Concentrate. Could he control it, and tune in? A dark shape moved in a tree by the arena. A crow, hopping from branch to branch, his glistening blue-black wings spread out, balancing on one foot, then another. He called… short, rasping cries. Trevor strained to see. Was the crow hurt? No, but was that something in his foot? Yes, it looked like a clump of grass and soil. A sudden 'chup' from Midge made Trevor jump.

"Crispin! That's mean!"

The crow called again, harsh and guttural. Trevor closed his eyes, determined. Come on, do it, focus. Midge shifted position on the glove.

"Seriously? Don't you have a conscience?"

Between the deep squawks and 'carks' in reply, words began to filter through. Trevor trembled. It sounded muffled, as though the crow was shouting with his mouth full.

"...keepers... tough. Her fault... lump it! ...should be more careful!"

Trevor opened his eyes and stared at Midge in delight. Not a clue what was going on, but he could hear and it was epic. The crow took off with a clumsy crashing of wings through branches, and headed over the valley, still yelling. He crash-landed at the top of one of the pine trees in the copse, and an angry-sounding bark echoed across the valley. Midge called again.

"Stupid, idiot bird."

Elise sighed.

"You're excited, I know, but I've tried to rush this. It's getting late. We need to stop. We can try again tomorrow."

She stood up and brushed her jeans, where some of the yellow-green catkin clusters of blossom from the oak tree had fallen. She looked at Trevor.

"This part is the biggest step forward, so don't be disappointed. As soon as he feeds his flying training starts, then it goes much faster. Come on, we'll take him..."

Midge suddenly lowered his head, opened his beak and ripped off a morsel of the raw meat from between Trevor's gloved fingers. He looked up at Elise, his tongue popping in and out of his beak as he ate the shred of food.

Elise's mouth opened but nothing came out. Trevor couldn't stop himself from gasping, and inhaled a mouthful of the pungent smell of raw rat wafting up from his glove.

They stared at Midge. The falcon clicked his beak as he ate. He kept his head down, focused on the food. He tore off strip after strip, more efficient than any knife, as he gripped the meat, steadying it under his talons.

Time stood still. Midge dealt with every bone, every bit of fluff, every part of the rat in a methodical, compelling way, until there was nothing left. Then he looked up, tiny shards of red meat dotted over his beak. Trevor held his breath all over again. Midge lowered his head and slowly rubbed his beak over the glove until the morsels were transferred from his beak to the leather. Then he gently hoovered up the bits, eating with precise, rapid nibbles.

Trevor and Elise beamed at each other.

"Oh my days... just... Trevor!" Elise could barely get the words out. "He cleaned his beak too! You've bonded!" She squeezed the arm of the bench with both hands. "I never get tired of this, no matter how many birds I train. Brilliant!"

Her face still aglow, she adjusted her bag and picked up the whistle.

"OK, he needs to rest on his new perch. Can you get here after school tomorrow, Trevor? Proper training starts!"

Trevor nodded so vigorously Midge tightened his talons on the glove.

"Take it easy, spellboda! You'll make me throw up all the rat!"

Midge looked tiny next door to the golden eagle. Tiberius kept his back turned, ignoring Trevor and Elise as they walked past his space. Midge hopped from glove to perch, his chest bulging with stored food. Trevor thought of his book. The store place was called a crop, like a hamster's cheeks, but further down the body. Midge would push it all down to his tummy next. The falcon's droopy eyelids reminded him of old Christmas dinners, when Dad dropped off to sleep after stuffing his face with food. Mum used to roll her eyes, then smile and ask him to help load the dishwasher. It felt so far off, like a dream of someone else's life. He shook his head. Get a grip. Stick to the plan, get back tomorrow and start investigating. He fished his notepad out of his pocket.

I'll come straight from school tomorrow, about 3.45 if I pedal quick. Is that OK?

Elise tilted the pad towards her.

"Don't bust a gut, Trevor, the afternoon will be busy. There's a group visit in. I'll wait for you. I promise."

Trevor looked at her, and returned her smile.

I know. I trust you ☺

13

Trevor ran down the path by the mews, his notepad ready. He glanced at his watch; he'd got the journey time right, it was just after quarter to four. School and Sykes had been boring and samey, but that was another world away. He skidded to a halt as he reached Midge's mews space, where the falcon was sitting on his perch. There was no-one around. Trevor grinned.

"You OK?"

Midge raised a foot off his perch and let it hang while he stretched a wing.

"Yep. Happy to see you. Flying time! When you stop panting."

Trevor laughed.

"If I'm always cycling and running like this I'll be fit as you are. I'll find Elise."

Trevor spotted her chatting to visitors beside Wol's aviary, next door to where the peregrine family had been.

He looked at her as he headed over. Her face was alive, hands flying everywhere as she talked.

"...yes, it's been my passion for ever. They're just amazing creatures. I can't remember ever not wanting to work with birds, I used to drive my family mad. They weren't surprised when I told them I'd be moving hundreds of miles to work here."

Trevor dawdled a short distance away, waiting for her to finish. At last she looked and waved. She walked over, but her hand was still up in the air in front of her as concern clouded her face.

Trevor raised his eyebrows.

"My ring!" said Elise, frowning as she lowered her hand. Her fingers were bare.

"It was a present from my gran..."

Trevor looked sympathetic, but she was miles away, thinking. Her face brightened.

"Oh yes – we washed those travelling boxes yesterday, I put it in the cleaning shed. Thank goodness! I'll grab it after the demo."

Trevor showed her his pad.

Demo?

"We do a late one, four o'clock on some group visit days," said Elise. "It keeps the golden oldies here for afternoon tea."

She looped some of the hair that had escaped her ponytail behind her ears.

"Come and watch. I'm doing it, though, Adam's day off today. His are miles better than mine."

Thinking fast, Trevor scribbled again.

I'll get your ring first, if you like?

"That's mega kind of you, Trevor, thanks," said Elise with a smile. "It's gold, with a ruby stone. On top of the cupboard where we keep the disinfectant. You're a star."

She called across the lawn. "Lennox!"

An answering shout came from one of the aviaries further down the row.

"You've got the caracara, right?" Elise checked her watch. "You'd better bring him now so we can start. It's nearly four. Make sure Rash brings Skye."

She turned back to Trevor.

"You're so red, you must be boiling. Get some water. I've got to hood the lanner falcon and get ready. See you after – for training Midge!"

Trevor watched as they headed out to the arena, and the last visitors melted away from the lawn like a mirage as they joined the others, herding themselves round to go down the path on the other side of the mews and watch the demonstration. Within a minute, the whole place was empty.

Trevor smiled. Clearance to get water. If there was an ideal moment to snoop, this was it.

But first the ring. He headed to the cleaning shed, pushed the door open and paused as the cloud of stale, stagnant heat trapped in the room broke over him. Taking a deep breath over his shoulder he walked in. He reached on top of the cupboard to pick up the ring but there was nothing there. His heart sank. He checked in the cupboard, around the cupboard, on the floor and even under buckets, but still no sign. No glint of red or gold anywhere. Trevor frowned. No-one came here except for falconers. Surely no-one, not even Lennox, would have taken it?

Elise's voice, amplified through the PA system, echoed around him.

"Good afternoon, ladies and gentlemen, boys and girls, and welcome to Flights of Fancy. We're going to fly some amazing birds of prey this afternoon, and tell you all about how we can help them in the wild..."

That gave him about half an hour to check the office. He couldn't waste any more time.

14

Trevor closed the door and looked around. Best to get water first, so he looked like he was on the level. He grabbed a bottle from the fridge and felt guilty before he'd even done anything. But it didn't stop the buzz running through him. He scanned the room. The shelves against the wall were boring, full of books and files dated from years earlier. He looked at Adam's desk. That was more promising.

Papers were stacked on the left of the desk in a neat pile. After a last scan to make sure no-one was around, Trevor began to leaf through them, trying to squash the voice in his head whispering that he was a stalker. All he could find were requests from schools and fairs, appeals for donations, and bookings for Adam to travel to events and give demonstrations. Trevor bit his lip as he bent down and looked below the desk, small beads of sweat tickling his forehead. He tried the top drawer of the three running down the left-hand side. It was littered with a snarl of elastic bands in a ball peppered with paper clips, some pens, a hole punch and a stapler. The second drawer was harder to open, but yielded after a struggle. Trevor looked inside and couldn't stop himself.

"Yes! Epic!"

The drawer was choked by a thick file that had 'Bird Records' scrawled across the front. Trevor wrestled the file out and sat on the floor. He flicked it open and ran his finger slowly down the dividers, all labelled. Buzzard, Caracara, European Eagle Owl, Golden Eagle, Harris Hawk. Trevor added organised to his list of Adam's attributes. He flicked the dividers over to reach 'P', sweat prickling his neck now too. There was an official-looking certificate showing registration of a male 'falco peregrinus' and a letter from Harry Neaves, Wildlife Liaison Officer. With shaking hands, Trevor unclipped it from the file.

'Dear Mr Shotlander,

    I write to confirm that Flights of Fancy is the approved rehabilitation point for the peregrine falcons recovered from criminal activity...

    ...to be kept until their release date, as approved by myself.'

That was it? No mention of the thieves' addresses? Choked, Trevor put the letter back and double checked the certificate. He downed a huge swig of water and sighed.

A loud ring came from nowhere, and Trevor jumped. Catching his breath, he curled up behind the desk. At the second ring his brain caught up. Of course, stupid, a phone.

One of those old ones that always stayed in one place. It was on the far edge of the desk. He sat up and jammed the file back, forcing the drawer shut. What was he thinking... that the person calling was going to see him? He had to be more on it if he was going to get this spellboda stuff right. After the fifth ring there was a click, and Adam's deep voice filled the office.

"This is Adam Shotlander at Flights of Fancy. I'm not available now. Leave a message after the tone."

Trevor closed his eyes as the high-pitched beep sounded.

"Good afternoon."

This was even worse. Trevor kept his eyes shut as he rubbed his face. He was earwigging as well as stalking now.

"This is Clive. Would you please return my call? My client Yousuf and I are staying at Willersley Castle. Thank you."

The voice was precise, soft. He wasn't local. Clive sounded like he'd swallowed a plum.

Trevor stood up and checked the window. All quiet still – except in the arena. If he stood on tiptoe he could see over the fence to where the demo was chugging along. The caracara strutted round, lifting up flower pots, jumping in a dustbin to find food, then chasing Lennox and Rash for more. People were shrieking with laughter.

He still had time. Elise said they finished with a falcon. He took another drink and tried to work out why he felt super-edgy. It wasn't just the phone ringing, or even this hunting around. Oh yes – the ring. Elise was going to be really disappointed he couldn't find it.

Maybe it had got knocked off the fridge and fallen somewhere outside? Someone could have handed it in. It might be in the office. The snooping urge kicked in for real... he could do something helpful today after all. He lifted the pile of papers off the desk and shook them vigorously, hoping a tell-tale 'ding' from falling metal would follow, but there was nothing. Crouching, he checked the floor around the desk and chair, but again, no sign. Plenty of dust and feathers, but no ring.

Trevor straightened up, leaning his elbow on the edge of the desk, and rubbed his face again. There must be a place for lost property. His eyes flicked over the desk again. He hadn't tried the third drawer yet. He opened it, expecting the same resistance as the second, but it slid out smooth and easy. Trevor tutted in frustration as he shivered. Apart from a large and hopefully dead spider curled up in the corner, it was completely empty.

Trevor sank down. That was that then, he was out of options. But... he focused on the bottom row of shelves on the opposite wall. Looking at them from a lower level, there was something there. Something more than books and files, wedged under a pile of oversized reference books. He scrambled up and over, and pulled the books aside.

It was a battered and peeling metal chocolate tin, the original contents of which someone must have stuffed themselves with years ago. Either that or the chocolates were still inside, growing something furry. The lid had a white label stuck on it with 'LP' written neatly on the front. Trevor brightened. Lost Property!

He worked off the lid with throbbing fingers, wishing he'd never started biting his nails. Inside was a collection of items, none of them chocolate. A couple of batteries, sun cream, a beanie hat, a packet of weird pills that said they ate fat and a pair of dirty purple gloves. Random. The ring was nowhere to be seen, but there was a cool little hardback book on birdwatching tucked inside the hat. He opened it and found 'Lennox Palmer' scrawled across the inside front cover in black marker. Trevor shut the book with a slap, dropping it back in the box like it was hot. LP. Right. He couldn't go through someone's private stuff. That was a snoop too far.

He picked up the lid and was about to put it back when something caught his eye. A sheet of paper was taped to the underneath of the lid. Strange. Trevor frowned and swallowed back his conscience... honestly, wouldn't anyone want to have a look?

He worked around the first of three tabs of sellotape that were holding the paper to the lid. He couldn't rip the paper and leave a clue that someone had touched it. He stiffened. Elise's voice was getting louder.

"Folks, I'm so excited to show you... you're going to be amazed by how this girl flies! Now we take the hood off so she can see. No, it's not a crash helmet, it's a way to keep her calm until it's time to take off. Did you know the word 'hood-winked' comes from falconry, putting the bird in the dark? Lanners are Mediterranean birds..."

So they were flying the falcon. Time was running out.

The first tab was free. Trevor moved on to the second, wishing again for longer nails. At last it was free, and the paper curled back, showing typed words underneath. Trevor held the lid above his head and craned his neck, trying to decipher it. Some of it looked like dates, but he couldn't be sure. He sighed, put the lid back on his lap and started on tab three.

A sudden eruption of noise exploded just outside the office door. A weird kind of bark, then shrieks; high-pitched squeals he'd never heard before. Trevor jumped and the lid flew into the air, clattering across the floor in a disjointed cartwheel. He crawled and fumbled to grab it back, jabbing the floppy flaps of sellotape back into place.

The birds were calling now too, but it was all noise, no words. Trevor didn't have a hope of being able to focus and hear. His chest got tighter. Any minute now Elise would rush back to see what was going on, and he'd be caught skulking around like this. He fought for even breaths as goosebumps spiked the hair on his arms, and pressed the lid back on the tin with shaking hands. He shoved it behind the books and stumbled towards the door, grabbing the thin windowsill for support with one hand and holding his water with the other. Any second now someone would come storming in.

Then the squeals and bird calls stopped, as suddenly as they'd begun. As if nothing had happened.

Trevor could hear Elise again now. She was still flying the falcon, her voice high and excited, not even needing amplification, while the audience clapped and shouted. She couldn't have heard anything then, not through that. Trevor gritted his teeth. So who was out there? What if it was *them*, back to finish the job? But no way would anyone come creeping in to steal Midge while they were open, or make weird noises like that... would they?

Fear and indignation was an interesting mixture. Trevor swallowed. This was all on him. He had to go for it, it was what he was meant for. Filling his lungs with a gulp of warm air, he opened the office door.

15

It was deathly quiet. For a moment Trevor imagined he was a meerkat scouting for the all-clear. He popped his head round the door, every nerve tense, on full alert. Elise was ending the demo, and any minute now people would be pouring back from the arena. Trevor stepped outside, clenching his fists to stop his hands trembling. Guilty conscience, that was all. He was spooked so bad because he'd been doing something he shouldn't.

"Trevor, you look a right mess!" Midge shouted from the mews. "He's over there, near the other end of the path."

Midge was fine then. Relief swept through Trevor as he stared down the mews path.

A dog fox sat, staring back at him; his flanks heaving, russet coat glowing and with one of the finest white-tipped, heavy brushes Trevor had ever seen curled round its haunches. A fat brown rat was dangling, lifeless, from his jaws. The fox got up, then trotted away, across the meadow towards the car park.

Trevor ran over to Midge's space and looked through the wire as he put his hands against it, his fingers poking through the gaps. Midge's head was tilted to one side.

"Roger," said Midge. "Dinner. Didn't you hear us all congratulating him?"

Trevor rubbed his nose. "Ah, right. I get it. And no, couldn't hear this time. I'm still working on it."

He looked down, avoiding Midge's stare.

"I reckon you just need practice," said the falcon. "Like me and flying. Anyway, did you find anything?"

"Nothing to help," said Trevor, looking back up with a frown. "You're right, though. I've got to sort myself out before I do anything like that again. I was useless."

Midge opened his beak to reply, then stopped. Visitors were back in the centre now, chatting and wandering. Trevor turned away, despondent.

The falconers' gate clicked open behind him, and he turned. Lennox and Rash, both flushed and panting, walked through with a couple of birds.

"Alright, Trev?" said Lennox. "It was stupid hot out there today, arena's in full sun. Birds flew well, though, they were exactly the right—"

He stopped and pointed at a small brown insect crawling up Rash's shirt towards his neck. It looked like a tiny armadillo.

"Bruv," said Lennox as he reached over. "Let me help you with your chisel pig."

Rash stared as Lennox persuaded the bug to crawl on to his fingers.

"My *what*?"

"Chisel pig. Look." Lennox held his hand out as the bug rolled itself into a tight little ball of intricately fitted armour in his palm.

Rash laughed. "Mate, what are you going on about? It's a woodlouse. What the heck is a chisel pig? Have you decided to start giving animals weird new names?"

Trevor grinned as Lennox rolled the bug into a pot plant with a sigh.

"They've got loads of names. Nutbugs, flumps, crunchy bats. I just think they're all nicer than woodlouse."

Rash was almost crying.

"Crunchy bats? Bruv, you don't get out enough."

"Oh, shut up," said Lennox with a grin. "I just like knowing stuff other people don't. Makes for interesting conversations, right?"

Trevor stared at Lennox. Would that include stuff you had to tape to a lid so no-one would find it?

"Ouch!" Elise struggled through the gate, a hooded falcon on her glove and a flying lure in her other hand. The thin white cord of the lure was hanging down and tripping her up. Trevor darted over. He took the lure and wound the cord in a neat criss-cross formation over the wooden handle.

"Oh… thank you." Elise was red, her eyes shining as she looked down at the lanner falcon.

"She flew like a dream. Did you see? Amazing. Man, I'm so hot! Any luck with the ring?"

Trevor shook his head. That was two friends he'd disappointed in less than two minutes.

"Really?" Elise's smile faltered. "That's so weird. I'll have a check later. It'll turn up. Maybe it got knocked off the cupboard or something. Come on, let's get sorted and tidy up."

As they worked, Trevor pondered again about how to hear. Midge's point was good, practice had to be part of it. He'd zoned in and done it with the crow in the tree, but that was when he wasn't trying to sneak through other people's stuff. He had to focus and stay calm, no matter what. No point having this gift if he just bottled it at the first sign of pressure.

He hung his clean falconry bag on a hook in the prep room, picked up his jacket and rucksack and walked round to the lawn, checking his watch. 5.10pm. Good, just enough time to spend with Midge before Sykes could get aggro about him being back late.

"Trevor." Elise beckoned him over to the mews as she put her phone in her pocket. A travelling box sat on the path beside her.

"Listen, we need to leave Midge till tomorrow. I've got to go to Castleton and rescue a buzzard that's in someone's garden. They think it's injured…"

She looked at him and sighed.

"I'm really sorry. Don't be too disappointed. You understand, right? This is how the job goes sometimes."

Trevor forced himself to nod as Midge called from his perch.

"No panico, Trevor. One more day… it's OK. If I can wait then you can."

"If you can't come tomorrow I'll start on Saturday," said Elise.

Trevor fiddled his pad out of his jacket and made himself look less gutted.

I get it. It's OK. I'm sure tomorrow is good.

"Great!" Elise grinned. "Come as soon after school as you can… it'll be worth the wait, promise." She picked up the travelling box. "See you tomorrow then."

Trevor trudged over the meadow a couple of minutes behind Elise, after a quick goodbye to Midge. The heat slowed him down too, and not just with walking. There *must* be more he could do, something he could think of. Just because today hadn't thrown anything up, it didn't mean there weren't other ways to help Midge. He'd go to the library again tomorrow. They might have that article about the thieves from last year's paper, or something else, even a way to find out where they were. He quickened his pace. Then he could—

Rustling from inside a nearby bush cracked twigs, and made its branches shiver. Before Trevor had time to think, a sharp, whiskered face poked out from the undergrowth and stared directly at him. Trevor froze, his senses sharpened. Now was the time to zone in, and it was like his whole body knew it.

"You are alone?"

Barely breathing, Trevor checked up and down the path. Elise was already in the car park, and Lennox and Rash were nowhere in view, probably getting ready to leave. He moved close to a large shrub brimming with purple flowers and walked round the other side of it, so they couldn't be seen.

"Yes."

Eyes bright and with more rustling, the owner of the face slunk his way out of the hedge and came to stand beside Trevor.

"Formidable. Allow me to introduce myself. Ginger. Roger Ginger. I do apologise for being indisposed with my snack earlier. I saw your glow clearly yet again. And may I also say that it is a privilege to meet another one of your kind. Garnell's prophecy foretold it would happen in our time, but to meet you myself, and talk to you. I am honoured."

Trevor didn't know what to say. Should he ask who Garnell was? Was Roger from another time or something? Should he try to talk back the same way?

"Er, thanks. I'm Trevor."

The fox licked his lips as he sat down. "I must be efficacious. Midge must not know that we have spoken – yet. That is vital. He is in danger."

"Yes, I know he could be," said Trevor, scratching his head. "We've been working out that he's—"

"No, Trevor, he is in real danger. Imminent danger."

Goosebumps prickled the back of Trevor's neck as Roger swished his brush across the ground, disturbing dry leaves and dust.

"What do you mean?"

"The men are returning. It will be tomorrow night."

Trevor's stomach twisted.

"Tomorrow? How… how do you know?"

"My range is many miles," said Roger. "I have many friends. I am told many things. And they are coming. They have hidden the other birds, but they know there is one more. Now you are here, Midge can be protected."

Trevor looked at his watch, then back at the centre.

"I can warn him now. I've just got time—"

"No!" Roger stood up, his paws leaving imprints in the dust. "There is nothing he can do, except be anxious."

He looked up at Trevor, his brilliant white teeth glistening as he opened his mouth and said exactly what Trevor was afraid of.

"Why leave him to fret? It has to be you. You must find a way, spellboda. You have to stop them."

16

Hello. Could we be friends? Thank you for letting me go to the bird centre. I love it. Is it OK if I stay late tomorrow to help more?

Trevor

It was nowhere near being anything he really wanted to do, but writing a note was something… and it kept his mind off the panic ballooning inside. Trevor stared at Mrs Bingo-Wings, curled up asleep by his feet, as he lay on his bed, chewing the end of his pencil. A flake of soggy wood worked itself free and the rough edge rolled against his tongue. He spat it out, and the miniature shard flew through the air and landed, sticking out of the rug like a tiny javelin. Mrs Bingo-Wings half-opened her eyes and stretched her legs.

"It's alright for you, being so cat and relaxing. I'm going loopy. I've got zero ideas on what to do tomorrow."

Mrs Bingo-Wings stared back at him, unblinking. Trevor reached over and stroked the top of her head.

"Can't you talk to me? Please? Look, why not? You could really help me. Am I doing the right thing with this note? Midge thinks I should try, and it's really bugging me."

The cat purred lightly as she pushed her head into his hand. Trevor stopped stroking her and ran his hand through his hair.

"Can you just help? I don't want Sykes poking his nose in, kicking off and causing problems. But I can't think of anything else to do to cover being there tomorrow." He sighed. "Look, I know you can hear me, so I'm just going to talk to you anyway. I don't get why I can't hear you. Is it me? I'm trying really hard."

Mrs Bingo-Wings stood up and pushed herself against him. Trevor ignored her. Why was this spellboda stuff not more straightforward? He read the note again. It was fake and rubbish, but what else could he say? He folded the paper in half. Midge could be right... Sykes and his tatty clothes, messed-up face and hair, he didn't look after himself. If he didn't care about himself then it wasn't just that he didn't care about Trevor, right? That was easier to deal with.

He slid off his bed, feeling braver, and padded downstairs bare-foot with the note in his hand.

The lounge door was shut, and the serious voice of a newsreader spilled into the hall. A glimmer of hope flared. Please let Sykes understand, somehow. So much was changing. It could be the time that Sykes would begin to like him again.

Trevor slid the paper under the door and went in the kitchen. Having a sandwich might stop his tummy from those crazy flips it had been doing ever since seeing Roger. The TV droned on as he buttered two slices of bread and slapped some ham in the middle. With a can and a bag of crisps in his other hand he padded back upstairs, and sat on his bed beside Mrs Bingo-Wings, who was sound asleep again. He spread dinner out around him and tried to detangle his mind.

How would he stop the men tomorrow? What should he do? Had Sykes seen the note? The bite of sandwich was a stiff ball in his mouth and jagged edges of the crisps caught in his throat when he swallowed. Trevor put the rest of the food to one side and got off the bed. Think about something else, anything. He walked in circles, willing his brain to spark up while his eyes skimmed the room. His old *Avengers* wallpaper was peeling down, curling forwards and drooping in defeat like... like Midge would if he got carried off by thieves. This wasn't helping.

Trevor stopped by his chest of drawers. He yanked one drawer open and fiddled around under jumpers until his fingers closed on the familiar, tatty cover. Back on his bed, he opened the book at his favourite chapter. Now, focus.

Falcons
Regarded by many as nature's most efficient predator, these birds are designed for high-speed flight and aerial hunting. Prey is mainly other birds such as grouse, pigeon and...

Trevor grasshopper-read down the page, jumping over waffle paragraphs to the interesting bits.

Falcons are flown to a lure, designed to take the place of their prey. The falconer swings the lure, evading the dives and twists of the falcon, and the game begins. After a shout of 'ho', the falcon is allowed to catch the lure, the game is over and he has won his prey.

Midge was going to do that. Unless... Trevor read on, making himself absorb information, re-reading sections when he caught his head wandering. Stop worrying about tomorrow. Then an answer would pop up, like bread in a—

"Boy! Get down here now."

Trevor sat bolt upright. Mrs Bingo-Wings lifted her head.

"Here. NOW!"

This was bad. But if he didn't go it would get worse. Trevor shoved the book under his pillow and went to the stairs. A random fly was bashing itself repeatedly against the bare light bulb on the landing, with an angry, whining buzz. Why was it called a landing anyway? Nothing ever crashed through the window and touched down on it. And do people always have random thoughts on the way to their execution?

Trevor's heart raced as he got closer to the lounge. But he had Midge now. It had to be alright, he could do this.

He opened the door. The heat from the fire was nothing compared to the blaze emanating from Sykes's face. His bulk was jammed into the threadbare armchair beside the fire, and the flames played flickering patterns across his face. Trevor felt like the fly, and right here was his personal light bulb. The room was boiling, like walking into hell. Sykes held a near-empty glass in one hand and Trevor's crumpled piece of paper in the other. Trevor had the strangest sensation that a second, detached shadow Trevor was standing right next to him, absorbing the scene… the real Trevor standing there, with his bare feet and his trembling hands shoved up his hoodie sleeves. He stamped down the urge to run.

Sykes threw the crumpled note on the floor.

"What is this? What IS this? Look at me, boy! You have no idea. No idea AT ALL, about anything!"

Sykes leaned forward in his chair and seemed to swell bigger. Trevor bit his lip. He didn't move or look up.

"You want to be friends?" Sykes howled, anger and anguish all mixed up in his voice. "Well, you can't help me. I want you to. So much. But you're the problem!"

The glass flew across the room, shattered on the wall, and shards tinkled down to the floor; a dark stain bleeding down the wall in its wake. Trevor stood his ground as the empty feeling consumed him.

"Don't write to me. Ever! I'm not interested, I don't care." Sykes's voice cracked. "Leave me alone."

Trevor lifted his head and stared at Sykes, watching his face crumple.

"Why do I have to deal with this every day? Her face. Remembering, every time I see you." Sykes stared into space. "Why? I could have helped her. I would have done if I'd had the chance."

Then he was back, eyes flashing, glaring at Trevor.

"I don't care how long you stay at that place. Keep those interfering idiots out of my life! Get out. I can't bear to look at you." His voice rose to a roar as he began to hoist himself out of the chair. "GO! Leave me alone!"

Trevor flew up the stairs. He shut the door and crashed onto his bed, his heart hammering. Mrs Bingo-Wings startled, jumped down and took refuge on the windowsill. Trevor stared at the wooden bed head, with its intricate swirling patterns and channels of trails carved out by long-dead colonies of weevils and woodworms. So it hadn't worked. Understatement of the year. He looked at Mrs Bingo-Wings and rubbed his eyes. The cat miaowed softly.

"I'm OK, I am. It's nothing new. Hurts less every time. And he doesn't care if I stay late tomorrow, so at least I've got that." Trevor sat up, frowning. "He did say something different. Me being like Mum. Reminding him. So… is that what this is about? Not just that he hates me?"

Mrs Bingo-Wings tiptoed along to the middle of the windowsill and crouched in her slow, deliberate way. Trevor scratched his neck and stood up.

"Look, Mrs B, I can't carry on letting him upset me. I'm a spellboda. Not a doormat. I have stuff to do. All that matters about Sykes right now is that he didn't stop me going."

The cat miaowed again, and an image of Midge popped into Trevor's mind: flapping, panicking, calling, as hands grabbed him and took him away. A sudden, white-hot fury burned him. He walked over to Mrs B and looked into her eyes.

"No way am I going to sit here and cave. I've got Midge to fight for. He's my friend! I might not have a clue how but I'm damn well going to think of a way to help him. It's my mission, and I'm going to do it!"

17

Resolve was all he had. Trevor thought it over again and again. When he walked to school, sat in lessons, all on autopilot, then when he pedalled out of town and across the country lanes. To top it all Miss Campbell's stupid bike had run a puncture, and he had to push it for the last half mile. Why couldn't he think of a plan? He was wading through cold porridge, the worst kind, thick and gloopy, shoving his brain into one dead-end thought after another.

He looked for Roger when he got to the centre, jogging his way over the meadow, desperate for another flash of red in the bushes, but the fox was nowhere to be seen. The centre was empty, but noise from the arena explained why. This time it was a man talking, not Elise. Trevor sighed. Much as he wanted to watch Adam in action it would have to wait. He looked at the first bird in the mews, the harris hawk he'd cleaned out and weighed the other day. He cleared his throat and kept his voice low.

"Um, Brock, isn't it?"

The hawk lowered its head as it stared back at Trevor.

"Look, I know you know I'm a spellboda. So will you talk to me? I need some help. Have you seen Roger?"

The hawk didn't move.

"You know, Roger. The fox?"

"Trevor!" a familiar voice called out behind him.

Trevor turned, squashing his frustration. Midge was perched on the weathering lawn, his wings stretched out.

"What are you doing?" said Midge. "Come here."

Trevor jogged over, then slowed his pace. The thought of tonight was lodged deep in his head, and he was tight and nervy. He mustn't show it. Roger was right. Midge could know later, when he'd worked out a plan. If he told him now they'd both be stressed. He made himself smile at the falcon.

"You're sunbathing."

Midge shook his feathers, making the buzzing noise Trevor loved. "Don't go off talking to other birds. You're my spellboda. Why are you so late?"

"School stuff," said Trevor. He sat down on the grass, his face flushed. "But I don't go tomorrow." He rubbed his forehead with the front of his shirt. "I tried writing a note to Sykes last night, like you said. It didn't go well. Although in one way it did: I get to stay here longer. He wants me out as much as possible."

Midge picked at his beak with a pale yellow talon. "Sorry. I thought it would make things better, but—"

"I think it did, weirdly," Trevor cut in. "Not how I hoped, but I understand him a bit better now. Thanks for trying."

Trevor chewed a fingernail while Midge flicked his head

from side to side in sudden, jerky movements. Whatever had been stuck to his beak flew off and landed on the grass. Trevor's brain ticked over. He'd never been a liar, he felt awful telling even little white ones, but over this week he hadn't had much choice. He rubbed his nose with his palm.

"I haven't found anything out yet, but I'm not giving up. I'll keep watch today, and we can talk later when I've got some ideas to work with."

"Yes, whatever," said Midge. "Don't worry about that, I've got my first flying trip! And I'm going to sort you meeting Roger properly today."

A loud and distinct 'humph' came from the mews, as Trevor felt hot, clammy and devious all over again. He looked at Midge and raised his eyebrows.

Midge fidgeted. "I'll talk to you about that later." He paused, tilting his head in the direction of the golden eagle. "It's awkward."

Trevor looked over at the mews. The eagle stood as high as possible stretched up on his perch, brown feather hackles raised. He pinned Trevor with an imperious stare, then deliberately picked up his huge orange feet, one after the other, and turned himself around to face the back wall.

Trevor looked at Midge.

"What have I done to upset him? Why doesn't he like me?"

Midge shook his head. "Later! Honestly, sometimes I wonder why you humans are called intelligent. Us falcons are way ahead of you!"

"Steady on!" said Trevor. "Us humans would call that being full of yourself."

"Like I said," Midge replied, "we grow fast. And *us* falcons are super intelligent. Fast learners, totally switched on, brilliant at everything!"

"Not arrogant then." Trevor raised his eyebrows. "Blow your trumpet, why don't you?"

Midge stretched. "Not arrogant. Confident, yes… sure of ourselves. We have to be. That's the biggest thing my dad taught us. We need it to survive. And I'm not sure what a trumpet is, but I'm pretty sure I couldn't blow anything very hard."

Trevor smiled and opened his mouth to reply, but footsteps stopped him. Elise was walking down the mews path, head down as she tapped her mobile. She looked up and stopped.

"Trevor, you made it – right on time for tea break! Come on, demo's just finishing. We'll grab the shady spot."

Trevor got up and followed her through the falconers' gate. They made for a grassy bank on the other side of the hospital shed. It was out of view from visitors, a little green island amongst the sheds and backs of aviaries between the centre and the arena. Elise sat down on the already flattened grass and got out her water.

"Man, do I need this! Sit down, Trevor. Let's cool off. Want some? You look like your face is going to explode."

Cooler air on his face was a relief after the bike ride. Trevor sat down and grabbed a swig of her water.

"Lennox and I were talking earlier," said Elise, as she grabbed her water back. "About you."

Trevor looked up.

"Don't look shocked," she laughed. "It's not bad. You're the fastest learner we've ever had. And potentially an incredible falconer."

Trevor felt warm all over again. He grinned, and got out his pad.

Thanks for teaching me so much stuff. I love it here.

"I can tell," said Elise. "And you're welcome. Next week you can learn how to swing a lure to fly falcons. If you pick that up as fast as you have with flying to the glove, you'll be working with them in no time. Especially as you seem to have a real connection with—"

"I can't cope with this weather. Alright, Trev?"

Trevor nodded and tried to control his bursting feeling as Rash and Lennox came round the corner, both emptying their bottles of water with huge gulps. Rash groaned as he sat down. Elise leaned forward.

"All demo birds sorted, yes?"

Lennox mm-hmmed as he chewed a piece of grass, then lay back on the bank and closed his eyes. Trevor stared at him and frowned. There was a link to something that he needed to make, but he wasn't getting it, there was something more to think about…

"Everyone good?"

Lennox sat up with a start as Adam's shadow fell over them.

"Yes, all good," said Elise, looking up and shielding her eyes. "When we've cooled down we'll get the last bits done. You off out now?"

"Yep." Adam scratched his arm. "Looking forward to the air-con!" He looked at Trevor. "Alright, lad? Very committed, that's what I like to see. You need it in this work. Keep it up."

Trevor opened and closed his mouth a couple of times, and finished with a smile that, judging by the look on Adam's face, he was certain was coming across as a weird grimace.

"He's doing well, I was just telling him the same." Elise saved him. "So see you tomorrow then?"

"Yes indeed. Bright and early," said Adam. "We need to sort the paperwork tomorrow for the conservation project in Pretoria. Can't wait to get into that with the vultures."

"Me too," said Elise with a smile. "Look forward to it."

"Can I be a part of that?" asked Lennox. "I want to find out more about that side of things, get involved."

"Sure," said Adam. He smiled. "The more the merrier. See you lot tomorrow then. Don't forget to lock the office door, and have a good evening."

Trevor raised his hand as the others replied, and Adam walked away. A good evening. His chest tightened. And there was that feeling again, a thought about Lennox that he couldn't grasp. He tried to zone in on it but Elise was getting up.

"Guys, can you finish off the mews bird feeds? Then man those two baby kestrels?"

She put her hand out to Trevor and hauled him up.

"We're going to train the peregrine."

18

Elise stopped on the way out to the flying ground.

"Sorry, drank that water too quick." She rubbed her tummy. "Gives me indigestion. Should have learned that by now."

Trevor's stress levels were too high to find it funny when Elise burped again. Midge was on his glove and fidgeting non-stop. The falcon was on full alert, his eyes darting in all directions. He threw back his head.

"This is going to be great!" Midge flapped his wings on the spot as his talons tightened their grip on Trevor's glove.

"I'm going to work these babies and show you what I can do!"

Trevor winced.

"Are you OK with him?" said Elise. "He's been so calm with you up to now."

She reached into her bag and pulled out a beautifully

stitched tan and green leather falcon hood, with a twist of tiny leather strands and a feather sticking out of the top.

"He really should wear this now. Maybe I should…"

She stared as Midge tucked his wings in to his body, fell silent and stopped moving.

"Hmmm, maybe not. I swear sometimes he could be…"

There was a pause. Elise shook her head.

"At least he seems happier to have me around him now."

Trevor frowned and bit his lip. They walked into the flying arena, their trainers clipping the tips off brittle blades of sun-dried grass.

"Damn it!" said Elise. "I forgot the creance. Stupid girl."

She pointed at the manning bench under the tree.

"Wait there, out of the sun. Won't be long." She shook her head as she walked back to the prep room.

"Can't believe I forgot the most important thing. It's this blinking weather."

Trevor sat on the seat and inhaled the mix of old wood and heated varnish, trying to breathe evenly. The night stress was creeping up on him and he couldn't stop it. He looked at Midge, who'd started bouncing around again.

"Can't you tone it down a bit?" he muttered. "That hurt when you gripped my hand, even with the glove on."

Midge bobbed his head. "You calm down! I can't help myself. It's not every day you get your first time flying."

"But you nearly blew it, didn't you?" Trevor snapped. "You'd better not stop whatever you're doing when she says something like that again. She's not stupid. You could give it away. Then we'd be in trouble."

"She is stupid, she just said so!" shouted Midge. "Don't

you get it? I'm about to take off, to be airborne, to start my destiny as a predator, to—"

Trevor snorted. "Why are you so full of yourself? From where I'm sitting, you're so flaming obvious, you're almost as close to letting humans in on the secret as dogs are!"

Midge drew himself up on the glove, his eyes flashing.

"Oh, really? I'm as dense as a *dog*? Well, you can shut right up, Trevor!"

The falcon stopped moving and stared straight ahead as Trevor stabbed at a splodge of dried bird food that had welded itself to his jeans from yesterday. The memory of the chair flying across the classroom replayed as he clenched his free hand by his side.

"Got it," shouted Elise from the gate. She walked into the arena.

"Bring him over to this perch, Trevor."

Breathing stiffly, not looking at Midge, Trevor stood up and walked to the tall wooden frame in the middle of the grass. It was shaped like a massive A, just with a longer top bit that had a strip of shiny green astroturf attached, making a perfect landing point for birds. Midge was silent and still.

Elise showed Trevor the creance.

"You know what this does, right?"

Trevor frowned, then shook his head. It was in his book, but his heart was hammering in his ears and he couldn't focus. Elise stared at him.

"Are you alright in this heat? So creance is a French word. It's a long piece of string attached to a piece of wood, like an oversized bobbin. It's the training line we use before a bird flies free. This way we don't worry the bird will disappear before it's able to survive on its own."

Trevor nodded. Elise moved to his side and opened her falconry bag, showing him inside.

"I'm not taking that flying lure out until I'm further away. See the bit of meat on the lure? Every time he flies he'll get a reward. The lure helps him get used to catching flying prey."

She moved in front of Trevor and undid Midge's leash. Slipping it out of its metal swivel, she replaced it with the string of the creance.

"When I say, you need to open up your hand and let the peregrine step onto the perch, OK?"

Trevor nodded again, as Elise walked away, unwinding the creance and leaving a trail of string behind her. He looked at Midge. The falcon was watching Elise intently, his head bobbing up and down. His body was tense and rigid. Trevor swore he could feel the falcon's excited heartbeat, and his own heart dropped like a stone.

"I'm sorry. I'm really flustered," he whispered. "Like she said, it's so hot."

Midge didn't take his eyes off Elise.

"It's OK. I shouldn't have stropped out. But you're not fooling me. Something's going on. And after this you and I need to talk."

"OK," shouted Elise, now halfway across the grass. She wedged the stick of the creance line under her trainer. "Let him step on the perch."

Trevor opened up his hand to free the jesses, so the falcon could go. Midge spread his wings and was there in one graceful movement. He looked at Trevor, his eyes sparkling.

"Later, right? It's all cool. But now is now."

Trevor understood, and smiled. He backed away from the perch and looked at Elise. With one easy movement, she pulled the lure out of her bag and began to swing it in wide circles. Midge crouched low to the perch and spread his wings out fully. Trevor held his breath. But after a moment, Midge drew his wings back in and stood up tall again, head bobbing. He shook his tail feathers.

Trevor turned a little so he had his back to Elise. Thoughts of the night to come were gone. "What you doing? Go for it!"

Midge didn't reply. He stared at Elise and the lure. His feathers began to fluff up and rise away from his body. Trevor took a step towards him.

"Don't move, Trevor," called Elise, as she swung the lure. "His rouse is the last thing before take-off, the pre-flight check!"

Trevor didn't even realise he'd moved, as he shivered with excitement. Of course. Every feather shook and vibrated in perfect order. In seconds, Midge's feathers were back to normal, like nothing had happened. The falcon crouched again, his wings stretched wide, and in an instant he was airborne. Trevor's heart was pelting. Midge looked amazing, his wings spread out, every part of him speed and precision. The creance line billowed out behind Midge as he flew towards Elise, with sure, steady wing-beats. She swung the lure up and let it fall to the ground in front of her. Midge hovered for a moment, then dropped down in one easy movement, like a massive butterfly. Trevor ran forward as the falcon gripped the lure in his talons, his wings spread out over the grass.

"Not too quick," said Elise. "Let him eat his food."

Midge bowed his head and picked his reward from the lure. As the last of the chicken disappeared into his beak and he folded his wings in, Elise crouched down, glancing at Trevor.

"Come here and take another little piece of meat, to pick him up with. He did so well, I reckon we can try it again."

Trevor bent down beside Elise and she handed him some chicken.

"We say 'make in' when we go to pick a bird up, so make in to him slowly. Put the meat in your glove, let him see it."

Trevor shuffled sideways across the grass, crouched like a crab, tilting his hand in Midge's direction. Before he'd covered half the distance between them, the falcon let go of the lure and half hopped, half flew to Trevor's glove. Trevor picked up the falcon's leather jesses and brought them under his thumb, while Midge ate the second tidbit.

"Nice job, Trevor. And what a little star!" Elise beamed. "He's so quick, he's learning fast. Pop him back on the perch, Trevor, this time I'll go further away. He can work harder for his dinner."

Midge's second flight was as textbook as the first. When Trevor made into him again, this time with a bigger chunk of food for a proper dinner, Midge reached the glove almost before Trevor had put the food in it. Elise couldn't stop talking as they walked back to the mews.

"I'm super proud of him. I reckon I can let him fly free soon, with a transmitter on, in case he flies off. In a few days. He's getting used to me too."

Trevor stopped walking. Elise grinned.

"Take that panic off your face, I won't fly him free without you. Let's up his exercise on the creance tomorrow. If he's this good then maybe even fly him free on Sunday. You'll be here, won't you?"

Trevor nodded, smiling as they walked on. It would be epic to see Midge have his first free flight.

But what if Midge wasn't here to have it? Reality crashed back in. No plan, nothing, and time was running out. But even if he thought of one and pulled off saving Midge tonight, would he get to come back here... would he get caught, or found out? What if Sykes worked out he'd lied? If he got hurt tonight, what then? His chest cramped. He didn't have even a beginning of an idea. What on earth was he going to do?

19

"Put him back on his perch for me," said Elise, as they walked in to the centre. "He can have a rest."

She took off her falconry bag.

"And if I leave this by the office, can you nip to the prep room and clean it? I need to make a phone call before we pack up and go. Thanks, Trevor."

Trevor was glad he didn't look as off as he felt. Every minute ticking by was bringing night closer. He put Midge back on his perch, only half-concentrating. The last visitors of the day were still milling around, watching him through the wire, so talking was impossible. Midge stared, tilting his head.

"Come over when it's quiet, right?"

Trevor nodded. At least he was off the hook for now.

He picked up Elise's bag and trudged to the food prep room, praying for an idea. The pungent smell of leather and over-heated raw meat hit him as he opened the door.

He wrinkled his nose. The plastic inner pocket of Elise's bag was sticky with warm leftover chicken pieces. He emptied them into the bin, turning his face away from the extra blast of stink when he lifted the lid, then went to the sink to wash the bag. Cold water played over his fingers, refreshing, and he stood for a moment, staring round, relishing the chance to cool at least one part of himself down.

Trevor's eyes rested on a red fire extinguisher leaning against the wall in the corner, dusty and forgotten. If it got any hotter maybe they'd bring that out… they could blast each other down with water. He gasped. Of course! He could use it – tonight. And why not find more stuff to stop them? There had to be other things round here that he could use. Why hadn't he thought of it before?

He turned off the tap and rubbed cold, wet fingers over his face. What else? He scanned the room. First stop had to be the cupboard by the fridge. He opened the door. Spare soap, toilet rolls, an incubator for eggs… and a weird-shaped torch. He lifted the torch out carefully. It was massive, and heavy. He'd seen one before. When Sykes used to take him hiking. It was one of those super-bright things, a million candlepower or something, whatever that meant. This could come in handy.

He put it back and shut the door as relief washed over him. The start of a plan. He was getting somewhere.

"Trevor… have you done my bag?"

The door opened and Elise popped her head in the prep room.

"Urgh, it stinks!"

Trevor showed her the clean falconry bag.

"Thanks for that. Will you hang it up it in the weighing room? I'm going to do a final bird check and we're all done."

Trevor's brain whirred as Elise walked away. Focus. He was pretty certain that the cleaning shed wasn't locked at night. It was full of old buckets and rakes. He could stash things in there. He could check there too for useful weaponry... and where else? He rubbed his arm, knocking off a fly. The only other place was the office.

He checked the centre as he left the food shed. Elise was walking into the mews. There was no sign of Lennox or Rash. He jogged along the path, trying to look casual. He'd just have to go for it.

Trevor walked into the office, his heart beating fast. He checked again, looking out of the windows on both sides. There they were. Rash and Lennox were by the flying arena. Lennox was locking the gates, and Rash was talking to a blonde-haired girl, one of the day's visitors, who looked about his age, and they were both tapping their phones. Good. First the desk. Not much to go on, though, he couldn't think of anything threatening he could do with a load of stationery, and scissors would definitely be pushing it. He scanned the bookshelves, and an image of the chocolate tin resurfaced with a ping in his head. He had to follow that up, but there was no time now. The shelves didn't throw up any bright ideas either... files weren't really weapons of mass destruction. There were jackets hanging from a hook, and the PA system equipment, which was flashing and winking yellow and red lights in the corner. Trevor walked over to it, thinking hard. Was there a way he could use it and get in here tonight? His heart sank. No, it would be locked for sure after what Adam said earlier. He turned away, but something registered in his peripheral vision. He looked back. That was a megaphone. Sitting by the PA system. It must be their emergency back-up. He picked it up and turned it over in his hands, his mind racing.

Elise was on her way around the aviaries as Trevor left the office, hugging the megaphone. He jogged to the food shed, his heart pounding. Megaphone in one hand, he opened the cupboard door with the other and lifted out the torch. Praying for invisibility, he ran back out, round the corner to the cleaning shed. Trevor put the torch and megaphone in the darkest corner of the shed and shoved a couple of overturned buckets on top of them. The buckets didn't quite reach the ground. They looked as if they were levitating, but it would have to do.

Sprinting back to the food prep room, he heaved up the fire extinguisher with a groan. Sweat prickled all over him as he staggered back to the cleaning shed. He dumped it in the dark corner with a dull thud. Trevor rubbed the back of his soaking neck, his chest heaving. That had to work. Surely they wouldn't come back in here again today. He closed the door and walked back into the main centre, puffing like a train. Elise was just walking back from the aviaries.

Trevor heaved a huge sigh of relief. Stage one, tick. Now to hold his nerve for stage two.

20

"Guys... come over. We're all done... let's cool down for a minute before we go. Trevor looks like he's run a marathon!"

Getting his pad out of his pocket, Trevor joined Elise on the weathering lawn just as Rash and Lennox came back from the arena. He sank down on the grass, trying to avoid the late afternoon sun and keep his breathing steady. He trembled. Did he really have the guts to do this? But there was no going back now.

Lennox leaned down beside him and gave him a nudge on the arm.

"You've done good again then, Trev. Nice one, coming in today."

Elise nodded, looking up from her bag as she pulled out a set of keys. "You made our lives a lot easier. Thanks a mil."

Elise smiled at Trevor as he nodded and forced a smile

back, then she leaned back on her elbows, her ponytail lifting behind her as a light breeze wafted by.

"At least it's a bit cooler. Could have done with some of this wind a bit earlier."

"You had some," Rash smirked, "at lunchtime."

"Oh, ha ha," said Elise, closing her eyes. "It's just a burp or two. Natural human reaction."

Lennox shook his head. "Always has to lower the tone. He's either had an overdose of heat, or he's too excited about his new blonde friend."

Rash snorted. "Another follower, one step closer to being an influencer. You're just jealous."

"Not me, mate." Lennox grinned. "Anyway, Trev, what were you doing in the office?"

Elise opened her eyes. Pink heat surged up from Trevor's neck. He bent his head and focused on his pad.

Just thought I should check - I saw some lights. I think the PA's been left on.

"Oh, thanks, Trevor!" said Elise. "Adam wouldn't be impressed if I left that on all night. I'll turn it off when I lock everything up."

Trevor could feel Lennox's stare as he kept his head down.

Elise sat up. "By the way, I still can't find my ring. Can you guys keep looking out for it?"

"Course." Lennox nodded, checking his watch. "Blimey, it's nearly six."

"Trevor!" Elise frowned. "What about your dad?"

This was it. Stage three. Trevor scribbled on his pad, praying his hand kept steady.

My dad's gone to a meeting. He's going to fetch me in a bit. I'll be fine waiting here.

Elise's frown deepened, more lines creasing into her brow.

"It doesn't feel right just leaving you here. What time is he coming?"

His heart thumping, Trevor wrote again.

He won't be long, by 7, he said. It's a fund-raiser thing. Don't worry. I'm used to being on my own. I'll walk up to the car park in a bit.

"But… I feel responsible," said Elise. "Can I give you a lift home or something?"

He knew this would happen. For the first time, Trevor was glad Sykes had never given him a mobile phone.

No thanks, there's no way I can get in touch with him, and I don't know what pub he's at. I'll be fine ☺

Elise scratched her head. "OK. I suppose. You'll have to climb over the gates, though."

She rummaged in her bag. Pulling out a bag of crisps and a chocolate bar, she lobbed them over.

"No, have them," she said as Trevor shook his head. "It'll make me feel better."

As Trevor reached to pick them up off the grass she

put her hand on his arm. "I can't leave anything unlocked, sorry. Especially after what happened with the peregrines. Just stay around here, and then the car park, right? Don't go wandering off."

Trevor nodded as another wave of relief flooded over him, this time soaked with guilt. He hated lying to her. But she'd forgive him if she knew why. Definitely. He got up and wandered over towards the mews as the falconers got ready to leave. A sinking feeling about tonight was crashing in. He had no idea what he'd do afterwards, if he even made it that far. What the heck would Sykes do when he didn't come home? But he'd got this far… and he had to keep going now no matter what.

A hand rested on his shoulder, and he turned to smile at Elise, and jumped. He was wrong. Lennox leaned over so his face was right beside Trevor's, and he got a blast of sweat and sweet stale breath in his face as Lennox spoke.

"Do me a favour, Trev, right? Don't go looking around in places you shouldn't be. You're a decent lad and I don't want to get upset with you."

Trevor froze. He stared at Lennox, his eyes wide.

Lennox grinned. "Enough said. I can see you understand." He stepped back and spoke loudly.

"Thanks again, Trev, have a good evening, mate."

The path shimmered in the heat as the falconers walked away, their figures growing smaller and wobblier as they neared the car park. Elise turned to give him a final wave.

Trevor's breathing was still choppy as he waved back. What was Lennox hiding? Was this an inside job, was Lennox a mole? There was no way of knowing unless he could get back into the office, or... if Lennox turned up here tonight. And that option wasn't something he wanted to face.

He looked round the centre. All was peaceful. Just him and the birds, and the glow of an evening sun. A kaleidoscope of sunset colours smudged the sky. Garden birds sang their symphony from the line of trees behind the aviaries. Trevor didn't bother to try to listen in. He stared across the lawn. A gnat cloud danced in a mini-rave over the grass, and tiny motes of pollen, illuminated by sunlight, grazed along lazily, buoyed by the gentle breeze that buffered them. All so calm, but reality refused to be subdued. With a feeling that it wasn't going to be the last time, Trevor checked his watch.

Night would fall about nine. Just under three hours to go.

21

"So," Midge rubbed his beak backwards and forwards over his perch, cleaning, "what's going on?"

Trevor sat down on the path next to Midge's mews space and leaned against the wire. Stage four was imminent... it was time. He couldn't bear the weight of it any longer.

"They're coming," he blurted out. "Tonight."

"What? Who?" said Midge. His head shot up. "The men?"

Trevor nodded.

"Tonight?" Midge gripped his perch. "How do you know?"

"Roger told me," said Trevor.

"Roger? So you've met him?"

"Only for a minute, last night." Trevor felt his face go red again. "He needed to warn me."

"If it's come from Roger it must be true." Midge fidgeted. "I knew it! What are we going to do?"

Trevor took a deep breath. "Don't worry. I've got a plan," he said, hoping he sounded confident. "We wait till dark, when they come. Then I'm going to stop them."

Midge turned his head away and didn't reply. Trevor guessed what he was thinking. Someone like him had no chance against grown men. He would be trying to think of a nice way to tell him to get some decent help. To get someone, anyone who could actually pull this off. Midge turned and looked back at him.

"I'll always be grateful to you."

Trevor blinked. "I didn't see that coming. What for?"

"For being here." Midge's dark eyes were fixed on him. "For stopping them. You're everything I was told a spellboda would be." The falcon looked down at the sandy floor. "And I'm sorry I got stroppy with you earlier, I was excited, and—"

"Don't say sorry!" exclaimed Trevor. "It's forgotten. And you're my friend, of course I'm here."

Midge looked up, his eyes bright. "Well, I'm thankful anyway, so deal with it."

Trevor grinned and pulled away from the wire. "Actually, I've had an idea. I think it could work. I'm going to proper scare them. But there is something you can help with."

"Of course it'll work!" said Midge. "And yes, name it."

"I need a lookout," said Trevor. "Someone... sorry, somebird, who can see far, down the paths, and over the fields." He looked over his shoulder. "I'd say Samson's aviary is in the best position, he can see in loads of directions. Do you think he'd help if you asked?"

147

"One way to find out," said Midge. He stretched up and called across to the redtail's aviary.

"Samson. Samson!"

Trevor concentrated hard. After a moment a reply floated back.

"Good evening, Midge. Congratulations on your flying today. Are you well?"

"Yes, thanks, Samson, but I've got a problem. I'm about to be stolen tonight…"

Trevor raised his eyebrows. Midge didn't muck about.

"…and Trevor, my spellboda, is going to stop them. Can you keep watch? Let him know if you see them coming?"

"Good heavens! Yes, of course. How dreadful. Is there anything else I can do? It would be wonderful to speak to the spellboda myself, if he is available."

A loud clicking noise came from the next-door cubicle. Trevor leaned sideways to see Tiberius standing on his perch, feet wide apart and his huge chocolate wings stretched out. He looked astonishing. The clicks weren't words as far as he could tell, but sounded disapproving, like a stressy teacher.

Samson's voice drifted over again.

"Ah, yes, maybe not. Not the right time, and all that. I'm a bit tired…"

"Oh man," drawled a voice from an aviary on the other side of the centre. "Not him again."

Trevor frowned and looked at Midge, who was jerking his head wildly in Tiberius's direction. Trevor couldn't help it. He leaned in, as close as he could to the mews wire.

"What's going on?" he whispered.

Midge bobbed from side to side. "You know I said before, about talking to you?" he replied, his voice just as low. "It's *awkward*. It's OK for me right now because I need you. *Sometimes*, talking is good. *Sometimes*, it isn't."

"What the heck are you going on about?"

"Don't worry." Midge huffed and shook his tail feathers. "Tell you later, after you've saved me."

Midge's total confidence made him relax – a little. Thoughts of Lennox crept into his head. What was he up to? Whatever happened later he was going to have to get to the bottom of that, there was definitely something weird going on. Lennox had seemed like a decent guy... ish. But then a thief wasn't going to go around just giving it away.

The sun drooped, dripping molten red rays through the trees, and the sky drifted into shades of purple as night crept forward from the east. Sitting beside Midge on the other side of the wire, talking, distracted, Trevor became increasingly fascinated with the glow, and looked round over and over again. The rich red fire of the sun hugged the tree-line like a blanket. Colours smudged as they crept upwards; ending with a swathe of deep lavender, tinged with carmine where the waning light hit a bank of rugged, cotton cloud. Small candy-floss plumes of vapour dotted the sky. It was breathtaking. But not quite enough to distract him completely. He turned over the objects hidden in the cleaning shed in his mind, and brightened as the idea began to take shape.

"Question," said Midge. "Your name's weird. Is it normal?"

Trevor snorted. "You say it how it is, don't you?"

"Isn't that the best way?"

Trevor laughed. "I don't know anyone else called Trevor. It's an old name, like Doris, or Maurice, or something." He nodded. "I like it. Mum said it was a family name. Important. Although she used to call me 'Fidget' when I was little. I have her last name too. Her and Sykes didn't get married. I'm Trevor Grainger, not Trevor Sykes."

He closed his eyes for a moment. "Thinking about it, maybe that's another reason I upset him."

Midge fidgeted.

"What happened to your mum?"

Trevor looked at the floor and picked at a few weeds sprouting between the join of the mews and the path. "It was an accident, near the sea. She was in a car. I don't want to talk about it."

Midge stared at him. "Fair enough."

Trevor turned away to the sunset again. It was weird… he didn't want to talk, but the moment she was in his mind memories of her grew so strong. He looked at the sky, ablaze with beauty, and her voice was clear.

"Always remember, Trevor, no matter what, don't just let life happen to you. Make it happen. And then… live it in colour."

Trevor was oddly reassured as silence stretched between him and Midge. He tried to think of something to say but couldn't. Anyway, he needed to work on the plan. He got up, stretched and checked his watch again.

"Where are you going?" said Midge.

"Just to get food."

Trevor took his time walking back to where he'd left

Elise's crisps and chocolate on the grass. He didn't feel hungry, but it would give him a chance to think without letting on to Midge that his plan wasn't fully-functioning yet. His watch read twenty to eight. He crouched down and opened the crisp bag.

Midge watched. "Wouldn't you rather catch it?" he called.

"What?"

"Your dinner. Wouldn't you rather chase it and catch it? Hunt it for yourself?"

"Not really." Trevor ate some crisps. He considered for a moment before swallowing. "Thing is, in my world, people do that, but some do it for fun," he mumbled through his mouthful. "Not because they're hungry. I don't think that's right."

"Same," said Midge. "If you just catch what you need, you don't kill more than you should."

"I get that." Trevor nodded, as he shovelled more crisps in. He was more hungry than he thought. "Trouble is, I don't think all humans do."

Midge stood on one leg, stretching the other, and slowly unfolded one wing to balance. Trevor paused to watch, the last crisp halfway to his mouth.

"Well, they should get it," said Midge. "I reckon spellbodas could change the world, if people listened to you."

Trevor smiled as he crumpled the empty crisp packet into a ball.

"Too much for now," he said, getting up. "Keeping this bit of world safe tonight would be a good start." He brushed crisp crumbs from his jeans. "Back in a bit. Got stuff to get ready."

"Oh. OK."

Midge bobbed his head as Trevor walked away, and the last wisp of tired sun slipped away and sank behind the trees.

Dumping the crisp packet in the bin, Trevor gulped a quick mouthful of cold water from the outside tap and headed to the cleaning shed. He moved the buckets off the torch and megaphone, and smiled. The plan was unfolding in his head like an old-fashioned photograph developing, shifting from a blur to a sharp-edged image.

He started with the fire extinguisher. Staggering back into the main part of the centre, he dumped it by the solid no-entry gate that led to the falconers' area. Perfect. He could crouch down and hide here, behind the gate. It was tall enough to hide him, but not too tall to lean over, and it was near enough a straight line from here to Midge in the mews. He leaned down and checked the canister in the fast-waning light. The instructions on the side were clear. Pull the safety pin, point the nozzle, squeeze the lever. Sorted. He jogged back to the shed and grabbed the torch and megaphone, examining them on his way back to mission central. They were both easy enough to operate. He switched the torch on, and its powerful beam spread across the grass. Epic. He flicked it off, and turned to the megaphone. The gun-like handle attached to the speaker had a button on it. He pressed it and held it to his mouth.

"HI... I... I... I." He boomed across the centre, echoing back from the tree-line, making birds call and hoot. Even

Trevor jumped, and he'd known it was coming. So weird, being super-loud when he was used to being super-quiet. But awesome. He stashed the extinguisher, megaphone and the torch in his base behind the gate, a thrill of excitement running through him.

"What in the sky did you just do?" called Midge. "Have you turned yourself into a giant?"

Trevor laughed as he jogged over to the mews. "Nowhere near. Just got my props to help out. You're not going anywhere tonight."

"Of course I'm not," said Midge. "But I wish I wasn't stuck in here and could help you. You've got this, though."

Trevor shoved anxious niggles to the back of his mind. No way was Midge's faith in him going to come to nothing. He sat down in his usual spot on the path.

"All sorted. Now we wait."

Darkness was drawing in. Trevor tried to relax, resting his head against the wire of the mews. He talked to Midge on and off, but silences grew longer as the night deepened. The warmth of the day was long gone, replaced by a sharp chill biting the air. Trevor wrapped his arms round his body. Waiting. The worst bit. Now there was time to think. To worry about when the men showed up. To wonder what Sykes was doing. If he'd realised Trevor wasn't home. How was he even going to get home after all this?

He stared up at the vast blanket of sky. It was clear now, as if the clouds had chased the sun below the horizon. A myriad of stars took their place, studding the dark in random patterns, like shards of diamonds flung across space. The new moon lingered at the edge of the horizon, as if waiting for an opening to join their dance. It was amazing. Trevor was filled with a sense of how massive it all was... galaxies, solar systems. And somewhere, in the middle of all that vastness, there was him. A tiny little pinprick in time. His eyes drooped and his head felt heavy, as the long day caught up with him. He was going to do this... a spellboda... and he wasn't going to let Midge down.

A low call sounded from the redtail aviary across the grass and Trevor snapped out of his doze, head up, wide awake.

"Trevor!" whispered Midge. "It's them. They're coming!"

22

Trevor sprang up, shaking off the stiffness in his bones as he stumbled to the gate. Samson called again, in a low voice.

"Two of them, with torches. They're switching them on and off. Climbed over the gate. Coming across the meadow now. I saw headlights in the car park."

A sharp 'chup' sounded from the mews.

"I am so sorry, Tiberius, sir," said Samson, "but I can't perch back and do nothing."

After all that time, suddenly there was none. Trevor vaulted over the gate and crouched behind it, fumbling in the dark for his cache of weapons. His heart thumped as his fingers closed on the megaphone, then the torch. The moon was higher, and now his eyes had adjusted he could see the shape of the fire extinguisher lying on the ground to his left. He moved them all out of the shadow of the gate, to where moonlight fell and he could see them more clearly.

How close were they? He raised his head above the top

of the gate, hoping against hope that they wouldn't spot him. His breathing quickened. There they were, halfway across the meadow now, torches flickering. A sharp noise of gravel being disturbed sounded behind him, near the food shed. Trevor froze. He stared into the shadows, his heart racing, willing his eyes to work better. Was there a third one? Lennox, here to make him pay for interfering?

Four red legs with black socks stepped out of the darkness by the food shed, and bright eyes flashed. Trevor wanted to cry with relief.

"Well met, spellboda," said Roger, his tongue lolling from his jaws and glistening in the moonlight. "Let's give these villains what for, shall we?"

Trevor nearly cheered as Roger leapt up and over the gate in one fluid movement, and silently melted away into the darkness, across the grass parallel to the mews. The men were through the meadow now and in the centre, starting their walk down the path running beside the mews. Trevor ducked behind the gate and forced his breathing to steady. He pulled the safety pin and released it from the fire extinguisher with a tiny click. As footsteps grew closer, the beams of the men's torches randomly flashed around. Iron strength grew inside Trevor. Fear was gone and absolute focus took over, the will to succeed. His hand closed over the torch, and he felt for the switch as the men drew closer.

The footsteps stopped.

"Which one were it? Next door to the eagle, right?"

The torch beams flashed again.

"Ay, that's it. Look, right there. Look at him."

"He's a beauty. Boss was right. 'Ere, hold this, Dad, while I cut the wire."

"Hurry up then, I'm mithered in this chill. Sooner we get home, sooner... uh?"

Light bright as day poured over the grass, spotlighting the two men like actors on a stage. The one crouching against the wire of the mews, wire cutters in his hand, froze, and the other dropped his torch on the floor, his mouth wide open. Trevor grabbed the megaphone in his right hand as he steadied the torch on top of the gate post, staying behind it so he couldn't be seen. He pressed the button and made his voice as deep and serious as possible.

"You are under arrest," his voice blasted across the centre, "for attempted theft of a bird."

"What? Hang on a minute!"

The men looked around, confusion on their faces.

"You are surrounded," Trevor bellowed out of the speaker, as he gripped the hose of the fire extinguisher in his other hand.

"Wait! We're just here to do repairs."

"Come on now," said Trevor, rather enjoying getting into his role. "The evidence is clear. You can't talk your way out of this. Put your cutters down."

He paused and then added the part he most wanted them to react to. "And don't even think about running away."

The man with the wire cutters stood up and looked at the other one.

"Sounds a bit weird, this. I reckon he's on his own. Let's find out."

Trevor trembled as they walked towards the beam of his torch. It was his turn to freeze. This wasn't supposed to happen. They needed to believe he was the police. They absolutely couldn't see him. His mind went blank and beads of sweat broke out on his forehead. He gripped the megaphone and fire extinguisher hose as if his life depended on them.

A menacing snarl sounded from the shadows and the men stopped. A precious beat of time to give Trevor the chance to react. Roger snarled again. He was closing in. Trevor raised the megaphone and pressed the button.

"If you resist we will set the dogs on you. And use the water cannon."

The men stared at each other, bewildered, wrong-footed. Suddenly, Midge called from his mews space, and one after another, birds joined him. A cacophony of calls, building louder and travelling across the night air. Trevor seized the moment.

He put down the megaphone and used his right hand to balance the extinguisher, then pointed the nozzle right at them. Roger's blood-curdling snarls grew louder as Trevor squeezed the lever and the stinging blasts of cold water hit.

"Ow! Aah!"

The wire cutters fell to the ground. "Dad... leg it!"

The bird noise was deafening now, the best alarm Trevor could have hoped for. The sodden pair took off over the grass, tripping as they ran full pelt across the centre and back over the meadow to the car park. Trevor put his hand over his mouth as he watched them in the beam of the torch, shouting and stumbling as flashes of red darted between them, nipping at their legs and shoes. Roger was a genius.

He climbed over his mission central gate and rushed to Midge.

"Are you OK?"

Midge was bouncing up and down on his perch. "More than. That was amazing."

"I know!" said Trevor. "Their faces when the water hit them! Epic."

"And Roger…" said Midge, as Trevor bent down and picked up the abandoned torches and the wire cutters. "I don't think they'll be back any time soon."

"No," Trevor agreed. His mind was still working at double speed. "But we have to be ready in case they do."

"I concur." Roger was back, panting lightly. "And I must confess, it has been a long time since I've enjoyed myself like that. I'd never go for a human as a rule, but those scoundrels will feel my teeth-marks for days."

Trevor resisted the urge to bend down and stroke his thick red coat.

"Thanks, Roger," he said. "You finished them off nicely. They'll never suspect now that we weren't the police."

"The pleasure was mine, spellboda." Roger blinked, his eyes glinting in the torchlight. "You glowed brightly this evening. What is your instruction? Shall I send scouts to follow, and remain near the house of the thieves?"

"Yes, great idea," said Trevor. Roger let out a series of sharp, clipped barks, answered by echoes from the woods.

Midge beat his wings and danced on his perch.

"What is it, Trevor?" he said. "Why are you pulling that weird face? We've just ruined them!"

"I'm just thinking. What if they come back? Should I tell someone, get help?"

"If they return it will not be tonight," said Roger, turning to face them. "They're drenched, and smarting from their wounds."

"And the scouts will know if they try to come back," said Midge. He stopped flapping. "We don't have to do this for long. As soon as I'm flying well Elise will set me free. Hopefully I'll be gone before they come back."

Roger nodded his sleek head. "If they are courageous enough to try. As for getting help, how will you explain to humans without giving us away? You're in our world now, spellboda."

Trevor scratched his chin. "You're right. And Midge, that sounds like the best plan. I just feel like I'm missing something." He rubbed his arms to drive away the chill, as reality set in. Stage four of the mission was a success, but there was one more stage to go. He clapped his hand to his head.

"Damn! I've got to work out how to get home. My bike's dead and my puncture kit's at home."

"What about your dad?" said Midge. "Can he fetch you?"

"Honestly?" said Trevor, straining to check his watch in the moonlight. "If Sykes has any idea I'm not home he's probably going to kill me. It's nearly two in the morning. He doesn't want to come and get me in the day." He sighed, suddenly feeling exhausted. Why was it that knowing the time when it was late always made him feel more tired?

Roger lifted his head. "I will gladly escort you home, spellboda."

Trevor smiled. "That's super kind, but I can manage on my own. And I live over fifteen minutes' drive away. Walking is going to take about two hours, and you've got better things to do."

"On the contrary," said Roger. "You are forgetting I do not travel by road. If you allow me to escort you home, we will go my way. Cross-country. Over field, peak and dale. And you will be home before the sun stirs."

Trevor brightened. "Wow. I hadn't thought of that. That would be epic, thanks." He paused. "Will you be OK, Midge?"

"Of course," said the falcon, fluffing up his feathers. "Fun's over now. Time for a roost, anyway." His eyes sparkled. "Got to have plenty of rest before I fly free."

Trevor grinned. "Not long to go, you'd better behave yourself for Elise. See you tomorrow." He looked at Roger. "I'll clear up and chuck my weapons in the shed. Then I'm ready."

★

The late night sky stayed clear and twinkling, and the glow of moonlight gave the countryside a pale brilliance. As he and Roger set off over the fields, Trevor had never felt more part of his new world. The walk soon drove away the chill, and Roger was a great guide, careful to lead Trevor over ground that wasn't too treacherous.

"Four legs may gain purchase where two legs cannot," Roger announced, as they crossed a field full of sheep. Whatever that meant. It sounded like a riddle out of *The Hobbit*. Trevor decided to google it in his next IT lesson. Woolly bodies shot past them as they realised they had company of the worst kind, and they gathered in a silent mass in the far corner of the field, each budging the other out of the way to get closer to the middle of the throng.

Trevor climbed over gates as Roger gracefully scaled the dry stone walls beside them. It was hard going navigating the peaks, but there were downs as well as ups. He could see the lights of town twinkling in the distance now. They picked up the pace as they went downhill, Trevor replaying the night for a second time in his head as they walked. It had been dodgy, but then come together like a dream. His idea, Roger turning up, those shocked faces. Trevor smiled as he pictured it. When the men were talking, just about to cut the wire, just about to… like a cog turning, the niggle slotted into place.

"That's it."

"What would that be?" asked Roger.

"The men, when they were talking. They said something. I didn't pick up on it at the time but now… I knew there was something else tonight."

Roger glanced up as he loped beside him.

"To what are you referring? They said many things, all concerning Midge."

"Yes," said Trevor. "But they mentioned someone. They said 'boss', remember? Something like 'boss is right.'"

He stopped walking and stared at the fox.

"Roger! There's definitely someone else involved. They must be working for someone. And I think it's Lennox."

Roger narrowed his eyes.

"I believe you could be correct. They did indeed refer to a boss. Who is this Mr Lennox?"

"Not Mr, just Lennox," said Trevor. "He's one of the falconers. He warned me earlier about keeping out of things." He slapped his hand to his forehead. "The first day, when the birds were gone… he didn't have his keys. But the next day he had them again. Like he'd got them back. And there's the tin too… why didn't I think of it!"

"This Just Lennox sounds suspicious," said Roger. "What is your plan?"

Trevor knew exactly what they needed to do. Warmth ran through him.

"I need to look in that tin again, his tin. I reckon he could be the one who's got the others, the rest of Midge's family."

"That would be logical," said Roger. "If he is—"

"Can you let your scouts know?" asked Trevor. "Ask your contacts to spy on Lennox? Find out where he lives? I can show you who he is tomorrow. Or Midge can, if it's too busy for you when the centre's open? It would be epic if we can stop him too."

"Of course," said Roger, and they walked on.

Trevor's legs felt lighter. This was good, really good. He was making a difference. And it was great to have Roger, who was fast becoming a friend like Midge. Unlike the eagle. He frowned.

"Roger, why aren't all animals friendly to me?"

"They should be," Roger said as he padded his way carefully through thistles. "Do you have reason to believe some are not?"

"Well, it's just one, really," said Trevor, "but yes."

He told Roger about Tiberius as they skirted the lower slopes of a peak. The fox threw up his head and showed his perfect teeth in a glistening smile.

"Ah, the golden eagle. I am foolish, I should have realised. You speak truth, spellboda, some will distrust you. But only alphas will show it, and those who harbour pride will doubt. Tiberius is both those things, the prize of his kind, and he is too aware of this to bow to anyone else."

Trevor thought for a moment. "Do you mean he's a jumped-up snob?"

Roger let out a sharp, laughing bark. "I think that could be an accurate summary of his character. But he, and those like him, will distrust and reject you and your precious gift at their peril."

They climbed over another wall and walked down the last hill. Houses on the outskirts of town loomed ahead, and the sky paled in readiness to welcome the dawn. Trevor was running out of time and suddenly desperate to know more.

"Do you know anyone else who's met a spellboda? Do you know any others?"

"I do not," said Roger. "I met one briefly only once. They were travelling north and could not delay. I do not have as much knowledge as I would like. What I do know is that your kind have good, pure souls. And you must keep your gift secret from all humans, except others like yourselves, who will see your glow as you see theirs."

That was good to know. Not that he was likely to go round shouting about it. They were coming onto roads now, into streets, and Trevor began to lead the way.

"So can I talk to any animal I want?"

"I cannot say. Everything I know I have told you. Your worth, the prophecy, how important—"

"Oh yes, the prophecy! You said about that. Who's Garnell?"

"Garnell is the wisest of animals. He has answers to all things, and all creatures in need turn to him. And indeed, if you are agreeable, I have a plan."

"What?" asked Trevor.

"Garnell should know that you are glowing, and that disconcerting events are afoot. I'd like to make the journey to visit him."

"OK… that sounds like a plan," Trevor said. "Why don't you go tomorrow? Is Garnell close to the centre too, near that copse where you hang out? Why don't I come with you?"

"He is past the copse, across the valley and a good way further than that," replied Roger. "He's in the high peaks. It may take me some time to find him. He is two nights' journey from here, I think, maybe more. Too far for you to travel. Your duty is here, with Midge."

"But then you'll be gone for ages," said Trevor. "What if word comes from your friends, the scouts? How will I know?"

"I will instruct them to report to you in the event of danger, now that I have knowledge of where you reside," said Roger. "I must also see Midge tomorrow, before I leave, and tell him of my journey. As you say, he can identify Mr Just Lennox, and we can brief the scouts. No harm will befall Midge that I can help you prevent, whether I am present or not. Of that I assure you."

They turned the corner into Trevor's road, and Trevor's mind shifted uncomfortably to Sykes. What if he was awake, waiting, furious?

"OK, I suppose. But come back as quick as you can. What is Garnell, anyway?"

Roger growled lightly. "Not the kind of animal with whom I'm accustomed to socialising. I hope he is calmer than he used to be and doesn't try to fight me again. I've only met him once, many moons ago. He made the prophecy when he was barely older than a cub. But he is advancing in years now, and hopefully enjoying a quiet life. Rather like me, before you appeared." His wide mouth lolled open again. "Garnell is a badger."

"Wow," said Trevor. "I hope it goes OK."

Roger looked at him "As do I. But it is necessary. He must know."

They paused at the gate. The house was in darkness. Trevor bit his lip. Could his luck hold out? He smiled at the fox and lowered his voice.

"Thanks, Roger. Be safe."

"Indubitably. Farewell, spellboda, and friend. *Adieu. À bientôt.* I will see you soon."

"Yes, soon," echoed Trevor. Roger pattered away, his claws tapping a rhythm across the pavement. Trevor watched his white-tipped brush disappear round the corner… and he knew he couldn't put it off any longer. He walked up the path. If there was going to be a storm to face on the other side of that door, then the sooner the thunder began, the sooner it would be over.

23

Saturday had only just begun and it was already a day of firsts and weirds, Trevor mused. First time he'd told whopping lies. And got away with it, amazingly. Not that he was mad keen on doing that again, especially to Elise. Guilt was weird, nasty. First time he'd gone to bed at four am, and still managed to wake up alert in the morning. His brain was wired after his mission at the centre, and he was desperate to get back. He shook his head as he grabbed his rucksack from the bed and gave Mrs B a goodbye stroke. His luck had more than held out. Last night he'd tiptoed through the kitchen and up the stairs so lightly he could've been on one of those hoverboards they'd been reading about in science. Judging by the strength of snores emanating from Sykes's bedroom, Trevor's worries were unfounded, but he couldn't shake the small cloud of sad shadowing him. Did Sykes really not care if he was even home or not?

Trevor padded downstairs to the kitchen to grab his usual two bags of crisps, and drew a sharp breath. He wasn't alone. For the first time in months, his father was up before him, and sitting at the kitchen table. Oh no. He must have known all along that Trevor had come in so late. Sykes pulled out a chair for him to sit down, passed him a mug of tea and undid the loaf of bread sitting in the middle of the table.

"Have a slice," he said, as Trevor lowered himself on to the chair, hardly daring to breathe. Sykes took a slice out and lobbed a huge splodge of butter over it. He bit a chunk off the corner and chewed heavily, his jaw chomping up and down as little white breadcrumbs bounced in his beard.

Trevor took a slice and did the same. He had to. The two of them sat in silence, eating their bread. Weird was an understatement. Trevor drank his tea fast, wincing as it scalded his throat. He had to leg it. The walk would take ages. Besides, this was unknown territory, anything could happen.

He put his empty mug on the table, got up and grabbed his rucksack. Sykes was silent, staring at the cooker, as he wolfed down another slice of bread. Trevor hesitated, wavering. There was no outburst – yet. If this was an outside chance that Sykes was making an effort, should he do the same? Pulling his pad out of his pocket, he ripped out a page, leaned on the dresser and scribbled a quick note.

Thank you.

He put the piece of paper on the table, resting it against the remains of the loaf of bread. Sykes watched him, then looked down at the note. He stopped chewing. Trevor walked to the back door, his unease growing by the second. This had not been a good decision. Any minute now he would kick off. Time to go – fast.

Sykes swallowed and spoke in a low voice.

"Keep writing me notes, boy."

Trevor froze, his hand on the door knob.

"I shouldn't shout at you. I'll try not to do that again."

Trevor turned around. Sykes was looking at the floor, his hair falling forward over his face. With a sudden rush of optimism he went back to the piece of paper.

Thanks. I'm going to the centre again today, OK?

Sykes looked up at the piece of paper and nodded.

"Right. OK." He rubbed his beard, dislodging crumbs that pattered on to the table. "I can give you a lift... if you want."

Not having to walk was too tempting. Plus this was a first and it couldn't be passed up.

Yes please. I was going to walk – need to fix the bike
– it's at the centre – puncture. Repair kit's in the
garage.

Sykes nodded. "Right. I'll get my keys. See you outside."

Trevor walked to the garage in a daze. Had that just happened? Was Sykes going out of his mind? It could have been a dream – just his own wishful thinking.

"Trevor," called Sykes, "you ready?"

Not a dream. And thankfully the puncture repair kit was easy to find. Trevor slipped it in his bag and headed out to the car.

The drive was uneventful. Sykes didn't speak again, instead he turned on the radio and the space in the car was filled with rock music and heavy guitar riffs. But that was a first too. When they arrived at the centre, Trevor showed Sykes his notepad.

☺

Sykes nodded. "OK, lad. See you later."

Trevor shut the door gently and breathed out as he watched Sykes drive away. Could his father actually like him? It made sense knowing he saw Trevor as a reminder, and that losing her was hard for him too. It didn't make things OK, but it made it hurt less. He walked down the path, taking another deep breath as the sun warmed his skin.

Elise was filling water baths, droplets ricocheting off the green plastic bowls and glinting in the sun, while Rash carried birds to their lawn perches. They both raised their hands when they saw him walking in.

"Morning, Trevor."

Trevor smiled and waved back, then tried not to look too hard as he walked past Midge's mews space. Midge gave him a welcoming chup.

"My spellboda! Everything's good. I saw Roger earlier, before he left, and the lookouts for the balds and Lennox are all in place. I just can't wait to fly!"

A warm feeling settled. There was no sign of anything from last night, other than a bit of scuffed lawn where the men must have tripped over. He'd cleared up well. The only niggle was Lennox… but he was nowhere to be seen, and there was no way he could link Trevor to anything last night. He'd be more bothered thinking the police had been here than to worry about anything else. So all Trevor had to do was make sure no-one came back before Midge was flying free and ready to be released, and back-up was in place for that. It was all covered.

"Trevor," called Elise. "Dump your stuff and come give us a hand. I want to get things done as fast as poss before it gets too hot. Then we can get Midge out for his first flight today, before we open."

Trevor grinned as he walked to the cleaning shed. Keeping Midge safe was going to be a piece of cake. In a few days they'd be planning his release, which should give him enough time to keep the thieves away, and to work out how to get Lennox found out. Everything was coming together.

24

"Know what? I've got a really good feeling about this. Plus the transmitter will be our back-up if it goes wrong. Which it won't! Take the creance off, Trevor."

Trevor's heart thumped as he fiddled with the knot. Elise pulled the cord part of the lure from her bag as she backed away and unravelled it to its full length. Midge shook his feathers, buzzing as he gripped the glove.

"OK, Trevor," she called. "There's his rouse. I'm ready too. Put him on the perch."

Trevor turned his back to Elise as he held out his gloved hand.

"This is epic," he muttered.

"Totally," Midge muttered back, his eyes shining. "Make sure we can talk after this, right?"

Trevor smiled and let go of the jesses. Midge stepped on to the perch, and the leather straps dangled free, with no creance line to anchor him.

Elise swung the lure. Trevor held his breath. Take-off happened so fast it was a blur. Midge flew straight at the lure, but banked round to the right as Elise let the line swing out to the side. Midge flew tantalisingly close. His feet shot out into grabbing position, and for a second Trevor thought the falcon was going to catch it, but at the last moment, Elise pulled the line in and snatched the lure away, back towards her and out of Midge's reach. Building speed, Midge continued on his flight path behind Elise and was caught up in the brisk wind. It raised him with a jolt up to about thirty feet as he flew out to the far edge of the arena. Elise walked across the grass, following him, and whistled – a long high note. She stopped swinging the lure when the falcon's wing-beats grew less rapid, and he glided and turned on the wind currents.

"He's a genius!" Elise shouted over her shoulder. "First time out, and he's starting to go up! Amazing!"

Trevor's mouth was open as Midge soared and twisted, making tiny adjustments to his wing and tail feathers. How did he know what to do? Of course, Midge had told him it was all in his blood, pre-programmed instinct. It was almost like he was soaring with him, living the moment, same as in his dreams, as Midge turned again, even higher, and began to coast in the direction of Roger's copse across the valley.

"Midge! Hey! Hey!" Elise shouted, and Trevor heard panic in her voice as she began to swing the lure again. "That's too far! Hey!"

Trevor ran across the field to Elise, as a page from his book sprung out in his mind. 'Hey' was the call to get attention, and 'Ho' would be the call to come for food. Midge turned and headed back to the arena, dropping height and flying at speed straight at the lure. As he drew close, Elise did the same thing again, letting the lure out and drawing it back.

"Ho!" It worked. Midge turned, more sharply this time, trying again and approaching on Elise's other side.

"HO!" This time Elise let the lure line up straight above as Midge flew towards her. His outstretched feet made a thud of contact. Elise let the lure fall to the ground, with Midge attached, wings spread as he descended. The falcon landed on the ground, gripping his dinner, beak open and panting, with his wings stretched out over the grass.

Elise's cheeks were pink and her eyes shone.

"Oh my days, Trevor, he is such a star! That was incredible!"

Trevor smiled so hard his cheeks ached. They sat down on the grass while Midge got his breath back and went on to eat his food. Elise was breathless.

"Did you see him? The way he had fun? He's brilliant! He's picking up exactly how to hunt. How to chase prey if it twists and turns out of his way, how to use the air currents."

Elise pushed wind-whipped hair away from her eyes.

"Just look at his wings! He's covering up his food, mantling, protecting it. Oh, wow, he's going to be great when he's free. He'll survive, no problem, if he carries on like this!"

Still beaming, Trevor nodded and gave a thumbs-up with both hands before he shoved his glove back on. He fiddled in his falconry bag for another piece of food, as Midge finished his lure-pad meal.

"That's it," said Elise. "You can pick him up now."

Midge looked up from the lure and across to Trevor's glove. He hopped over with a single wing-beat and stepped on. Trevor took hold of his flying jesses and tucked them between his fingers.

"Can you beat that?" Elise said, as Midge clicked his beak and started on the second course of his meal. "Having a peregrine falcon wander over to you and choose to be with you, when he could just take off and please himself. Best feeling in the world."

Trevor couldn't stop smiling as he attached Midge's swivel and leash. Together, they walked back across the field. The centre was open now, and a few visitors were watching them, hanging around by the arena entrance gate.

"They're a bit early," said Elise in a low voice. "And they look like the sort who want to talk and take pictures. You keep going, and I'll field them. The peregrine needs a rest before we fly him again."

Trevor nodded and walked on as Elise stopped to talk. As he went round the path past the office, the door opened and Adam popped his head out.

"Good flying, that was," he said. "He's a stonker of a bird. And that was some great handling, lad. Keep it up."

Trevor nodded, feeling like he could burst. Adam thought he was good. He smiled stupidly at Rash as they passed each other in the mews, then waited till he was out of the way before he crouched to put Midge on his perch.

"You were amazing," Trevor whispered as he tied the leash.

Midge stepped on to the astroturf. "I know," he said, sounding smug. "Seriously, Trevor, that was the most fun! You should have wings, you're missing out."

Trevor grinned, remembering his daydream. "I wish I did, trust me. How did it feel?"

"Like… like freedom. All I can see, the colours, the speed. When I felt the wind for the first time, that was crazy. There's no limits."

"Why did you fly off?" said Trevor.

Midge looked over Trevor's shoulder and bobbed his head. "Shh."

"What?"

"Trevor? Did you say something?"

Trevor turned with a jump. Elise was standing just outside the wire.

He shook his head and coughed, pointing to his throat.

"Oh, right," said Elise. "I just wondered. Because it sounded like you were." Her eyes crinkled as she smiled. "I talk to the birds all the time, so if you did, I wouldn't think it was strange. Just saying."

Trevor stared at the ground, wishing it would swallow him.

"And if you ever feel like you want to speak to me, you know you can."

A happy-sounding tune rang out from the depths of her falconry bag. Elise fumbled inside.

"Damn, sorry, it's Lennox. Got to take this."

Trevor breathed out as she walked away. Midge stared at him.

"Why has your face changed colour?"

Trevor smiled and shook his head. He'd have to be more careful. He turned to leave the mews, wondering what was going on with Lennox and where he was. This could turn out to be very interesting.

The office door banged as Trevor left the mews, and Adam walked over, wearing a massive glove that came up to his elbow.

"Working with the Goldie this morning, lad. Have a look."

Trevor watched from the path. It was amazing how fast Adam picked Tiberius up and untied the falconer's knot. Almost too fast for the eagle to react, but not quite. As Adam straightened up, Tiberius took a swipe at him with his huge talons, only just missing his hand. Hackles up, the eagle spread his wings and opened his massive beak. Picking up his feet, one after the other, he gripped Adam's glove harder each time he slammed them back down. Adam glanced at Trevor.

"Got to watch those feet, lad, when you work with the big birds." He moved closer to the mews wire and lifted his right arm. Three raised white circles glowed on his skin, about halfway between his elbow and his wrist.

"See that? Harpy eagle. Belongs to a friend of mine in Saudi. Talons went right through my jacket. I lost a pint of blood to that."

Adam shut the door to the mews and looked across the grass.

"Elise, I'm going to fly him in this morning's demo. He needs more training."

Tiberius threw back his head and called sharply as Elise walked towards them. There wasn't time to tune in, but

Trevor didn't have to be a spellboda to work out that the eagle was stropping out.

"Rather you than me!" Elise grinned, putting her mobile in her bag. "That was Lennox. He's seen a doctor. Nothing serious, but he needs to be out of the sun. He's happy to come in and get stuck in to paperwork, so I said that would be fine."

"It's better than nothing, but we could have done without it." Adam frowned. "Going to be busy, and I'm already pushed as it is." He leaned his head towards the meadow, where groups of visitors were working their way in. "It'll be all hands on deck."

"This one will be a great help." Elise threw a smile in Trevor's direction. "I'll get Rash sorted to take on some of Lennox's stuff, and Trevor can fill in with the cleaning and tidying. That's OK, right, Trevor?" Trevor nodded as Elise turned back to Adam. "We'll cope."

"We'll have to." Adam checked his watch, leaning to his right as Tiberius lunged at his face, which he completely ignored. "And it's only ten minutes to the demo. Don't be late." He glanced at Trevor. "Appreciate your enthusiasm, lad."

"OK then." Elise shrugged her shoulders as Adam walked away. "I'll get Rash and sort the other birds. You prep the flying food, Trevor, and I'll see you in five!"

There wasn't a spare seat around the arena. Trevor handed food bags to Elise and Rash, and found a shady spot on the grass. No way was he going to pass up the chance to see the eagle fly. Besides, Lennox turning up and finding him alone was the last thing he wanted to happen.

He sighed. Typical that Lennox was going to be in the exact place he needed to go. The tin would have to wait.

Adam walked in with Tiberius, his arm muscles straining through his T-shirt. He was wearing his PA headset and sunglasses, and there was a buzz of chatter from spectators as he walked past them. When he reached the centre of the arena, Tiberius called out. Trevor concentrated. He had to hear this.

"Yes. I have the starring role in this display, and I will allow the man in charge, the only human worthy, to touch me."

His attitude was unreal. Tiberius puffed out his chest feathers as Adam spoke.

"Ladies and gents, welcome to the unforgettable experience of seeing the king of the bird world fly. The golden eagle is our nation's second largest bird of prey, with only the white-tailed eagle bigger. These incredible birds were hunted almost to extinction in our country, but thanks to conservation work we now have over 400 pairs of breeding birds. A success story."

Tiberius called again. "Correct, I am incredible. Wise words, human."

Like everyone else, Trevor absorbed every word, his eyes wide. Even children were quiet. Seeing Adam and Tiberius in action was something else.

Adam opened his glove and the eagle launched into the air, a great leap using Adam's arm as a springboard. His huge wings spread so wide one of them bashed Adam on the side of the head as he took off. Adam didn't register it touched him. The majesty and power of the eagle in flight was crazy. He soared on the wind, his wings steady and his tail spread wide. And Trevor understood why Tiberius was the way he was. A bird like him had every reason to be.

A gust of wind raced through the arena, bending the branches of the trees. Adam held up his glove and whistled, a large piece of meat visible, even without Tiberius's eagle eyes. Trevor held his breath as the eagle turned and folded in his wings, making a 'w' shape in the air. Tiberius approached the glove at what seemed an impossible speed, but he raised the tips of his wings, lowering his huge talons like landing gear from his body, and held them out. He hit the glove with a thump, but Adam stood strong and solid like the trunk of a tree. Trevor joined the rest of the audience as he clapped enthusiastically. They were amazing.

Adam smiled at the crowd, as chilled as if he'd just had a cup of tea and a biscuit.

"So today the wind is strong, and you see how eagles love to soar on the currents. But Tiberius here is still quite young, and that's why he struggled."

Tiberius threw back his head, his huge beak wide.

"What? How dare you!"

"As he gets older, he will become more confident in the air…"

"More *confident*? Are you serious?"

"…and his flying ability will improve."

Trevor pressed his lips together.

"This is outrageous!"

"So ladies and gentlemen, I hope you enjoyed meeting Tiberius today."

Adam dodged just in time as the eagle took another swipe, this time at the top of his stubbly chin. He grinned at the audience.

"And if you'll excuse me, I'll leave you with Elise and put this youngster back in the centre, before he takes a chunk out of me. Don't worry, he'll grow out of it."

The visitors laughed their heads off, clapping again as Adam walked back to the centre. The eagle roared at him all the way.

"Human weakling! Upstart. Bumbler... Halfwit!"

Trevor pressed his hand to his mouth to stop himself from laughing out loud. Hearing everything was so cool. It was kind of sad people didn't know about spellbodas, but then again maybe more sad if they did. Then they'd understand how much they'd lost. As he watched Elise fly the wood owl a realisation hit. It wouldn't be possible to go back to normal, ever, after discovering this gift. But he knew now he'd never want to.

As the demo came to an end Trevor jumped up to help. He gathered up loose equipment and tidied litter left lying around seats, while Elise and Rash took birds back to their perches. Mid-way to picking up a chocolate wrapper he paused, with a funny feeling he wasn't alone. He looked up, straight at the office window, where Lennox was standing, looking out at him. Hairs prickled on the back of his neck as he grabbed the wrapper and jogged back into the centre. All he had to do was stay near Elise.

He found her near the caracara aviary, on her mobile again, with a huge smile on her face. She put her hand up as Trevor got closer, gesturing to wait. Trevor looked at

Austen inside his aviary, and the caracara hopped over to the wire.

"Hey, dude. Nice work last night. And don't listen to that funky eagle. His manners are jank!"

Trevor grinned. He was getting so good at tuning in now, it was coming naturally.

"Thanks so much, Harry. Great! So we'll speak tomorrow? Cheers then, bye!"

Trevor turned to Elise, who was still beaming. "You'll want to know this. Come on, we need Adam."

Trevor matched her stride as they headed across the centre to Adam, who was locking the mews. He turned to walk towards the office.

"Adam!" called Elise.

Adam looked round. "Can it wait? I've got a ton of paperwork."

"This won't take long," said Elise, as she and Trevor caught him up. "I've just had a call from Harry."

Adam kept going. "Wildlife liaison Harry? Walk with me."

"That's the one," said Elise. "He had great news." She looked at Trevor. "Do you remember the two guys I told you about? The ones who stole the peregrines?"

Trevor put his hand to his mouth to hide a gasp and faked it into a sneeze.

"They've been arrested," said Elise, her eyes shining. "This morning, around—"

"What for?" asked Adam.

"Nothing bird-related this time," said Elise. "But just as bad. They were caught on CCTV snaring a badger, last weekend, on the Chatsworth Estate."

"Fools," said Adam, opening the office door.

"I know," said Elise. "Harry said they're in custody. I didn't catch it all, the phone cut out a bit. He said something about repeat offences."

"Well, it's what they deserve," said Adam shortly. "Unbelievable."

He made to walk in the office and Elise put her hand on his arm.

"Just a sec. There's more. I told Harry about the peregrine, told him how well he's doing. He's coming tomorrow to watch him fly!"

Adam frowned, as Lennox emerged from inside the office. "He's doing great, I'll give you that, but is that a bit soon?" He glanced as Lennox edged past him. "Where are you off to?"

"Just the loo," said Lennox. "Back in a minute."

Adam turned back to Elise. "I mean, he won't be ready for a bit. Won't it be a waste of Harry's time to get him out here?"

Elise grinned. "I think he's excited to see him. Says he has an idea."

Adam rubbed his head. "Fair enough then." He walked into the office and called over his shoulder.

"Can you and the lads do the afternoon demo? I need to get on with this paperwork. Think I'll nip home and get it done somewhere cooler with a glass of beer. And before I forget, well done for locking the office door last night. I've finally got through to you!"

Elise laughed. "No problem. And fine for later too. Thanks, Adam."

Adam shut the door and Elise smiled at Trevor.

"Good news, right? They so need putting away."

Trevor nodded. A huge load had left his shoulders. Midge was safe. But a sick feeling grew in his tummy. Was Garnell the snared badger? Chatsworth wasn't that near the high peak, so hopefully not. And there were loads of badgers out there. But even so, none of them deserved to be strangled in a wire. Elise was right, men like them shouldn't be free. He looked over his shoulder while Elise checked out the contents of her falconry bag. Midge stared out at him from the mews and Trevor raised his eyebrows. Had the falcon heard? Midge stared back and bobbed his head deliberately, three times.

"Come on," said Elise. "Rash can do his training here, on the weathering lawn. You give the feed room a quick clean while I do the cleaning shed, then we can go back to the arena with the peregrine. He'll be ready for another fly."

Trevor followed Elise, relief overcoming niggles – mostly. The thieves were off the radar. Sykes was bearable. And flying Midge again would be awesome. But there was just one thing. The boss. He had to work out a way to find out for sure if it was Lennox, without making him suspicious. How much of the conversation had Lennox heard, when Adam opened the office door? He shivered and his arm hairs prickled, despite the heat. With the two balds in custody, the boss would have to come and take Midge himself. Would any of the scouts realise in time? And anyway… if Lennox was the boss, and had keys to get into the mews, who could possibly stop him?

25

Midge's second flight of the day was textbook, another step closer to his release. Although it was amazing, it didn't stop Trevor's brain working overtime. The next step all hung on Lennox, and proving he was involved. He had to get in the office, find that tin, have a proper look... and get the megaphone and fire extinguisher back in their usual places before anyone noticed they were gone. Especially without Lennox knowing. But there was no chance of that, not while Lennox was hogging the place with his 'illness'.

By lunchtime the heat was relentless. Visitors clustered into groups, standing under trees to escape it. They reminded Trevor of shoals of fish, mouths opening and closing as they gulped from bottles and cans. He grabbed his rucksack and went to join Elise and Rash at their usual grassy spot in the shade behind the cleaning shed.

"Chuck us another pasty, Elise," said Rash, his mouth full. "They're well nice."

Elise raised her hand.

"Get in line. I'm older. There's a pecking order!"

"Oh yeah, very funny," Rash said.

Elise reached over and picked up the bag.

"There's only two left. That'd be your second. I've only had one, and Trevor needs one." She lobbed a pasty to Trevor. "We should see if Lennox feels up to the last one before you filch it."

"Stuff him!" said Rash, reaching for the bag. "He's wriggled out of all the jobs today because he's not well. That means he doesn't get the Saturday pasties. And as next of kin I get his share."

"Speak of the devil, bro."

Trevor stiffened and forced down a mouthful of pasty, as Lennox sat beside them.

"Alright, Elise? Alright, Trev?" said Lennox. "For the record, no food for me. Not feeling up to it." He snatched the bag from Rash, and his brother scowled. Lennox got the pasty out. "But I nominate Trev to have it. It's only fair. If he hadn't come in today you'd be twice as boiling now without him to help you."

Trevor eyed the pasty as if it was poisonous. Lennox smiled at him.

"Go on, Trev. You deserve it."

What was he playing at? Trevor stared as he reached for the pasty. Lennox looked perfectly innocent, as if nothing was wrong. But then he'd looked innocent last night too, after warning him off. Well, two could play that game, and he wasn't giving anything away. He returned Lennox's smile and took a huge bite. Lennox laughed.

"I know they're good, mate, but don't forget to finish your other one first!"

Elise laughed too, as Trevor's face grew hotter. "They're good pasties! Adam's started a tradition now, bringing them in."

She took a swig of Coke.

"He should bring more than four in," said Rash. "Where is he, anyway? Isn't he doing the second demo?"

Elise shook her head.

"He's not back today. He's got paperwork, and as he was leaving he said he'd just had the nod to go and look at a new eagle. One he might buy. Bald, I think."

Rash nodded as he chewed. "That would be cool."

"Yeah," said Lennox, "but where does it fit in with the conservation stuff we're working on? Balds are North American, not African."

Rash sighed loudly. "Will you give it a rest? Can you stop finding things to argue about for a change, and talk about something interesting?"

Lennox leaned over. "Like what? Something worthwhile, like texting the blonde girl from yesterday?"

Rash rubbed his nose. "Nothing wrong with that, bruv. She's peng. Besides, blondes are the thing right now. Ask Elise. She's all out for that blond teacher from Trev's—"

"OK, OK, lunchtime's over!" Elise got up, sweeping the crumbs from her jeans. "We need to get ready for the demo." She rushed on. "And can you keep looking out for my ring? Hope you're feeling better, Lennox. Come on, let's go!"

She walked off, and Trevor scrambled up to follow her, shoving remnants of pasty into his mouth. No way was he going to end up with Lennox. But Elise and who?

"Nice one, bro, as usual," said Lennox, rolling his eyes at Trevor. "I don't think she appreciated that."

"Oh, whatever," said Rash as he got up. "She'll get over it."

Trevor walked into the centre, his head whirling. Blond teacher? No way. Just no. It couldn't be.

He stuck by Elise like a shadow as they got ready, and kept an eye out for any sign of Lennox. Besides seeing him go back in the office, there was nothing. So he was keeping out of the way too... or up to something. By the end of the sweltering demo the visitors were at their limit. Fanning themselves and downing drinks, a mass of people left straightaway, leaving only a straggling few flaked out under trees. Elise walked out of the arena with the last demo bird, a panting saker falcon, sitting on her glove.

"Trevor," she said as she passed him. "Can you check the mews birds are OK while I cool Simba down and give him his last bit of dinner?"

Perfect. Trevor gave her a thumbs-up and set off to the mews and Midge. He might not be able to get in the office, but there were other things he could do.

After his walk past each mews cubicle, Trevor crouched at the edge of Midge's mews space and pretended to tidy up some of the stray old feathers that dotted the sand.

"Is everything OK?" he whispered.

Midge barely looked up as he preened his chest feathers.

"Of course," he said. "Why wouldn't it be?"

"No problems?" Trevor persisted. "No weird visitors or anything? Or any word from scouts?"

Midge paused, his beak half-hidden in his feathers. "No. Why would there be?" he repeated. "The thieves are shut away. You know I heard, don't you?"

"Yes, but I just wanted to check nothing else's happened," Trevor replied. "This afternoon."

"No." There was a tinge of frustration in Midge's voice. He raised his head. "Stop worrying. My flying is going brilliantly, that bloke's coming tomorrow, I'll be free soon, and I can find my family. It's all good. Plus I'm tired. All that energy I used, being up there. Don't stress, Trevor, OK?"

Suddenly Trevor knew it was better that Midge didn't know anything about the boss. Why should the falcon feel on edge too? It had been a long hot day after a crazy night. Trevor yawned and stood up.

"OK, it's all cool. I'll see you tomorrow."

Midge bobbed his head as Trevor walked out of the mews. This was on him now. Lennox must be using his time in the office to plan his next move, now he knew the thieves had been arrested, so Trevor had to work out his next move too, and quickly. He had to get proof. And getting into that office was the only way to do it.

26

Trevor pressed the tyre. It was firm, pumped up and good to go. He packed away the repair kit and checked his watch, yawning again. Five thirty. The others were finishing off in the centre but when Elise told him to go he hadn't argued. He didn't have the energy to lift another broom or bucket today.

Slinging his rucksack over one shoulder, he grabbed the handlebars and was just about to go when a large crow landed with a flutter and a clunk on the car-park gate. His deep blue-black plumage was so glossy it made Trevor think of shoe polish. The crow leaned its head, first to one side, then the other, looking hard at him. Trevor frowned. A scout? He concentrated, as the crow opened its dark wedge of a beak.

"Alright?" he said. "Saw you from the top of the tree, what ya doing?"

"Sorting my bike," Trevor replied, after a quick check for people. "Repairs. Have you got news?"

The crow's black eyes shone.

"News? No, mate, they don't give me jobs like that. Just thought it was time I said hello. I'm Crispin. Top crow round here."

Trevor remembered him. It was the crow Midge called to in the arena, the first time he ate his food on the glove.

"Oh, right. I'm Trevor."

"I know that," said Crispin. "Heard them talking. Nice glow. You're the spellboda then?"

Trevor nodded.

"So you can help somebird like me?"

The crow hopped clumsily along the gate towards Trevor.

"I can try," said Trevor. "What's up?"

Crispin's head drooped and he studied his silver-grey feet. "Can you talk to them raptors? Them birds of prey? They're horrible."

"Really?" said Trevor. "What's the problem?"

"They're idiots, is what the problem is," said Crispin. "I'm not so far off being the same as what them lot are. I eat meat. I'm big. But they all hate me."

"Why?" said Trevor.

Crispin looked up.

"Dunno," he said, dark eyes glinting. "I do loads for them. I tell them things. Like what that dozy caracara gets up to, who's said what about who. I'm, like, the daily news, I am."

Trevor rubbed his chin.

"Well, I'm no expert, but could they think you're being nosy? Maybe—"

"Nosy? No way," said Crispin. "Can't you talk to them, tell them to stop? If they don't I might have to move tree and find more polite neighbours."

"I can have a go… but it might not help," said Trevor. "They don't all talk to me either. But I could do with your help. Can you—"

"Mate! Knew I liked ya! You'll sort it." Crispin flapped his wings and jumped backwards and forwards along the gate. He puffed out his chest and began to strut.

"They'll see!" he crowed. "I'm the bird, top of the murder! The one with all the bling."

"What are you going on about?" said Trevor, laughing. "What do you mean, bling?"

"You know, bling!" Crispin jigged on the spot. "I've got it all, mate. Magpies, shmagpies, they've got nothing compared to me. I get all the best wrappers, the sparkly foil stuff the kids drop, and some of them lovely round things from off the top of a can. Mate, they sparkle like you wouldn't believe. Can't resist them. Last week I found the ultimate bling, mate, the top banana. If I carry on like this I'll have—"

"You know what I think?" said Trevor with a grin. "Maybe if you didn't brag so much they'd listen to you more."

"What?" said Crispin. "But they need to know how amazing I am."

"So show them, by being helpful," said Trevor. "You can keep them safe, same as I do. I could tell them you're doing it."

"I'm up for that. Pukka idea."

"Great. So I have a job for you," said Trevor. "Perch in that big tree in the flying arena, as often as you can. You'll see everything. Let me know if you see anything weird, especially when the other humans are there. You know who they are?"

Crispin nodded. "I know. Three blokes and a bird. The one with the horse tail."

"Horse tail?" said Trevor.

"The one coming out of her head. Weird things, you humans. No offence."

Trevor laughed again. "Ponytail. Epic. So you're up for it? And I'll help you back?"

Crispin tilted his head and looked over the meadow.

"Deal. I'll spy. Especially on that bloke who brings his mates in after everyone's gone home. That one in the office today."

Trevor drew in a sharp, hissing breath. "Lennox. I knew it! Look, Crispin, you need to watch everything he does, OK, until I'm back tomorrow. Every single thing. I need to know if he—"

"Alright, mate, calm! I heard you first time." Crispin stretched and tilted his head. "Isn't the white car with brown and grey dirt something to do with you?"

"Sykes's car? I guess so, if that's what you mean."

"So why do you need your bike?"

Trevor frowned. "What?"

Crispin took off and circled overhead, with steady wing-beats.

"It's coming now… up the drive," he shouted. "And I get it. Every single thing. Laters, mate."

194

Trevor's feet were glued to the gravel as he watched the car approach. Sykes drew to a stop next to the bike. Trevor opened the door cautiously and jumped back. Was that Sykes?

"Thought you'd like a lift. Put the bike in the boot, the back seats are down. Don't look so shocked. I've only got a haircut, boy."

Understatement of the year. The wild dark waves were gone. In their place was a short, neat cut, and his beard was trimmed close to his face. No breadcrumbs or other remnants of food. Trevor's mouth hung open. Sykes looked less like a bear and more like a… a dad.

"Come on then, get on with it."

Trevor pulled himself together as he loaded the bike into the car. He sat in the passenger seat, bracing himself for some sort of catch.

"We need to crack on home, boy. I've put a big ready meal in the oven."

27

Sykes didn't talk during the drive home, and rock music filled the silence again. Trevor got his head together as the landscape of fields and farms slipped by, changing to houses, people and shops as they neared town. He shot a sideways glance at Sykes. On top of all the Midge business, it was almost too much to process. It was good Crispin was keeping tabs on things… as long as he didn't forget and decide to show off or steal a sweet wrapper or something. Sorting the office sneak-in was priority, as soon as Lennox was out of the way. Trevor stifled a yawn. There was too much backed up in his head and not enough energy to think about it all.

Sykes pulled up outside the house.

"Get your bike out, lad. I'll check the food."

Trevor wheeled his bike up the path. By the time he'd stowed it in the garage and got to the kitchen, Sykes was clattering plates and forks on the table, where dinner sat steaming. Mrs Bingo-Wings curled her tail around the table legs, and Trevor reached down to give her a stroke.

"Come on then, get a drink, sit down."

Trevor grabbed a mug, filled it with tap water and sat at the table. Sykes took a bottle of red wine from the side and poured a glass, smaller than his usual size.

They ate in silence. Lasagne in a foil tin might not be homemade, but it was a massive upgrade from a sandwich. Trevor realised he was starving, and between them the tray was soon empty. He kept glancing at Sykes, getting used to his facial upgrade. Strange to see him looking so… normal. It was weird. But good… hopefully. Swallowing his last mouthful, Trevor leaned over and pulled the pad out of his rucksack. Why not give it another try? He wrote, then pushed the pad across the table.

Thanks for the lifts. And the food. I had a good time at the centre today. Is it OK if I go again tomorrow?

Sykes looked at the pad, nodded and took a gulp of wine.

"You can go." He got up and fiddled with the dials on the oven. "Get to bed then, you look tired. Clear up all this first, can you?"

Trevor got up and ran the hot tap as Sykes picked up his bottle and glass, retreating to the lounge. Trevor shook his head, as Mrs B rubbed against his legs, purring. They'd just had a meal together, like a normal father and son. Sykes had been OK. Could he be a proper dad again? Even if he couldn't, this new version of nearly pleasant and less hairy Sykes was so much better than the old one. A hope seed began to grow.

Leaving the dishes to drain on the side, Trevor went

upstairs, Mrs B close at his heels. He grabbed his book from the drawer and flopped down on the bed. His tummy growled, and he chuckled. It was probably as much in shock as the rest of him after having hot food. Mrs B jumped up with a miaow, sank down on the covers and started a meticulous clean of her paws.

Trevor opened the book and scanned the list of chapters. He stopped at thirteen. He hadn't read that section before: it always looked too boring. But now the title leapt out at him. He turned to page ninety-eight.

BIRD THEFT – FALCONRY AND THE LAW

Years ago, it was customary for a falconer to trap a wild bird for a season, and to train and hunt with it over that time. This was a partnership of bird and man, when the bird would catch prey to be shared with the man, who in turn sheltered and protected the bird. It was a relationship of trust, and at the end of the season, the bird was released. Today, it is illegal in the UK for any bird of prey to be taken from the wild. Sadly, however, this practice still occurs. Eggs and chicks are stolen from nests. Adult birds are trapped. Some are taken by ill-informed individuals who think it would be fun to 'own' a bird of prey. Others, however, are professional 'bird rustlers', people who will sell a wild bird to a falconer, or use a wild bird for breeding purposes.

Trevor nodded, glancing at Mrs B. "This is exactly what the thieves have been up to." He read on as she purred.

The offspring of wild birds are highly valuable to such criminals. Known as F1, or descended one generation from the wild in their bloodline, these birds are sold for much higher sums of money, sometimes four or five times as much as their captive-bred counterparts. We can all play our part to stop this. All captive-bred birds are given leg rings and certificates to prove they have not been 'wild taken', so never agree to purchase a bird if it is offered without a leg ring and paperwork.

Trevor's brain whirred. He shut the book and ruffled Mrs B's head.

"This is why they came back, Mrs B. Midge is too valuable." He stopped stroking her and frowned. "Do you think Midge's family are long gone? Like sold already, to someone who wants an F1 bird?"

Mrs B pushed her head back into his hand, but Trevor ignored her.

"What if they're miles away, or in another country? How can I tell Midge? I can't do that to him. There must be a way to find out first. I need to stop Lennox." His tummy clenched. "And I'm scared I'm running out of time."

28

Sykes was still snoring when Trevor left. If he got there early he should have more time to do some sniffing around. He wheeled the bike down the garden path and checked the tyre. All good. The morning air was fresher as he built up speed, but the sky was already a flawless blue, with heat steadily building. Trevor couldn't keep a fast pace. By the time he made it to the centre cars were already parked there, and he walked across the meadow hot with frustration.

Loads of the birds were in peaceful early mode as he passed the mews, heads under wings and roosting, but Midge was awake, his eyes bright and head bobbing up and down. Trevor checked round for other falconers and stopped.

"Hi," he said. "Quiet night?" He tilted his head towards weathering ground. "Who's in?"

Midge stretched. "All quiet. You mean other humans? I've seen them all, except Adam."

"Dammit."

"What's up?"

Trevor could have kicked himself. "Nothing, just wanted to get stuff from the other night back in the office before anyone notices."

"Oh, don't worry about that," said Midge. "Today is my big day. Remember?"

Trevor made himself grin. "Couldn't forget that. I can't wait."

"It's going to be… what do you say?" Midge flapped his wings. "Epic!"

"Haha!" Trevor turned around just as Elise was closing the falconers' gate, a rake and bucket in her hand. She looked up and stopped.

"Oh! Trevor… that was you laughing, right?"

Trevor raised his eyebrows and tried to look convincingly confused as he shook his head. Elise laughed.

"Don't even try that with me. It's good to hear you happy. Come and help me clean when you've stashed your rucksack. Harry's in at half ten so we'd better hurry up!"

Trevor jogged to the cleaning shed and dumped the rucksack. The fire extinguisher, torch and megaphone were still where he left them in the corner. His luck was holding for now. He grabbed another bucket and rake and joined Elise.

"Birds will stay in the mews today," said Elise, as she shovelled dirty sand into a bucket. "Too hot for them in this sun."

Trevor nodded and raked over the poo-free sand as Elise moved to the next cubicle.

"And there's another visitor today."

Elise's voice had changed. Trevor looked at her. She was frowning at the ground in deep concentration, as she picked up more bird poo.

"Your teacher's coming in. Wants to see how you're doing."

Trevor stopped raking. Was she going pink?

"But that's not till this afternoon. So plenty of time. Come on, keep up!"

They powered through cleaning in record time, and Elise was her normal colour at the end of it. She grinned as she locked the mews door.

"Brilliant! Not many visitors yet either. Lennox and Rash should be nearly done on the aviaries too. He's back to normal today, thank goodness... let's grab a break."

She called to Rash and Lennox, who caught them up, deep in conversation. Trevor sighed. It was going to be impossible to avoid Lennox. That would be more obvious than asking him when he was planning to steal Midge.

"Bruv, she's not going to meet you, you haven't got the magic touch."

"Yes she blinking is." Rash held up his phone as they reached the falconers' area. "See? She DM'd me."

"She's out of your league, mate. Wait till you're older, you need a bit of experience with the ladies."

"Get stuffed, Lennox. You don't know what you're talking about."

"Oh, shut up, you two." Elise lobbed an apple in Trevor's direction. "Here you go, one of your five a day."

Rash huffed as he tapped his phone.

"Anything going on today?" said Lennox.

Trevor stared hard at his apple. Lennox knew. He'd heard Elise with Adam yesterday. Slimeball.

"Heat is the key thing today. We need to be careful who we fly," said Elise, between mouthfuls. "If the forecast is right it could be too much, especially for Justin, Aerosol and Dolly. Just be aware."

Lennox nodded. "I'm on it."

"And Harry's coming to see the peregrine fly," said Elise. "In about an hour."

"Great!" said Lennox. "So has he decided when the peregrine goes?"

Trevor clenched his fists against the grass to stop himself from throwing the apple at Lennox's face. Elise shook her head.

"Not yet. But he says he has a plan."

Lennox smiled, as Rash took a selfie. "Exciting." He glanced at Trevor. "You eating that apple then, mate?"

Trevor nodded and pulled his pad out of his jeans pocket.

In a minute.
Why hasn't he got a name?

"Who," said Elise. "The peregrine?"

Trevor nodded again.

"We don't name birds that we know are going," said Lennox. "We get attached if we do."

Trevor took a bite of apple, wishing Lennox would disappear. Elise stared at Trevor.

"You've named him, haven't you?" she said.

203

Like they would believe him if he told the truth.

"Midge," said Elise. "I like it." She looked at the others. "Tell you what, seeing as Trevor is the fastest learning falconer we've ever had, let's bend our rule for once. You two OK with that?"

Rash grunted, without looking up from his phone.

"Alright with me," said Lennox. "Midge it is."

"Blimey, you lot, how many breaks do you have?" Adam came round the corner and stood over them. "Is everything done?"

Elise grinned and stood up. "Morning, guvnor! Yep, cleaning all sorted and we're good to go. Just got to get demo food ready."

Adam nodded. "Good. Make sure it's spotless, right, with Harry in. Always good to keep the powers that be happy."

"Of course," said Elise. "I'll double check everywhere. Are you on demos today?"

Adam nodded. "Yep, I'm good for that." He grinned. "Unless you want to do the afternoon one? Maybe you have someone you want to impress."

Elise flushed bright red as Rash snorted. Lennox looked away, his shoulders shaking.

"Seriously, you lot, stop it! Sorry, Trevor, don't take any notice of them! I'm going to check your aviaries!"

Trevor shadowed Elise while firmly shutting out the possibility that this afternoon could be one of the most awkward of his life. At ten thirty exactly the centre was spotless, and Elise raised her hand as a ginger-haired man wearing khaki shorts walked towards them.

"He's always on time. Trevor, can you go and get your Midge? Weather's perfect for him."

The familiar thrill bubbled up as Midge stepped on the glove. Trevor carried the falcon to the prep room for his weight check.

"Just go for it," he said.

Midge bobbed his head. "For sure I will," he said. "You should see those thermals."

"I read about them," said Trevor. "Warm air, right? That lifts you up?"

"That's it," said Midge. "Easy to fly when you find one. Just soar and they lift you higher."

Trevor followed Midge's stare, out of the window. "Can you actually see them?"

"Yes, in a way," Midge replied. "The air changes shape, the pressure does things to my ears, then to my eyes. Hard to describe."

Trevor opened his mouth to ask more, and stopped. Midge was somewhere else, his body tense, his eyes on the arena.

"Sounds epic."

Midge stayed still and silent as they walked to the arena, his talons gripping the glove harder than normal. They went through the gate and Trevor realised there was an audience. Rash was sitting on one of the demo seats... next to Lennox, of course. Adam stood beside Elise in the arena, leaning against Trevor's bench and talking to Harry. Both men were wearing sunglasses, but Harry didn't have Adam's cool image. His knobbly knees didn't help.

Elise turned and smiled. "So this is Midge, and Trevor, our volunteer, who's done loads of work with him. Trevor, Harry."

"Hello, Trevor," said Harry, with a nod. "Good work so far, I hear."

Trevor smiled as Elise continued. "Let's see what Midge has got today. Conditions are perfect." She looked at Adam. "You OK for me to do this?"

"Sure," said Adam. "I get to watch and enjoy it."

Elise nodded. "OK, Trevor, get him into position."

Midge took off as soon as Elise swung the lure. He flew close, the same as yesterday, with the lure just out of reach. But this time he didn't turn back. He kept going, like a bullet, straight out across the valley.

"Hey!" Elise shouted, but Midge didn't waver. He stayed on course until he reached the centre of the valley, and there he caught the wind.

"Oh my days!" Elise's voice shook. "He's looking for a thermal!" She let the lure pad fall to the ground.

Trevor could barely breathe as Midge began to glide and work his way across the valley. What did it look like when a bird found a thermal... would he be able to tell? His heart thumped. A moment later and it was obvious, like the falcon had hit a solid wall of air. Midge jolted, then climbed, without seeming to fly at all, just hanging in the air. With wings stiff and outstretched, feathers fanned out like fingers and his tail spread wide, Midge rested on the warm current. It lifted him at juddering speed. Elise gasped as he soared up. Time stopped. Midge climbed higher and higher, until he was no more than a black dot in a blue sky.

Trevor was in shock. He didn't have a clue how long he stood there, his face fixed skywards. His neck ached. He tore his eyes away from the dot for a moment to glance at Elise, and realised she was doing the same. She glanced over at him briefly too, shaking her head as she looked up again.

"I daren't let him go any higher. I can't believe this is happening. It's so soon."

Still gazing up, she fumbled around for the lure line and began to swing.

"Whatever you do, just don't look away."

Elise gave the lure another circuit and yelled up at the sky.

"HO!"

The dot turned and became a speck. For an awful moment, Trevor thought he was just getting higher and further away, but then realised Midge looked smaller for another reason. A stoop. The falcon had drawn his wings in tight to his body, clamped his tail feathers together in a short, stiff bar and had literally turned himself upside down. Every moment the bird grew closer and larger, Trevor found it more impossible to believe. Midge was dropping vertically from the sky, head-first, in freefall. His speed was phenomenal, his aim deadly as he shot directly towards Elise and the lure.

Trevor felt like his heart had stopped beating. As Midge drew closer, he didn't slow down, and he looked like he was going to crash straight into the ground. But at the last moment he flipped up, out of his descent, and powered in at an impossible angle, hitting the lure with both feet as

Elise launched it up to him. The falcon fluttered gently to the ground, gripping his prey. Within seconds that felt like forever, it was all over.

Trevor looked at Elise as Midge ate his food. Her green eyes glittered back at him. There were no words. Tears suddenly pricked the back of Trevor's eyes too. He'd never seen anything like this, ever. Breathtaking. Humbling. Whatever he had to deal with – his gift, Midge, even Sykes – at least he would always have this amazing memory inside. He scorched every detail of it deep into his heart.

"That's an exceptional falcon," Harry called.

Elise beamed at Trevor. "When he's ready, can you make in to him and pick him up?"

Trevor wanted to speak so badly, and tell Midge how fantastic he'd been. He gave Midge a meaningful look as he stepped on to the glove. Midge replied with a victorious-sounding 'chup' as they walked over to join the others. Rash and Lennox both clapped as they got up and walked back to the centre.

"Wasn't it just?" Harry was saying, as he nodded vigorously, sending more ginger curls of hair to join the others over his forehead. "What an amazing bird. I've never seen a stoop like that in my life."

"He's quick to learn, outstanding," Adam agreed. "Elise has done a grand job." He glanced at Trevor. "The lad's done well with him too. Good handling."

Harry looked at Trevor. "You're well into this, aren't you? I can tell." Trevor nodded.

"Keep that up then, son. One day you could be the kind of person we want on our team."

Trevor's cheeks burned.

"I have to say," Harry turned back to Adam, "I didn't expect the falcon to be this proficient with his flying yet. He's about ready for us to take him."

"Not long," Adam agreed. "If he carries on like this, I'd say he'll be ready in a week or two."

Harry shook his head. "Too far ahead. If you keep him here that long, he's going to become too socialised to people. He's ready – or near enough."

He scratched his neck. "Damn gnats. No, this week will work."

Trevor's chest tightened. This week? That was brilliant, hardly any time for Lennox. But… that was only a few more days. That was hardly any time before Midge went. They needed to work out a plan, decide when and where to meet when Midge was free. They had to do that today, like now. It was so sudden. Panic swept through him.

"Amazing!" said Elise. "How about—"

"That's maybe a bit quick, Harry," Adam said. "He could do with more exercise time."

"He looks fit to me," said Harry. "We have the feeding platform up there now. And the GPS tracker means we can check his movements and find him if anything goes wrong. I can be back here Tuesday."

"Right," said Adam. "Well, if you're sure, we'll sort it. I'll say cheerio now, got to get on to the never-ending paperwork."

"Good good," Harry replied as they shook hands. "Nice to see you again. I'll be here around ten on Tuesday to pick him up."

Elise looked at Midge as Adam walked away. She sighed.

"I'll miss him like crazy, but I know it's right."

"Of course," said Harry. "It's why you're a good falconer. This work should always be about getting them free, increasing wild numbers. Give him more flights today and tomorrow before he goes, build him up. He needs that freedom."

"I know," said Elise. She glanced at Trevor. "Can I ask a favour?"

Harry raised his eyebrows.

"Could we both come with you, when you release him? Trevor's done so much with him too, and I can ask his teacher for permission. I think we'd both like to see Midge go free."

Trevor nodded hard as Harry laughed.

"Is that all? I think we can manage that."

He raised his hand and kept talking as he walked away.

"Tuesday. See you then. Good to meet you, young Trevor. And keep it up."

Elise's smile lit up her face. "Can you believe it? Your falcon is such a success story! Come on, let's get him back to the mews."

Trevor put his foot up on the bench. He fiddled his pad and pen out of his falconry bag and balanced the pad on his knee as he wrote, trying not to wobble Midge on his other hand.

Can I just go for a walk with Midge before I put him back?

Elise sighed. "This is hard, I know. You've done so much with him. But he's flown. He's hot. He should chill out on his perch now."

Please? ☺ Won't be long ☺ Please???

Elise groaned. "Alright, but only if you stay in the arena. You've got ten minutes, OK? That's it." She laughed. "Don't look so triumphant, I'm not a complete soft touch. I'm timing you!" Her face softened. "Your Midge'll be fine out there, you know?"

Trevor did know. He wished he could tell her the real reason for the walk. The stupid thing was if he told her the truth, she'd only think he was lying. Midge was calm as they walked, dark eyes bright as his head bobbed, taking in every movement across the valley. They stayed quiet until they reached the far side of the arena. Trevor leaned against the wooden railing of the fence and rested his left arm along it so that Midge was at eye level.

"Two days till I go free! Mental!"

Trevor checked over his shoulder, but there was no-one in sight.

"That flight was amazing, Midge. Your stoop was—"

"Incredible. I know," finished Midge. "Best feeling ever."

"Was it how you imagined?" said Trevor.

"Better." Midge stared hard at Trevor, his head tilted so sharply he was almost looking at him sideways. "Imagine falling, straight down, but you can control it. The wind screaming, the ground rising towards you… it's beyond brilliant."

"It's your instincts, like you said."

"I know." Midge preened himself lightly, running his beak through his flight feathers. "I hope Roger's back before I go. I need to sort out where to meet him, work out how to find my family."

"Totally," said Trevor, feeling on edge all over again. "What shall we do? Meet near my house? When?"

"In the town? I saw the brick and cloud from up there," said Midge, tilting his head at the sky. "Too busy for me, I'm not going near all the choky town air, not when I've got the peaks to whiz round. I've got a better idea. Let's meet here."

"Here?" said Trevor. "Why not? It's easy, I guess."

"Exactly. Keep a look out for me on Wednesday, when people get ready to go home, tell Elise you need to go for a walk or something. I'll hang around in Roger's copse."

"Could we meet Roger there too, if he's back?" said Trevor.

"That's what I'm thinking," said Midge. "By then I'll have had a chance to zip round and see if I can find news on my family myself. And we can make plans."

"Great idea," said Trevor, as Midge stared out over the fields. Tuesday wouldn't be goodbye. And it gave him time to do more checking on Midge's family. He looked out across the valley, and beyond, where the peaks glowed purple in the sun.

"You're going to have the best life out there."

"Amazing."

Trevor tried to imagine it. Being wild and free, no limits to what you could do, to how high you could go. He smiled. Tuesday didn't give Lennox time to do anything. They'd nearly made it. A call drifted across the field. Elise was waving and beckoning. Trevor sighed.

"We have to go. But I'll be back tomorrow, after school."

He turned and walked slowly across the grass. Midge lowered his head and rubbed his beak across the glove.

"I won't forget what you've done for me, ever. You're more than my spellboda. You're a true friend."

29

Trevor turned as Sykes walked into the kitchen.

"Morning, lad. Bread and butter before you go?"

Yes.
Great.

He shouldn't feel optimistic but he couldn't help it. Could this be their new normal? He'd give anything not to go back to the old. Sykes said keep writing notes, so he pulled the pad back across the table and sat down. Sykes pushed a mug of tea in his direction and buttered bread as Trevor wrote.

I've cleaned up the bathroom.
Mrs B's had her breakfast.

Sykes nodded and handed him a slice. "Good. Thank you, son."

Trevor looked out of the window as the bread stuck in his throat. Did that really just happen?

He cycled to school, warmth spreading through him that had nothing to do with the heat. There was no word from Roger's scouts. This time tomorrow he'd be watching his best friend fly to safety. Even Elise's chat with Mr Mac yesterday afternoon had seemed normal... alright, only a bit cringey. And on top of that, Sykes... after all the hurt, it was like the sun was starting to rise.

He stowed the bike in the shelter and was about to walk away when a tapping noise sounded on the corrugated iron roof. A bird was perched on the edge, its jet-black head and back a sharp contrast with the snow-white tummy underneath. Black wings were so defined into the white plumage it looked like someone had drawn them in with a marker pen. The bird stared down at him in the way he knew too well. His shoulders tensed as he tuned in and waited.

"Hello... Trevor?"

The bird hopped closer, its feet making a tap-dance sound along the roof as Trevor nodded. "That's a relief. I mean, I didn't think I was wrong with your glow and all, but you can never be too careful."

It fluttered down from the roof and rested on a handlebar of Trevor's bike. "I'm Charlotte... Charlie. Friend of Crispin's. He sent me."

Hairs prickled on the back of Trevor's neck and he looked around. No-one was close enough to hear, as long as he made sure he was quiet.

"What's wrong?" he said, as his heart slammed against his chest.

Charlie tilted her head. "Don't look like that. Crispin says to tell you Roger is back. Well, nearly. And he has good news."

Trevor let out a long breath. "That's amazing! When? I'll see him later and we can—"

"Slow down! Like I said, he's not actually, totally back," said Charlie. "He was about four fields away when Crispin saw him. Roger said to tell you his visit to Garnell was very… what was the word… oars-fishers? Ummm, horse-pishuss?"

Trevor smiled. "Knowing Roger… auspicious, maybe?"

"That's it!" Charlie hopped onto the other handlebar. "At least one of us knows what we're talking about."

"I know the word," said Trevor. "I'm not certain but I think it means good things are going to happen."

"There we are then." Charlie clicked her beak. "Crispin said Roger said to tell you he's making one more visit today, and he'll either see you at the centre tomorrow, or if he's quicker than he expects, he'll run over to see you this afternoon."

"Really?" said Trevor. "That's amazing."

Charlie nodded. "From what Crispin told me, Roger's very excited."

"So what's he seeing someone else for, if he's so excited?" said Trevor. "I need to know!"

Charlie bent her head lower, looking furtive.

"Well, I didn't tell you this, but I can't help myself. Us corvids are all the same with news. He's got a… you know."

Trevor frowned. "You know what?"

"Yes," said Charlie. "A you know what. You know!"

"No, I don't," said Trevor. "What are you going on about?"

"Gah, this is awkward!" Charlie threw her head back. "A special friend. You know… a vixen-friend."

Trevor laughed, and stopped short. He was too loud. He checked round again and said a silent thank-you that his luck was holding.

"Aah, so he has a date? Isn't he a bit old for that?"

"Listen, I've seen five seasons now," said Charlie as she puffed out her chest. "And you're never too old."

Trevor grinned. "I get it. Well, I suppose I can wait for Roger's social life if I have to. Just about." He glanced at the school building. "Listen, I have to go in now. Thanks for the news. Will you say thanks to Crispin?"

"Sure," said Charlie. "It's a treat to meet you, spellboda Trevor."

"Same," said Trevor. "Until next time, right?"

"Right!" Charlie took off, her wings spread, flashing vivid blue stripes. "Until then!"

Trevor walked up the path as the lightness inside him spread all over. If only Roger could get to him today, life would be—

"Trevor, wait!" Miss Campbell was hobbling up the path on her crutches. "How's my bike? Everything OK?"

Trevor smiled and nodded, as Charlie circled round them with massive squawks of goodbye.

"Good, well done." Miss Campbell looked up. "Noisy one, isn't he? We could do with seeing another."

Trevor looked at her.

"Haven't you heard the old magpie saying? One for sorrow, two for joy?" said Miss Campbell. She laughed.

"Clearly not! Anyway, have a good day, Trevor. And keep looking after my bike!"

School was the worst kind of drag when there were so many good things hanging around the edge of it. Like the day before a holiday. Anticipation swallowed up concentration, and Trevor couldn't control it. By lunchtime every teacher had snapped at him for looking out of the window. He was even worse in the afternoon. Biology was his last lesson, and all he could do was chew a biro and keep staring, despite Mr Mac's interruptions. The lesson droned on for ever, until a glimmer of red slinking behind the school bins outside caught his eye. This was it! Trevor jumped up, knocking his chair backwards on the floor with a clatter. He ran to the window and hammered against the glass. The fox's head darted up, then it turned and shot away into the bushes. It wasn't Roger. Trevor bashed the glass one last time in disappointment, and cringed as a sharp line spread two ways from his impact point, like a crack travelling across ice.

"Trevor. TREVOR!"

Mr Mac had never shouted at him before. Trevor turned to face a bunch of sniggering students and the stony glare of his teacher. So much for the low profile. They would all think he was completely off his face now.

"What on earth are you doing?" said Mr Mac. "Pick up your chair and sit down. My office – after class."

Great. Now he would be late to the centre. The bell sounded, and chattering students piled out of the building like ants streaming from a nest. Trevor nipped to the toilets and splashed his red face with cold water. He wiped the drops away with scratchy green paper towel, got his notepad out of his rucksack and jogged down the corridor to Mr Mac's room.

"Come in." Mr Mac was looking at a file. "Sit down, Trevor."

His teacher leaned forward, elbows on the desk and hands linked together as he looked at Trevor.

"What happened?"

Trevor shrugged his shoulders.

I was a bit hot. I was having a daydream. Sorry. It was an accident.

"Trevor, that was some daydream." Mr Mac wasn't smiling. "And sorry doesn't cut it. That's school property you've damaged. Again." He sighed. "You know, I heard nothing but good reports about you from the centre yesterday. They're so pleased with you. I take it you're happy going?"

Trevor nodded.

"That's good," said Mr Mac. "You look happier. So I don't understand…"

He leaned back in his chair.

"This afternoon's antics are unrepeatable. And you have to make amends. Detention. In the classroom, now."

Trevor shook his head violently and scribbled on his pad. Mr Mac put up his hand.

"Stop. No excuses. Where's the work on the Biology project I asked you to start?"

Trevor's heart sank.

Sorry. I'm starting it this week. But please don't give me detent

"Trevor. You were supposed to start last week. No. This is happening. You can start it now." Mr Mac stood up.

PLEASE! I need to go to the centre.

"Come on." Mr Mac shook his head as he opened the door. "You can't damage school property and disrupt a class, Trevor." He motioned Trevor to go through first. "And you don't *need* to go to the centre now. I've already OK'd for you to be there and out of school tomorrow morning at El… Miss Lowry's request, and you're not doing that unless you make amends for today and give me some of your project. So get on it. I'm here till five. Now so are you."

30

Trevor hammered out three pages of his project, spouting facts on bird weight control and training, in the time it took for the clock to tick to five and for the heat trapped in the classroom to douse him with sweat. He stabbed his pencil into the last full stop so hard it broke the paper and the lead.

"Come on now, Trevor. No need for that." Mr Mac stood at the door. "You can go."

Trevor shoved everything in his rucksack and got up. He might make it to see Midge, even just for ten minutes, if he rode fast now. But it was so hot. Head down, he walked to the door. He wasn't in the mood to be grateful, whether tomorrow morning was sorted or not.

"I called your father," said Mr Mac. "He's sorting out payment for the window."

Trevor stopped dead.

"Don't look at me like that," said Mr Mac. "You know we

have to do this if school property is damaged." He reached over Trevor's head to grab the edge of the door. "It's done, though your dad said to tell you to come straight home. Go on, get off and forget about it."

Forget about it? Mr Mac was so far off the planet he might as well be living on Mars. Trevor pedalled across town, dread growing heavier on his shoulders. How could he have let this happen, when Sykes was actually becoming OK? He'd been so stupid to lose his head over seeing Roger. He shook his head at the traffic lights and groaned loudly, making an old lady jump as she crossed the road. There was no way he'd make it to the centre before Elise went home, and she'd probably flown Midge already. Besides, even if there was the remotest chance new Sykes would be OK about the broken window, he'd blow his stack if Trevor ignored him and cycled off now. He was stuck. At least he could go first thing in the morning and get out of school.

He coasted round the corner into his road, slowed up and got off by the front gate. He hesitated, checking for Roger and then peering in each window, as if they could reveal a clue about the mood of the man inside. Please let him be OK. He pulled his sweat-sodden shirt away from his back. The heat still sweltered, but something was different. He looked up. The air was heavy, humid, and the sky was changing, the old relentless blue littered with new, smoky clouds.

He closed the gate, walked the bike up the path and propped it against the wall. As soon as he opened the back door, his stomach plummeted. *The Little Mermaid* was playing in the lounge.

Trevor was filled with an urge to leg it, but it was too late. The kitchen wasn't empty. Sykes looked up from his seat at the table, holding his knife and fork and eating a mouthful of dinner. Trevor had no choice. He put his rucksack down on the floor and looked up just in time to see a white plate fly across the room, shedding its leftover load as it travelled. It bounced off a cupboard and exploded onto the floor like a little bomb. Baked beans, remnants of scrambled egg and droplets of orange juice from an overturned glass sprayed in its wake. Trevor froze.

Eyes flashing, red-faced, Sykes slammed his dirty knife and fork down on the table. More bean and egg fragments stuck to his beard, stabbed by his shorter whiskers as if every part of him was in attack mode. Sykes got up, and Trevor shrank back, as close to the back door as he could get. He couldn't breathe. Fury was etched all over his father's face. But Sykes wasn't looking at him.

"I can't do it," Sykes shouted into the air. "It's too much! I can't…"

Trevor forced his legs to move and tried to edge round him little by little, as Sykes tailed off, mumbling. If he could just get to the hall… but Sykes focused. He looked into Trevor's eyes, and his face softened. He held out his arms, and for a wild moment Trevor thought that he was going to hug him. Sykes's eyes filled with tears.

"Clem? It's really you? Are you… no, no, it's not, it's…"

Sykes stopped and shook his head. He was back in the room. It was like a button had been pressed in his head, flipping him to meltdown mode.

"Get out!" he bellowed, moving towards Trevor and

engulfing him in bean and wine fumes. "You fool! Another bill to pay thanks to you! And today of all days. I don't want to see you. Go!"

It took less than a second for Trevor to find his feet. He shot through the hall door.

"And forget that bloody centre! You're done!"

Trevor pelted upstairs, shaking. He slammed the door and took a running jump onto his bed. His heart hammered as he ground his fists into the pillow and squeezed back fury. Sykes was a pig, a mental pig. And he could dream on if he thought he was going to stop him going tomorrow. Trevor's face burned. No way was he going to miss seeing Midge go free. And this time, he would leave too, just like Midge. Sykes could do one, get stuffed.

The DVD blared on, a constant reminder of who was down there. Trevor leaned back on his bed and looked out of the window. Clouds were banking up, and a deep grey gloom built; an unnatural darkness. The heat was still stifling, pushing down, and he felt his arms prickle. Tiny black bugs were creeping over his skin. He lifted his arms and blew them away. Thunder bugs, Mum called them. She said they showed up before a storm. Trevor clenched his fists again, fury boiling back up. Those bloody insects should be in this house all the time. There were loads of them crawling over the window too. The concept of establishing a thunder bug colony in the house suddenly seemed like a good idea. Trevor was just planning to make their crawling, seething base camp right under Sykes's pillow when he snapped back to reality. Where was Mrs B? He sat up. She was always in his room, every night. His heart clenched. Had Sykes done something? He'd never, ever forgive him. He got off the bed. Nothing else for it, he had to find her.

The DVD was finishing as Trevor walked to the stairs, and the house fell quiet, except for one welcome noise. Sykes was snoring, yet again, great rattling thrums echoing through the hall. Trevor tiptoed downstairs. The lounge door was shut, another bonus. He crept down the hall to the kitchen, taking his time, listening for any tell-tale meows between snores.

Mrs B wasn't in the kitchen, so he opened the back door in case she was hanging around outside, but there was no sign of her. The tinkling music of a distant ice cream van was intercepted by a low, deep growl, and Trevor jumped. Ah, right. Thunder. Not an animal. He left the door ajar for Mrs B and picked his way over the fallout: shards of plate fragments that crunched under his feet. He glanced at the table and shook his head as his tummy rumbled, a pocket-sized echo of the thunder. Time for a ham sandwich. No chance of an oven meal tonight. Or probably ever again. He went to the fridge and threw some ham between slices of bread, not bothering with butter. He checked the door again. Still no sign.

On his way to the cupboard to grab crisps, he realised something was different, not just the carnage on the floor. It was the calendar hanging on the cupboard door. The month was changed. It was the right one for once. Sykes never ripped the months off in time. Usually only the last couple of days were on view in time before the month changed again. But June was gone, much earlier than normal, and

July was on display, with a picture of a sunflower. Trevor peered at it, frowning. There was something written on it. On today's date.

Wedding anniversary.

Oh. Trevor sat on a chair and rubbed his forehead as he bit chunks out of his sandwich. Today wasn't a good day then. Understatement. Not the best day for him to break a window. Trevor gritted his teeth as his temper threatened to flare again, but he controlled it and forced himself to think. What was the last thing you'd need when you'd lost your wife? On your anniversary? Being around someone who looked like her must be high up on your 'last thing' list. He glanced at the half-empty wine bottle on the table. Seeing someone like that, who did something to annoy you… that could push you over the edge.

But it didn't make any of it OK. There were no excuses. Sykes was horrible, he was wrong, he was an idiot. But… these last few days. He'd started to change. Hadn't he? Trevor put his head in his hands as another violent snore emanated from the lounge. Was it enough, a haircut, a few kind words and a ready meal? He'd so wanted it to be. But it wasn't. He didn't feel like eating any more.

He lifted his head and looked at the door. His rucksack was still there, leaning against the wall. He got up and fetched his pad and pen. One last note then, before he went.

He picked up the pen, put it down, then picked it up again and bit it. Should he, though? The old Trevor would just walk away. But now he was a spellboda. He stared at the wall, and an image of Midge sitting on his perch, waiting for freedom tomorrow, filled his mind. Midge was focused on his family, and he wouldn't give up. He'd try everything. Trevor took the pen out of his mouth. It was now or never. If this didn't work he'd have no options left. He'd need to leave, for good. He took a deep breath and began to write.

31

A violent crash of thunder sent tremors through the house. Trevor sat up, disorientated, eyes heavy. He couldn't remember falling asleep but it must have stolen up on him and taken him unawares at some point after he'd finished the note in bed. Heart thumping, he fumbled for the bedside light and picked up his watch beside it. Six thirty. He switched the light off again and sank back on the pillow, pulling the warmth of the covers around him. Funny how hearing thunder made you feel like the world was about to end. And on top of his weird dreams… Midge in a stoop, a ham sandwich talking to him, the slices moving around the ham tongue, telling him he was a spellboda, a break-dancing badger, his father hugging him, then the badger pushing him away… his eyelids drooped. A second crash rattled the window in its frame, and Trevor jumped all over again. No way was he going to get back to sleep.

He slipped out of bed and crept to the bathroom, feeling

his way in the dark that should have been chased away with the sun by now, another effect of the storm. Was Sykes in his bedroom or still crashed out downstairs? He stopped outside Sykes's room on his way back and peered round the door. There was a definite mound under the covers, rising and falling, accompanied by a gurgling snore. He didn't hang about. Sykes couldn't be too deep asleep; the thunder was loud enough to wake dead people.

Just before Trevor got to his bedroom, a vivid fork of lightning shocked the landing into eerie light. The fork was framed by the window, where it hung and shone, a snapshot of time standing still while the sky was torn in two. Thunder crashed, the floor trembled and Trevor ran. He flew into bed and pulled the covers back, tight round his neck. He lay still, then shook his head. For goodness sake, it was just thunder. Silly being jittery over a night storm. He should get up, check for Mrs B again and get ready to leave.

He sat up, brushed his hand through his hair, and looked up as a tapping sound came from the window. At last, rain was coming.

Tap tap tap.

Tap tap tap.

The rain was constant, regular. Too regular. The thunder rumbled on, less noisy and frequent as the storm rolled on into the distance.

Tap tap tap.

That wasn't rain.

Trevor leapt out of bed, rushed across the room and drew back the curtain. He stifled a shout. A white ghost was sitting on the sill outside, staring at him. Black eyes blinked twice, and the beak tapped again. Trevor's breath came out in a rush. Of course, a barn owl. These stupid night frights had got right under his skin. His fingers trembled as he slid the window up. The bird stepped in to the inside sill.

"Greetings, spellboda." The barn owl spoke in a whisper, but even so its voice was high and shrill. "I am a scout. There's no time to waste. The falcon is in trouble."

The chill iced Trevor's bones. "What? What's happened?"

The owl spun its head in a half-circle over its shoulder and back again.

"This is all I know. I left the centre when there was torchlight, and two legs coming."

Trevor shook his head hard, as if he was trying to clear his ears. "I don't understand. Where's Roger? He's supposed to be—"

"I have not seen Roger. We are looking for him. You must go. I had to check many windows in the storm, before I found your glow, too many." The owl stepped out of the window. "Please. Don't delay."

With a silent, graceful leap, the owl soared into the night. Trevor stumbled as he shoved his clothes on, his foot caught up infuriatingly inside a trouser leg. He snapped his watch round his wrist with shaking hands. Nearly seven. Cycling there would take until seven thirty at least. As he was about to leave the room, he remembered. His treasures. With badger, book and photo clutched firmly under his arm, he rushed back to the door.

Sykes's room was quiet. Trevor ran down the stairs, banging against the banister. He skidded to a halt in the kitchen, his trainers scraping over plate fragments. Too bad if Sykes woke up; he was long past worrying. He put his photo, book and badger in the rucksack and looked around. This could be the last time he would be here, and it was OK. He had all he needed. He pulled the note out of his pocket. There was nothing more he could do.

Dad,

Please read all this before you get more angry. I need to say some stuff.

I know why you were nasty yesterday, and I wish things were different. I wish Mum was here. I know you do too. I wish we were all still together. I know I remind you of her, and you're unhappy. I wish we could have been friends, and that you could be my dad. You could be, if you wanted to. The last two weeks I hoped and hoped things were changing. But it's too late. I hate you when you're like this.

I'm not the failure you think I am, Dad. And you're not one either. Please don't be like this. I'll come back after school, and if you want to see me, meet me in the front garden. I'm only coming in if you don't blow up and throw things. Otherwise I'm done, I don't want to be here anymore. Please give me and you a chance. Get some help, do something, just stop being angry. Please.

Your son, Trevor

A floorboard creaked upstairs, followed by a groan. Trevor propped the note up against the half-eaten loaf of bread and raced out, slamming the back door. He slung his rucksack over his shoulder and jumped on the bike. As he picked up speed down the road, something lurched out of the darkness in the bushes and ran across the pavement. Trevor slammed the brakes on and the bike screeched to a halt with a sideways skid.

"Oh, Mrs B! You're OK!" Trevor jumped off the bike and ran to her. Mrs B meowed and wound herself round Trevor's legs.

"I'm happy to see you too," said Trevor. "I thought you'd run off." He crouched down to scratch the top of her head. "I wish we could have talked, but you know what I'm saying. I might not come back." Mrs B looked up at him, her eyes like two little lamps. "I have to try to rescue my friend."

Mrs B rubbed her shoulder against him, then turned and put her front paws on his legs, so her head was almost level with his. She leaned forward and her whiskers tickled his neck.

"You have found your destiny, Trevor."

Trevor gasped, leaning back, his eyes wide.

"You can talk! You really can!"

"Yes, being able to talk hasn't been the issue. It was about when to talk. Now is the right time."

Trevor shook his head. "But you could have helped so much, if we'd talked sooner."

Mrs B sighed. "Believe me, Trevor, I would not have helped. You needed time, and you're starting to understand why, aren't you? Roger will talk to you very soon."

"You know Roger?"

"Of course. But now, your destiny is to help Midge. Go quickly, be a spellboda and achieve all you are gifted for. We will talk again."

Mrs B leaned forward and planted a snuffly kiss on Trevor's forehead.

"Yes, I have to go." Trevor picked up his bike. "But my head's exploding. I can't believe it! You won't leave, will you?"

"Trevor, I have never left you. And I never will."

Head down and pulse thumping, Trevor put his head down and gritted his teeth as he pedalled like mad down the grey, cloud-heavy streets. He'd taken too long already. Please, please don't let it be too late.

32

Red-faced and gasping, Trevor shoved the bike between two bushes in the corner of the car park. He stood for a second. The single car there was Elise's. She said she always got in before the others, but he didn't think she meant this early. He chanced a low call.

"Crispin? Are you here?"

Nothing. He vaulted over the gate and ran down the path, his chest hammering. So far nothing was different. A wild hope grew… the person with the torch could have been Elise, starting super-early because of the thunder. It was the sort of thing she'd do. Maybe the barn owl had got it all wrong. There she was, sitting with her back to him, on her coat spread out over the dewy grass. He slowed to a walk, his chest heaving, desperate for Midge and a normal day, as distant thunder growled on. Elise brushed her sleeve across her eyes and looked round. Trevor's heart plummeted.

"Trevor." She stood up. "I can't believe this has happened. Someone was here. The mews have been bro—"

Dread hit Trevor's stomach with the impact of an anvil. He stumbled forwards, missing his footing on the path as he ran to the mews.

"Trevor!" Elise shouted, but he was gone, sprinting at Olympic speed. He skidded to a halt at Midge's mews spot. His breath coming in painful rasps, he forced himself to look.

The perch was empty.

Trevor sank to the ground, his head in his hands, as Elise caught up with him.

"I'm so sorry. I've called the police." Her voice broke. "And Adam. They're on their way. I hope they can get fingerprints, anything, to help find them and bring them back."

Trevor looked up at her. Who else had been taken?

Elise read his thoughts. "They've got Tiberius too."

Trevor leaned sideways. The golden eagle's perch was empty. As if he needed to check. He looked across to the open mews door and the broken, twisted padlock lying on the ground. Tears stung his eyes.

Elise sniffed and cleared her throat.

"We need a cup of tea and chocolate. I'll make a brew."

Trevor shook his head, two treacherous tears spilling out as Elise went to the office. He'd never be able to find Midge now. Why hadn't he done something sooner about Lennox? If only he hadn't cracked that window he could have been here and stopped him... everything was crashing down around him and there was nothing he could do to put it right. It was too late. Sykes was probably picking up the note now and trashing the house in a rage. And Sykes had been right all along. He was useless, a failure. What was the point in trying? His shoulders slumped and his head sank further as he drove the tears away.

Elise put her hand on his shoulder as she bent down and clinked a mug on the path beside him.

"Drink it. It'll make you feel better. There's a piece of chocolate too, sorry it's not much." She straightened and looked across the grass. "I think I hear a car. I'll go check." Her mobile rang and she fished it out of her pocket. "Back in a minute."

"Hello? Oh, Harry, thanks for calling back so quick." Elise started to walk away. "We had a break-in last night, the peregrine was one of the birds taken. So we can't… yes, I've called it in…"

The tea scalded Trevor's throat, but it was sweet and strong, and it fired up his brain. This was the moment Midge needed him most. Was it too late? For a spellboda? He could sit back and give up, but was that who he was now? The boy who hosed down thieves with a fire extinguisher, the boy who made plans with falcons and foxes? Do spellbodas give up?

Like a match striking, a flame started to burn inside. Trevor stood up, the chocolate forgotten as the words of Midge, Mrs B and Roger bounced round his head. His destiny. He had a friend to rescue, Lennox to stop and somehow, he was going to do it. He scanned the centre, pinned under the dense blanket of sky, gathering his wits. What on earth was holding up Roger? And still no Crispin.

That bird was useless. Trevor needed clues, ideas, anything. Then it was time to write it all down for Elise and convince her of a way he'd worked it out without giving his gift away. While his mind went into overdrive his eyes rested on a nearby aviary. Help had come from there before.

Trevor walked across and leaned over the railing.

"Samson. What did you see? What happened?"

There was no sign of the redtail, and no answer. Samson had to be behind the bushes at the back of the aviary. Trevor thought for a moment.

"Tiberius is gone too. If you talk to me, I can help them both."

There was a rustle, and Samson flew across the aviary to rest on the closest branch, his chestnut wings shining in the sun. His deep brown eyes pierced Trevor's.

"This is terrible. I did see. There was a man, spellboda. He took Tiberius, then came back for Midge."

"What did he look like?" said Trevor, holding his breath.

"That was the strange thing," said Samson. "I didn't realise humans wear them. I thought it was just falcons."

"What are you talking about?" said Trevor. Had the trauma of everything got to him?

"Hoods," said Samson. "The human was wearing a hood. I didn't see his face." He looked up and raised his voice. "Did anyone see the human take off his hood?"

A chorus of calls echoed across the centre.

"No sign of his face."

"He was all in black."

"Gloves on both his hands."

"He hooded Midge too."

Trevor suddenly realised what they meant.

"A balaclava, right?"

Samson drew himself up tall and puffed out his feathers.

"With respect, spellboda, I know you're upset, but I would appreciate it if you don't use bad language."

"No, no, I mean…" Trevor thought better of explaining. "I mean, thank you for telling me." He was about to turn away, then stopped.

"Did he say anything?"

Samson moved along the branch, one foot at a time, eyeing up a piece of food on the floor of the aviary. "No, spellboda, not a word. I'm sorry. I wish I could be of more help."

Trevor sighed. This wasn't going anywhere. He picked up his mug and took another gulp of tea.

"Alright, geezer?"

Trevor looked up to the oak tree and sighed. Finally.

"Crispin."

The crow bounced jerkily across a couple of branches towards him.

"Did you tell 'em?"

"What?"

"Did you tell 'em? About me watching? You know, like you said."

"Not yet, no. I haven't had a chance."

"Well, when's you going to?"

"When I've got time. Look, everything's rubbish right now."

Crispin nodded his head.

"No offence, mate, but could you get a shift on and do it? I've thought about what you said, see? I want to make a change. Be a better corvid."

Trevor couldn't stop himself. "Well, why couldn't you have worked that out sooner? I wish you'd spent less time thinking about yourself and more time keeping an eye on things. It's not enough to say you want to be better, you have to show it."

"Caw, someone got off the wrong side of his perch this morning," said Crispin, bobbing up and down. "I *am* showing it, see?"

Trevor was about to snap again, but the crow held out one of his feet, curled up.

"What's that?"

Crispin hopped lopsidedly towards him.

"It's me best bling. To show you I'm changed."

The crow opened up his foot and something round fell to the floor with a glint of gold. Trevor bent down and picked it up. A red stone glowed back at him. Elise's ring! It had to be. He looked at the crow.

"This is a good thing, Crispin. It'll make a difference. I really will let them all know."

"Knew it would!" Crispin bounced through the tree. "It's why I'm top crow, see? I know everything."

"I wish you did," said Trevor, as he put the ring into his jeans pocket. "I mean, this is great, but I wish you'd stayed awake last night, like I asked you. I needed you."

Crispin clattered his clumsy beak through his feathers, tidying up.

"Last night? What, when the man came and took the falcon and that jumped-up eagle?"

239

Trevor's heart missed a beat. "You saw him?"

"Course I did. I said I'd watch. I'm a changed bird. Don't you listen?"

"What did you see?"

Crispin raised a foot and scratched his head deliberately with a claw. Trevor felt like climbing up the tree and throttling him.

"Well, I was awake. Couldn't sleep anyway for the thunder. All that noise. And still no rain."

"Crispin. What happened?"

"I'm getting there. He went in the office, then he took old Talons of Terror out the mews and went to the car park."

"He went in the office? That makes sense. There's no break-in there. Then what?"

"Then he came back and picked up your mate. That falcon. Took him off too."

"Did you see anything else?"

"Nope."

It was like someone had stuck a pin into Trevor's hope balloon. He could almost hear it deflating inside him.

"Oh, OK. Thanks for letting me know."

The crow hopped down to the railing by Samson's aviary.

"I didn't *see* nothing else, did I? It's what I heard that got me thinking."

"What?"

"In the car park. I followed him when he took your mate. He put him in the car, and his phone thing did a ring. He pressed the button, said hello. That he wasn't expecting a call this early, bloke must be up with the lark, that kind of thing. Not that larks are up earlier than crows."

Trevor held his breath.

"What else?"

"He said the birds were ready. And he'd meet him this morning, at ten."

Trevor punched the air. Crispin jumped and flapped back to the tree. "Oi, mate, don't do things like that, I'll have a funny turn!"

Trevor kept his voice low.

"Crispin, did he say where? Where he was meeting him?"

"He said something." Crispin tilted his head. "He said see you later, that kind of thing, and then something I didn't get, I haven't heard it before."

"What? What?" Trevor gritted his teeth.

"Let me think."

A bang of thunder crashed violently in the sky, making them both jump. Crispin eyed the sky.

"It's going to rain."

"I don't care," Trevor hissed, clenching his fists. "What did he say, after see you later?"

"Alright!" Crispin looked at Trevor. "I think he said something about eggs. And then he said see you there you stuff. Look, I gotta go, spellboy. Get myself roosted up and stay dry under a big tree." He took off and flapped towards the copse, shouting over his shoulder, "Good luck!"

"I need it," said Trevor. "That makes all kinds of no sense at all."

He checked his watch as the first drops of rain splashed on the dial. Eight fifteen. He looked up. The air was different, sinister. A gust of wind blew through the centre, as cloud after cloud rolled in and took root, backing up in muddy peaks across the sky. The real storm, not last night's electric warning, was inexorably advancing across the sky like an enemy invasion, with staccato thunder cracks and flashes of lightning. A blue-green colour he'd never seen before spread across the horizon, and all trace of the sun was snuffed out.

Trevor shivered. Focus, it was more important than anything. 'See you there you stuff?' Meeting who and where at ten? And eggs... did they have more birds? After Lennox met whoever that person was, Midge and Tiberius would be even harder to find. He groaned. Where was Roger when he needed him? He had to work this out before it was too late. And there was less than two hours to go.

33

Elise walked across the meadow with two police officers on one side of her and Adam on the other. They stopped on the path by the mews, and Trevor got as close as he could without being weird. It was a long shot, but someone might say something to give him more to go on. The older, official-looking policeman was talking, his hands waving around.

"And when you've done that, make sure you don't touch the door or padlock. Can you cordon that area off for forensics?"

"Lennox or Rash can do that." Elise nodded. "Falconers. They'll be in soon." She looked at Adam as Trevor pressed his lips tight together. "Is that OK?"

Adam nodded, his face grim. "Do you need me to give a statement?" he said.

The other officer shook his head as the first one turned away, bending his head to his shoulder as he spoke into his radio. "Not yet, sir. But we'll need the young lady here, as she was first on the scene."

The first policeman turned back. "Forensics should be here in about an hour, but you'll need to keep the centre closed till they're done. Not much more we can do here, except have the fingerprint people in. As you don't have CCTV, it means we're unlikely to find them any other way, I'm afraid."

Adam frowned and nodded. "Fair point. I'll look at getting some." He glanced at Elise and tilted his head in the direction of the office. "This storm's going to hit. I'll grab some paperwork and head off if I'm not needed. I can put updates on social media to delay visitors, and I'd rather work from home if it's going to pee down." He glanced at the officers. "Is that alright with you?"

The older officer nodded. "Be careful what you put online. Word it 'due to unforeseen circumstances', something like that. We don't want to give these people any information."

"Absolutely," said Adam. "Good idea." He looked up as a couple of fat rain drops bounced off his wax jacket. "Thank you, gentlemen." He shook hands with the first officer. "I'm on the end of the phone if you need me."

The younger officer turned to Elise as Adam walked to the office. "We'll take a closer look just in case, but as Doug says, there's not much else, except for you to come down the station later, sort the paperwork and make a statement." He smiled. "Can you show me around, miss? Just quickly, before it chucks it down? They're beautiful, but a bit of a rum lot, with these big beaks and claws."

"Of course," said Elise. "No problem." She looked past his shoulder.

"Trevor, don't touch anything, right? Best you wait in the office. I'll see you in a few minutes."

Trevor nodded and turned away. As he neared the office, the door opened and Adam emerged, leaning against the door to keep it open as he wedged a load of paperwork into his satchel. He nodded at Trevor as another growl of thunder rolled across the sky.

"Go on then, keep dry, lad. You don't want to get caught in this."

Trevor shut the door and watched Adam jog across the centre, as he replayed what was said. Don't touch. Forensics. Statements. Paperwork. He bit his lip. There was a memory, just at the edge of his mind. He needed his head to catch up. There was something else too that he needed to remember, but his panicking brain was porridge.

He had to think straight. He walked to the desk, where a couple of yellow pieces of paper sat under an empty mug. And at last it slotted into place, twisting into focus like the colours in a kaleidoscope. The page in his falconry book.

All captive-bred birds are given leg rings and yellow certificates, called A10s, to prove their bloodline and that they haven't been 'wild taken', so never purchase a bird if the seller doesn't provide an A10.

Paperwork. Tiberius was a captive-bred bird, and so was Midge, even though his parents had been wild. Both birds had worn leg rings. So they both had to have A10s. Trevor moved the mug, but the A10s underneath were for a couple of kestrels that had just hatched. He rubbed his chin. The bird file. As only the mews had been made to look like it had been broken into, and not the office, it followed that Midge's and Tiberius's paperwork should still be there. But if the A10s were gone, then Lennox would have slipped up, maybe not thinking anyone would make the connection. Had he been clever enough to cover himself? Trevor took a quick breath. If not, this could be the way to catch Lennox out and prove he was the thief.

Please let the bird file be there. Trevor slung his rucksack on top of the desk, crouched and gave the handle a pull. It was still hard to open... a good sign. His breath hissed out as he hauled the drawer open and the file slid into view. Pulling it out, he opened it and ran his finger down the index, to G. The section was empty. Hands trembling, he counted the sections along to P. Empty. He checked both sections on the other side of each letter, and F and E, in case they were logged under Falcon or Eagle, just to be sure. Nothing. The papers for Tiberius and Midge were gone.

"Trevor! What on earth are you doing?"

Elise was at the door. Trevor jumped up; the file fell off his knees and clattered on the floor. Elise stepped inside and shut the door, as a fork of lightning illuminated the celadon sky, and another crack of thunder shook the office windows. She walked over, her face clouded.

"What are you thinking, going through files? There'd better be a good reason!"

His heart racing, Trevor reached to his rucksack and yanked out the pad.

I needed to check something.

"Like what? Why would you need to look at someone else's stuff?"

Trevor paused. She had to believe him. He looked out of the window as rain spattered the glass with angry force. "Well?"

I wanted to find Midge and Tiberius's certificates. I want to help.

"What? Their A10s?" Elise raised her eyebrows as Trevor nodded. "How is that helping?" She groaned. "Look, Trevor, I get it, but you just can't go through other people's things without asking."

She leaned her forehead on her hand. "God, Trevor, I know how awful this is. I'm on autopilot right now. I can't stop thinking about what's happening to them." She closed her eyes. "And feeling so useless about not knowing, not being able to get them back."

Trevor stared at her as rain battered down. He checked his watch and panic bubbled. Eight thirty. Hardly any time left, and all he had to go on was the A10s. A fat bluebottle whined drunkenly past him, bouncing off his knee. Trevor closed his eyes too. Time. The one thing Midge didn't have. He didn't either. And even if he did, if he could work this out, how would he get to Midge? On a bike, in a hammering rain storm?

Snapshots of more time, spent with Elise, filled his mind. She'd made him welcome, believed in him, trusted him with Midge. He couldn't stand her thinking badly of him. She cared, and he'd only known one other person like that in his life. Determination swept through him, and he knew what he had to do. This was for Midge. It was time.

He leaned over and tugged Elise's jacket. She lifted her head off her hand and opened her eyes as she spoke.

"You OK?"

Trevor took a deep, ragged breath.

34

"Do you trust me?"

Elise stared at him, her eyes wide.

"What the hell is going on?"

"There's... stuff I need to tell you."

Elise shook her head. "Is this is a dream? Are you actually talking?"

Trevor made himself carry on. "I need to tell you, then you have to talk to the police. And you need to trust me."

"Trevor, I'm gobsmacked. Yes, of course I trust you. This must be important."

Trevor took another deep breath. His mouth was thick and dry, his hands clammy.

"OK," he said. "You're going to need to. It's Lennox. Lennox has got Tiberius and Midge."

Elise's mouth fell open.

"What?" she said. "Lennox? What on earth are you talking about?"

"I've worked it all out. He's stolen them." Trevor forced words out of a mouth that felt like it was full of cotton wool.

"It doesn't make sense," said Elise. "He already works with them. He's around them all the time. Why would he?"

"Think back to when I first started," said Trevor. "When the wild peregrines were found and brought here. Those two gits were working for someone."

"Were they? I didn't know," said Elise.

"I read it in the paper," fibbed Trevor. There was no other way. Even if he had time, or was allowed to explain his gift, she'd never believe him.

"Then they all got taken," he carried on. "Except Midge. And you didn't think it was a fox."

Elise shrugged. "But we all wondered about that. And then the police checked the thieves out. The birds weren't there. There was no sign of them."

"Lennox was bluffing you. He's working with the thieves. The birds were with him all along. He must have thought his luck was in when they first got brought here. I bet he's sold them now. And now he's got Midge and Tiberius. The A10s, their certificates." Trevor showed Elise the file. "Gone. Only a professional falconer would know to come in here and find their papers."

Elise gasped, eyes wide as she looked at Trevor.

It was getting easier now he'd got going. "Lennox bodged it. He should've made it look like he'd broken in here, as well as the mews. But the door wasn't damaged, right?"

"No. It was locked when I got here."

"Lennox has keys to the office." Trevor thumped his fist

on the desk. "But he didn't have them the day the peregrines were taken." It was all falling into place now. "He had to borrow yours, remember? Because he must have given his keys to someone the night before. Then the next day he'd found them again. And last week he told me to keep out of things, when he thought I was being nosy."

"What? He did that?" Elise sank to the floor, shock etched over her face. "This is mad. Why didn't you tell me? I have to talk to him."

"And warn him that we're on to him, so he can move the birds quicker?" Trevor leaned forward. "You have to go out and tell the police, now."

"But they've gone, Trevor."

"What?" Trevor ran to the window. The rain was so heavy everywhere was a blur, but the centre was empty. Elise got up and followed him.

"They had a call about a lightning strike and had to leg it." Elise got her phone out. "I'll call them. They need to know about the paperwork, that's for sure." She shook her head. "But God, I still can't believe Lennox would do this."

Trevor leaned against the wall and fiddled with his sleeve as she fetched her phone from her back pocket and began to scroll. He wanted to scream. How could he explain everything he knew without giving himself away? And get her to believe they only had until ten? What else could he do, so she'd realise it was—

"The tin!"

"What?" Elise jumped and dropped the phone.

"Don't call yet. There's something else." Why had his stupid brain taken this long to click? "I haven't looked at the tin! I meant to, ages ago, but then Roger... er, other stuff happened and I didn't get a chance."

"What tin? Who's Roger?"

Trevor ran to the bookshelves.

"This one," he said in triumph, as he dragged book after book off the bottom shelf, to get to it, shoving them out of the way.

"Look, LP. Lennox Palmer." He banged the tin down on the floor. "There's something in here." Trevor worked his fingers round the lid. "And it wouldn't be hidden if it wasn't important."

"How do you even know about it?"

"Doesn't matter now. Yes!" The lid came loose, sending batteries, bird book, sun cream and pills clattering across the lino. He flipped the lid over.

"No! It's gone!"

"What are you looking for?"

"I knew it was important. There was a piece of paper taped on the underneath of the lid. He must have taken that too." He groaned as he slammed the lid and tin down.

"Do you mean this?" Elise reached down to the bird book lying by her feet. A piece of paper was poking out from the pages.

"Yes!" Trevor snatched it from the book and unfolded it. At last he'd find out what Lennox wanted to hide. "It's a list," he said, glancing at Elise. She was staring at him, her hand over her mouth.

"It's got a date in June," he said. "Then '£12,000. Newport Pagnell Services. Saturday 1pm'. Look."

Elise crouched beside him. She read aloud.

"'Two untrained mature adults as a breeding pair, one tiercel, one female. (Fledglings – no sale – died in transit.)' Oh no." She looked at Trevor. "A tiercel is a male peregrine falcon. It's Midge's parents. Which means the other babies… this is insane. How could he do this? I mean, working with animals doesn't pay much but to steal them and stop wild ones from going free." She groaned. "I can't believe this. I feel sick."

Trevor's heart plummeted. How was he going to tell Midge? He read on.

"But then… Elise, look! This one's today's date!"

One Mature Male Golden Eagle £10,000
One Trained Juvenile F1 Tiercel £25,000
Egginton, Tuesday 10am

"Let me see." Elise grabbed the paper, then let it fall to the floor, her face white. Trevor put his hand on her arm.

"We have to call the police. Now."

Elise nodded, fumbling for her phone, while Trevor breathed a silent thank-you to fate as he picked up the paper and put it in his pocket.

"If Midge and Tiberius are being sold at ten this morning, then there's only an hour and a half to go."

"Yes, and Egginton is about an hour away," said Elise.

Trevor looked at her, hope ballooning. Crispin. Eggs… of course. That's what he'd meant. "It's a place? You know it?"

Elise nodded. "Near Derby. It's not a big village, but it would help the police to have an address to go to."

"They'll just have to find him," said Trevor. "He must be driving there, you can give them his car details."

"Yes, it's a start." Elise unlocked her phone, then looked up.

Steady thumping noises were coming from outside, and getting louder. They both got up and looked out of the window. Two sets of long legs were hammering down the path, feet slapping on concrete, sending water flying from the puddles. The office door opened and Lennox skidded to a stop, his hair all over the place, as Rash followed, bumping into him.

"Careful, bruv," he groaned. "Alright, Elise... Trev. Blinking awful out there. What's up with you two?"

35

Trevor's mouth was dry. Elise's was opening and closing like a fish.

"Lennox. What are you doing here?"

The brothers took their coats off and hung them, dripping, up on the hooks. Lennox snorted. "Well... I work here. Remember? You OK?"

A red flush crept up Elise's face. "But... I don't understand." She frowned and her expression changed. Trevor clenched his fists. Don't do it.

"Look, Lennox," she said. "I need to talk to you. What's going on?"

Lennox grinned, gesturing at the window. "Well, this is the mother of all storms. It happens a lot after hot weather." He looked at the floor and his eyes widened. "Oh my God, you found it! Where was it?"

"What are you talking about?" said Elise.

"My tin! I've been looking for that everywhere!"

Lennox crouched down, gathering up his things. "Where was it? It's been driving me crazy. Not that most of it's important, but the bird book is. It was a present from my grandad."

That was it. He couldn't stand there and listen to Lennox lie.

"I bet the book was really important."

"Trev! You're talking, mate – brilliant!" Lennox reached for the book as Rash's mouth hung open. "Have you two both got zapped by the storm or something?"

"It's not there."

"What's not there?"

"What you're looking for. Where are they, Lennox?"

"Trev, you're not making any sense. Are you alright?"

"Don't try and pin this on me!" Trevor's voice rose. "You know what you said to me the other day. So where are they?"

Lennox shook his head. "Seriously, I don't know what's going on. What did I say? Where's who?"

"The peregrine," said Elise. "And the goldie. They're gone. Stolen. Last night."

"What?" said Rash.

"And you'd better be quick if you want to pick them up from wherever you've hidden them, and get to Egginton on time," said Trevor.

"You think I've taken them?" said Lennox, eyebrows raised. "What the hell would I do that for?"

"That's what I said," exclaimed Elise. "But we found your piece of paper… in the tin."

Lennox looked at the floor again. "You mean the tin I

lost weeks ago?" He frowned. "Look, I'm not having this. Where do you get off accusing me?"

Trevor clenched his fists. "Gone out of your head that you warned me to keep my nose out of things, has it? Do you think I'm stupid? Where are they?"

Lennox put his hands up, palms forward. "OK, stand down, Trevor. I get this. You mean after I saw you in the office?"

"Yep. And then you stared me down when I was out in the flying ground. Don't pretend you didn't."

Lennox snorted as Rash and Elise looked from one to the other like they were watching a tennis match.

"Mate, you've got it all wrong. You need to calm down. Your face'll be purple in a minute. Let me show you."

Lennox walked to the shelves and pulled a file off the very top of the shelving. He opened it up and took out a sheaf of papers.

"Look." He held them out to Elise. "I've been doing a load of extra work on the conservation project for Pretoria." Elise took the papers and leafed through them. "Didn't want you to know until I'd finished. Wanted to surprise you." He looked at Trevor. "So when you were hanging out in here I just had a word, joking more than anything. I didn't mean it seriously."

Trevor looked at Elise and she nodded. "The papers are like he says."

"What about staring at me?" said Trevor.

"Mate, I've watched you a couple of times, cos I think you're a really good volunteer. Not just with the birds either. Hardly anyone thinks to pick up litter. Look, I can just about see how you thought it, but I haven't got those birds. If I did, why the hell would I be here now, explaining myself to you?"

Silence filled the room. Trevor fished the paper out of his pocket and held it up.

"So this isn't yours?"

Lennox leaned forward. "Never seen it before."

Elise smiled at Lennox. "I couldn't believe you'd really do it."

"But the tin," said Trevor, looking at the paper again.

"Like I said, not seen it for weeks."

"So then…"

Trevor gasped and looked at Elise. It was in her eyes too. "Oh God. It can only be Adam." He thumped the desk again. "Of course it is! Where is he? I'll bet anything he's not at home. He's gone to Egginton!"

Elise rubbed her eyes as thunder crashed again. "This has to be a nightmare."

Trevor stared at the tin lid on the desk, as he shifted into a memory of another day. The picture came into focus, and it all fell in place. Crispin. You stuff. The plummy voice sang clear in his mind, after the beep of the answerphone.

"*This is Clive. Would you please return my call? My client Yousuf and I are staying at Willersley Castle. Thank you.*"

"Willersley Castle! He's there!" yelled Trevor, making them all jump.

"Who, Trev? Adam?" said Lennox.

"The buyer! It was on the answerphone, that day I was in the office." The words were falling over themselves to get out of Trevor's mouth. "He's meeting someone called

Yousuf. He's staying there." He looked at Elise. "Just trust me, I know it's him."

Elise looked at the floor, frowning.

"I can't remember Adam ever mentioning that name. Shouldn't we just—"

"There's no time," shouted Trevor, over another explosion of thunder. "I just know. Quick! Call the hotel! We have to find him too!"

Elise grabbed her phone again, fumbling over the code. "I don't know the number, I'll—"

"Call the number-finding people!" yowled Trevor, his heart racing. "Quick! Put it on loudspeaker. Say anything, find out if he's still there!"

Lennox looked at Rash, who was leaning against the office wall looking like he was going to pass out. "Bruv, this is not panning out to be the usual morning."

After a minute of scrabbling that felt like an hour, the calm voice of a hotel receptionist sounded across the office.

"Willersley Castle, good morning."

Elise's best telephone voice shook as she clutched the phone.

"Hello, I need to speak to one of your guests, um, a gentleman called Mr Yousuf. I'm from the falconry centre. He's left some, um, falconry property with us that we need to return. Please can you put me through?"

There was a pause.

"I'm afraid *Sheikh* Yousuf checked out, about an hour ago."

Trevor's heart missed a beat. Elise looked frantic.

"Ah, er, that's a problem. I'm sure he would be grateful

to have his property returned. It's very precious. Do you have any idea where I might contact him?"

After another pause, and a rustling of papers, during which Trevor wanted to leap down the phone and yell at her, the receptionist replied, "I'm afraid we can't give out information about our guests."

Elise's face turned beetroot. "Look, it really is important. I'm sure the sheikh would be very upset if he was unable to get it back when there was an opportunity. He gave me your details himself in case I needed to contact him."

Trevor held his breath. He could almost hear the receptionist thinking.

"I'm afraid you'd have to be quick to catch him. The sheikh is returning home today by private jet. I can call him for you, possibly?"

Elise's hand shook. "Oh, I see. Well, yes, but maybe I could get it to him before he leaves, if he's not too far away. Do you know where he's flying from?"

"Well, this is a little unorthodox, but I would imagine that will be where our driver has taken him. Bear with me."

There was another pause. No-one breathed. Trevor was about to explode. He looked at Rash and Lennox, who could only stare back. Elise's forehead was shining, and she held one hand to her chest.

"Yes, here we are. He's being driven to Egginton Airfield."

"Oh!" Elise dropped her phone, and scrambled to pick it up. "I'm so sorry, my service is bad. Thank you so much, Sheikh Yousuf will be delighted."

"You are most wel—"

Elise pressed the end button and looked at them, her eyes flashing.

Trevor looked at his watch again. It was 8.45. "Come on!" he yelled, as he grabbed his jacket. "We might just make it! We can call the police on the way."

"We're coming!" said Lennox.

Elise stopped beside him. "You know what? Can you stay here?" Lennox started to speak but she put her hand on his arm. "Someone needs to. The forensic guys are coming to do fingerprints. Not that it matters now, but at least you can tell them what's happening." She sighed. "Truly, though? I'm worried he'll come back for more. I want you here just in case."

Lennox nodded. "I get you. But you have to let me know—"

"Elise!" Trevor pulled her arm. "Come on!"

"Of course I will. Wish us luck!"

Lifting jackets over their heads, Trevor and Elise raced past the mews. A stab of pain shot through Trevor as he passed the empty perch. Everything was hanging on this for Midge. They just had to make it.

36

Rain swiped them as they sprinted across the meadow. Drops flung sideways in the wind, stinging like angry bees. Elise beeped the car open, and they piled in, rain hammering the roof. They looked at each other, chests heaving, rain dripping from hair and clothes into little puddles on the floor. It was like getting to a safe house in the middle of a war.

A harsh, guttural bark sounded and Trevor sat bolt upright, peering through the passenger window. Roger Ginger was standing beside the bushes, his brush rigid, chest heaving, eyes glinting bright.

At last. Trevor opened the door.

"What are you doing?" said Elise, as she started the car. "We've got to hurry!"

Trevor put one leg out and Roger barked again.

"No, spellboda, this is your time. It's meant to be. Go with honour and valour. Our hearts are with you. Win our friends back."

Elise started the engine as Trevor sat back and shut the door.

"Was that a fox?"

Trevor nodded, wiping an eye. "Let's go."

Elise stared at him for a moment, as if she was going to say something. Trevor looked straight ahead, not catching her eye as she half drove, half skidded down the track. She unlocked her mobile and thrust it into Trevor's hand as she turned onto the main road.

"Call Harry." She raised her voice over the hammering of the rain on the windscreen as the car picked up speed. "Put it on loudspeaker and hold it up for me. He's in recent calls."

Trevor pressed Harry's number, then groaned.

"It's not connecting."

"What?" said Elise. "Stupid mobile! Keep trying."

Elise was grim-faced, concentrating on the road, while Trevor pressed redial over and over.

"I think your phone's frozen."

The car jolted as Elise took her foot off the pedal.

"Give it to me," she said, holding out her hand.

"No! Just keep going."

"Well, hold it up so I can see it."

Trevor lifted it up and gripped the seat with his free hand, his knuckles white.

"OK," said Elise, "it's service drop-out as we go through the peaks. It comes and goes. Check the service bars when we get closer."

Trevor was lost in thought as Elise focused on the road, her face grim with concentration. The road went on forever. He looked for signs to the airfield at every junction, and as they got to the edge of Derby sweat began to prickle the back of his neck. He checked his watch for the millionth time, and grabbed the seat again. Nine forty five. They had to get there. He glanced at Elise's phone again.

"It's back!" Trevor shouted, pressing redial.

"Great," said Elise. "Not far now."

Ring after ring, and the sinking feeling grew. "He's not picking up."

Voicemail kicked in, and Trevor held the phone up at the beep.

"Harry, it's Elise. Call me urgently. We know who's got Midge and Tiberius, we need help. We're on our way there now, Egginton Airfield."

"Elise, look!" Trevor pointed. Egginton Airfield was signposted half a mile ahead.

"This is it," said Elise, then gasped so hard it made him jump. Trevor looked at her as she indicated left.

"What's wrong?"

Elise pulled into a petrol station and stopped by the air and water machine. She wrenched up the handbrake.

Trevor was frantic. "What's going on? What are you doing?"

Elise put her hand to her forehead. "Trevor, I'm going mad. What was I thinking? I can't possibly take you to this airfield and put you in danger." She reached over for her mobile and put her hand on his arm. "We need to wait for the police, or Harry, then go in after and get the birds when they've dealt with Adam."

Trevor shook her hand off. "If you think I'm going to sit back and wait, and let them take Midge away, you must be mad!"

"Trevor, think about it. Your dad would be furious. And school."

"I don't give a stuff what they think!" Trevor shouted. "Just tell them I had to come with you because I couldn't be left alone at the centre. And that we did wait for the police! I'm not going to tell them any different!"

Elise half-smiled. "I know how important this is, it's the same for both of us. But I can't risk your safety. I'm sorry. There's enough time before ten. We'll wait here and I'll keep trying Harry."

Trevor looked down, with everything he wanted to say churned up somewhere inside. This couldn't happen. They were so close… so close. He was meant to do this. He looked at Elise.

"OK, I understand. We'll wait."

Elise sighed. "Oh, I'm so glad you get it. But I am sorry." She unlocked her phone.

"Could you do something, while we're waiting?"

"What?"

"I'm starving," said Trevor. He tilted his head at the petrol station. "Could you get me a hot drink and a pasty? It won't take a minute. You could phone from the shop."

Trevor waited until the shop door closed behind Elise before he whipped the car keys out of the ignition and opened the door. Shoving the keys in his pocket, he ran back on himself, out of view, then crossed the road, before walking past the petrol station with his jacket over his head. He didn't look back. Nine fifty-five. As soon as he was level with the sign for the airfield, he threw his jacket back on and ran faster than he'd ever run in his life.

37

Trevor raced into the airfield entrance and down the drive, heading towards an ancient-looking control tower. More of the airfield came into view as he rounded a corner. He skidded to a stop, chest heaving, wind whipping his face. A handful of lights were on in the main building. There was the runway, and—

"YES!"

Not far from the hangars, a sleek-looking jet hummed on the tarmac, light pouring out from the open door at the top of the stairway. A familiar white four-wheel drive was parked behind it.

Trevor slowed to a jog and tried to look purposeful, stopping when he reached the back of the jet. Where was Adam? Where was anybody? He looked up the stairs at the open door. They must be on board. Adam would be pocketing all the money. Trevor frowned. Think. If he was lucky Midge might not be on the plane yet. He could grab him and make a run for it. He walked to the Land Rover, as at last the rain stopped. A dull thumping noise was coming from the boot. Trevor tensed. He tried the handle and the boot opened easily.

"Midge," he whispered, "is that you?"

There was no answer. There was a plastic box in the boot, a blanket draped over it. Trevor held his breath as he reached out and pulled off the blanket, then let out a squeak of triumph. The dark, hulking shape with huge unblinking eyes staring back at him was unmistakable. Tiberius! Standing in a massive box with an open front, like a cat carrier for a tiger.

Suddenly Trevor knew exactly what to do. It was laid out like a map in his head. He leaned into the boot and reached for the door of the travelling box.

"Tiberius," he whispered. "I know you understand me. Maybe you already know what's going on. I need your help. We've got to stop Adam before you and Midge are taken away. I'm going to let you out. I know you don't think much of me, but please don't go for me!"

Tiberius made one sharp, angry noise as Trevor swung open the door. He stepped out and walked across the boot floor to the edge of the car, his massive feet and razor-sharp talons clicking over the metal. Trevor backed away, praying the eagle's next move wouldn't be to pin him to the ground. Tiberius stared at him, holding his elegant head high, his huge brown eyes glittering like jewels. He opened his beak.

"Leash."

Trevor understood immediately. He moved forward, his heart hammering. Trying not to focus on the huge talons, he took off Tiberius's leash and swivel as quickly as trembling hands would allow, so he was free to fly. Tiberius immediately launched himself up and out of the back of the car. With huge, powerful wing-beats, he flew directly up to the roof of the jet, landing near the cockpit.

"Clever eagle," murmured Trevor as he walked back to the aircraft. This could work. Keeping low to the ground, he stooped beneath the undercarriage and crept forward to crouch under the stairway. Perfect timing. Voices sounded above, and the tap of feet descending the metal steps soon followed.

Adam's deep voice drifted down. "What sort of bird would you like me to source for your next visit? I can get kites for you?"

"No, no," another voice replied. "I fly only falcons and eagles. Clive knows. You speak to him."

"I'm glad you're pleased with them," said Adam. "I'll be able to find you more that are just as good. I'll fetch the eagle."

As the men reached the bottom of the stairway, Trevor gripped his hands together to steady the shaking. What was he thinking, going up against Adam on his own? How could he possibly stop this? He looked down, and fear vanished in an instant. His hands were glowing... really glowing, he could see it. Determination swept through him. He stepped out from under the stairs, and the two men jumped in surprise.

"You can't take these birds," Trevor said. "It's illegal."

After a moment's shocked silence, Adam laughed. But there was no humour in the sound.

"Silly lad, how did you get here?" he said, reaching out his hand to try and pat Trevor's head. Trevor dodged him. "He works at my centre, got attached to the falcon. It's alright, lad, sometimes they just have to move on."

"Not like this," said Trevor. He turned to the sheikh. "This man is trying to trick you. The peregrine is a wild bird. You can't take him."

The sheikh turned to Adam. "What does the boy mean? I am confused. Clive told me the birds are captive-bred. This is the only way I trade. Never wild. I do not want a problem here."

"There's no problem," said Adam. "You have the papers. It's all organised. Everything is fine, I can assure—"

A whine of sirens drifted over the air, getting closer. Trevor wanted to cheer as the flashing blue lights of two police cars screamed onto the airfield. Nice one, Elise.

He grinned. "I think you'll find it's not fine!"

"What is going on?" Sheikh Yousuf's face was turning red. "What have you done, Mr Shotlander? Mr Shotlander!"

As the sheikh's voice and police sirens grew louder, undisguised rage spread across Adam's face. He shot Trevor an evil glare, so venomous it paled all of Sykes's rages into insignificance. Trevor backed away over the tarmac but Adam followed, his eyes flashing. Suddenly, he didn't look like a hero any more.

"You'll regret this," he spat the words out as he got closer. "Interfering little git!" He grabbed Trevor by his jacket and pulled him close, and his breath steamed hot in Trevor's ear. "So that stunt the other night was something to do with you then?" Trevor struggled but Adam's hold was too tight. "I'm going to—"

Adam looked over his shoulder as a harsh call sounded, coming from the roof of the jet.

"What the—"

Tiberius launched off the roof, his wings at a tight angle, calling again, flying at Adam like a bullet.

"At last! My chance has come!"

Adam froze, his face a picture of shock. But only for a moment. As Tiberius put his feet forward ready to strike, Adam turned and ran, straight to the first police car as it stopped on the runway.

"Let me in, let me in!" he shouted, wrenching the car door open as the eagle descended on him, talons aiming for his head. "I'm giving myself up! Just get me away from that bird!"

Trevor couldn't help laughing at the surprised face of the police officer through the car window as Adam threw himself onto their back seat. Tiberius landed on the car roof, his talons scraping across the metal. Trevor winced. He looked at the sheikh, whose mouth was open, staring at all the craziness. Elise got out of the other police car and started shouting about getting Tiberius back. The sheikh walked towards her, and Trevor turned back to the jet. One last thing to do.

He clattered up the stairway. It was jaw-dropping inside. The fuselage was empty, swathed from roof to floor in ivory leather, with only lines of polished dark wood panels and tables to break up the pristine brightness. Trevor walked further in, the commotion unfolding below

271

forgotten. There was a door, set in more dark panelling. Trevor opened it. It was more like a normal plane on the other side, with tables and chairs, less posh... and it wasn't empty. A bulky-looking man took out his earphones and rose from his seat.

"Who are you, lad?"

Trevor ignored him. On an ornate perch fixed to a table, a stunning cream and brown bird was sitting, with a leather hood on his head. Without thinking, Trevor stepped forward, loosened the hood braces and took it off.

"Oi!" said the man. "What are you playing at?"

The falcon's head bobbed, and his gleaming bright eyes stared at Trevor, as he spread his perfect wings wide and called in delight.

"Trevor! I knew you'd make it. What took you so long?"

"I said... who are you?" The man stepped closer.

Trevor looked at him, as voices grew louder, and footsteps sounded in the cabin.

"I'm Trevor. And I'm getting my friend back."

38

Elise and Trevor sat on the floor of the airfield office, each holding a mug of steaming tea. Trevor checked his watch. Still morning… just, but it felt like days later.

Elise shook her head. "You know, Trevor, I should be hauling you over the coals for what you did."

Trevor looked at his tea. "I'm sorry."

"You're not, though, are you?" said Elise. Trevor looked up. "You got there in time and stopped them. In style! I mean, setting Tiberius free, then him going for Adam." She grinned. "Genius. I can't be angry with you for that. I have no idea how you did it, but I'm so glad you did."

Trevor returned her smile as he dug into his pocket. "Here you go." He reached over to her and handed her the car keys. "Just knew I had to. Can't explain it."

"Instinct!" said Elise. She sipped her tea and winced. "I don't think I'll get over the look on Adam's face as he ran to the police car. You know what?" She laughed. "Lennox isn't going to believe any of this when we tell him."

"It's crazy," said Trevor. And she didn't know the half of it. "I feel bad about Lennox. I need to say sorry." He frowned. "But what will happen now? With the centre, I mean?"

"I asked Harry that when we were putting Tiberius in his travelling box," said Elise. "He thinks there's a way. As it's a charity we could carry on, maybe link in to another centre or a zoo. Hopefully it'll be OK, especially if we up our conservation work." She huffed. "Ironic, right? I thought conservation was really important to Adam, until today. And it was all a front." She shook her head. "I reckon he'll go to prison. Specially if the sheikh presses charges. He was really upset."

"That was the great part, though, wasn't it?" said Trevor, swallowing tea. "I mean, what a top bloke. Did you hear him saying to that policeman about bringing the other birds back? About it being a matter of honour?"

"Yes, brilliant," said Elise. "Midge's parents will be coming home! We'll be able to sort their release. And Harry said as long as Midge and Tiberius clear their vet checks this afternoon, we're OK to stick with the plan and release Midge as soon as possible."

"When will they be back from the vet?" asked Trevor. Except for Midge managing to shout, "Trevor! You're talking!", he hadn't had a chance to speak to him. "They won't just release him, will they? Before we get to say goodbye?"

Elise shook her head. "Don't worry. Harry said as long as they're fit, and I'm sure they are, we'll have both birds back at the centre later. No-one wants them to have any more stress. I reckon Harry will want to do it tomorrow."

She smiled at Trevor. "I'll clear it with your teacher, of

course. After all this, there's no way on earth you're not coming with us."

Trevor sighed with relief. Elise's phone beeped and a message flashed up.

"That's Lennox," said Elise, draining her mug. "We need to get back. Come on, he's going mental." She got up, putting her hand out to Trevor and hauling him to his feet. "I'll call him on the way and—"

They both stopped. Voices were at the door.

"In here, sir. Thank you for getting over so quickly."

"Of course. Thank you."

It hadn't entered his head the police would do that. Trevor froze. Sykes walked into the room, with Trevor's note in his hand. It was like he'd written that years ago now. Sykes stared at Trevor, then nodded to Elise.

"I'm Charles Sykes, Trevor's dad. Seems you two have had a bit of a morning."

Elise held out her hand.

"I'm Elise. Good to meet you, and I'm really sorry it got dramatic. The police didn't get here quite as quick as I expected them to. But your son has been amazing."

Sykes shook her hand and nodded, as Trevor held his breath.

"So I hear."

Elise smiled at Trevor. "I'll see you for the release then? I'll call Si... er, your teacher, when I know a definite time." She went a little pink and turned to Sykes. "If that's OK?"

"Yes, do," said Sykes. "Actually, please call me too. I'm interested to hear more about what's been going on. You do have my number?"

"Yes, on my forms," said Elise. "Of course, I'll be in touch."
She walked to the door and stopped before going out.

"Trevor, you're a hero for today. I'm proud to count you
as my friend."

The door shut, and Sykes moved closer. Trevor's chest
tightened. His feet felt stuck to the floor. He put down his
empty mug and balled his hands into fists as Sykes stared
at him.

"Trevor. I'm not a good talker. It never has come easy.
You must get that better than anyone. But I've read your
letter."

He held the note out, as if he wanted to prove it.

"This made me think. And then you went and pulled a
stunt like this."

Trevor braced for the rant. Sykes spoke in a low voice.

"I know I've done so many things wrong by you. I know
it. Yes, you remind me of Clem... your mum. So much it
hurts. I thought it would be easier having you around less,
but when you started going to the centre, I missed you.
Then after acting the way I did last night, and when I read
your note this morning, I just knew I've got this all wrong."

He reached over and rested his hand clumsily over
Trevor's. Warm, chunky fingers over skinny, tense, cold
ones.

"I've been so stupid, Trevor. I could be close to her
again, if I let myself be close to you. I'm the loser. You're a
part of her world and I hardly know you. And then, after
what you've done today."

Sykes's voice was trembling. Trevor looked up.

"The police ringing... took me right back to when we

lost your mum, when they said she was gone. It made me realise how awful I've treated you. And how much worse my life would be if I didn't have you. And it's not me, son, it's not who I really am. I just couldn't see straight after your mum was gone."

Sykes paused, his eyes shining.

"I'm proud of you. What you've done, how brave you are and you've put up with all my crap." He glanced at the note again. "I know I don't deserve it, I know it will take time, but if you really want to, I want that chance to start again. To make changes and put things right. For good. I messed up. I'm so sorry, son."

Trevor looked at Sykes for the longest time, and hope fluttered like a butterfly. He smiled.

"Yes, Dad. Let's do it. I'm not saying it's all forgotten, but I want to try too."

A slow smile spread across his dad's face, lighting him up. He opened his arms and dragged Trevor into them. Trevor leaned his chin on his dad's shoulder and breathed in the woolly smell of his jumper. He closed his eyes for a moment, then leaned back to look at him.

"But you have to promise me. Don't be cross with Elise. It wasn't her fault. And I have to keep going to the centre."

His dad laughed shakily. "Trevor, after what I've been like, it's the least I can do. And in time I can prove to you that I mean it. Fresh start, clean slate, right?"

They walked out to the car, and Trevor looked up at the sky. The sun had broken through, dappling the steaming tarmac, and a crisp breeze was chasing the clouds away. The storm was over.

39

Elise looked up from raking sand in the mews as Trevor walked across the grass. She waved.

"Hey! All ready?"

Trevor smiled. "Hi! Hundred per cent. Is Lennox still asking loads of questions?"

"Loads. Rash just keeps snorting. They still don't believe it. But I can't tell them any more than I already have. Anyway," she paused and checked her watch with a grin, "now you're here, I'm guessing there's something you want to do? We've only got half an hour before Harry gets here."

Trevor beamed. "Thanks, Elise, you're amazing. I'll go get a glove," he called over his shoulder as he ran to the prep room.

Midge stared at Trevor as he stepped off his perch. Trevor stared back, taking everything in. It could be a while before he'd get this close to Midge's dark, sparkling eyes again. Trevor walked their usual route to the arena. When they reached the far edge, Trevor leaned up on the barrier fencing with both arms, just like before. They looked over the valley.

Midge tilted his head.

"Don't tell me you've gone all quiet again. You can't now! You're talking to everyone!"

Trevor laughed.

"No way. I'm just happy you're safe. I couldn't wait to see you."

"Well, I have something to say. Two words doesn't cover the feeling, but thank you," said Midge. "The story of what you did is big news. Tiberius is telling everybird about it."

"Is he OK with me now?"

"I wouldn't go that far," said Midge. "He's saying he could have done it without you. But he did call you a hero, someone fitting for an eagle to be around. Now he'll be fine about talking to you."

Trevor went pink. Midge flapped his wings as he gripped the glove, working his muscles. "I heard Elise talking about my parents coming back. That's amazing."

Trevor frowned. "I'm really sorry about your brothers and sisters."

"Me too," said Midge. "I'd kind of got used to the idea I might not see them again. And if we were wild and free from the start we wouldn't have stayed together, but I wish they'd made it."

"Me too," said Trevor. "But I'm so glad about your mum and dad. Wouldn't it be epic, though, if you just see them flying around?"

"Epic," said Midge. "How's your dad?"

Trevor grinned. "More like a dad."

"That's a result," said Midge.

"I stress a bit about it not lasting," said Trevor, "but so far he's OK. We're talking. He's letting me come here as much as I want. So that's cool. He's not perfect, but he's trying, and that's a million times better than he was. And he's promised to stop watching *The Little Mermaid*."

Midge tilted his head. "What's that?"

"It's a film. He likes it so much because it was Mum's favourite. I remember her saying that now, when she made me watch it. So it makes sense, finally. He says he always thought she was extra special, like a mermaid, or an angel or something. Like she was almost too good to be real." He looked across the valley. "I can understand that."

Midge nibbled a talon. "I told you. If you spoke to him, he'd—"

"Yeah, OK," said Trevor, smiling. "I know, I owe you one too. That's what friends do, right?"

"Too right," said Midge. He stared at Trevor. "What are you going to do next? You can't go back to normal."

Trevor sighed. "I don't know what normal is, really. It's all been so…"

"Epic?" said Midge. "Well, you're a spellboda. It's who you are, and what you do now, right?"

"I guess," said Trevor. He smiled again. "I haven't really thought about it much, it was more about getting you free."

"Trevor, this is just the start," said Midge, still watching him. "There's more you need to know."

The peregrine looked across the valley and gave a series of sharp calls.

"Roger! Rog! Over here!"

Trevor stared in delight as a streak of russet shot out of the copse and ran up the hedge line.

"Finally! What happened with Garnell?"

"Ask him," said Midge, as Roger trotted over, hidden from the centre by the bushes below the barrier fence. "You should hear it straight from the fox's mouth."

"Good morning, Midge, good morning, spellboda." Roger sat in front of them, panting lightly, his fluffed-out brush curled round his back legs. "Well met, as ever. And my compliments on a fine rescue mission. I had no doubt in your ability."

"Thanks, Roger. I wish you'd been there," said Trevor, beaming. "It's so good to see you."

Roger tilted his head. "Spellboda, that was your mission to own. And own it you did. You have proved your mettle beyond doubt."

"Thank you," said Trevor. His face felt hot again. "So, you found him?"

"Garnell?" Roger inclined his head. "I did indeed. He lives in the forest of Goyt, by Errwood, in the shadow of Shining Tor. And he was most interested to receive news of you."

"What did he say?" said Trevor.

"Garnell became overly excited," Roger replied, "which is unsettling to see in a badger, especially one as big as him. He wishes to meet you. He declares the prophecy has come to pass with your arrival."

"Really?" said Trevor. "He wants to see me? Not sure if that's exciting or scary. Both, actually. So what does the prophecy say?"

Roger scratched his flank with one of his back paws.

"Garnell wishes to talk with you himself. He said you must visit him at your earliest opportunity."

Trevor frowned. "Did he say anything else?"

"He said he has much to tell you. That there is more, much more for you to know, and much more to come."

"What does that even mean?" said Trevor.

"That there's something to do?" said Midge.

"I concur," said Roger. "This is your purpose. Your destiny. The meaning to your life."

Trevor considered. Alarming? Or an amazing opportunity? Like meeting Garnell, probably both. He jumped as a call carried across the field. Elise was at the gate, waving. It was time. He waved back and lifted his arms off the barrier. Midge leaned closer to his face.

"I think you'll need help finding Garnell. Me and Roger are up for that, aren't we?"

The fox drew himself up tall. "Indubitably, Midge, indubitably."

Midge bobbed his head as Roger stood up and shook the corn dust off his coat. His eyes gleamed.

"A new mission, spellboda?"

Excitement beat fear, hands down. Without hesitation, Trevor nodded.

"Indeed, Roger!"

He smiled at them both, and his thrill for the future grew.

40

Trevor picked his way over rough ground, careful not to trip on tufts of coarse grass that were scattered over the slope. Midge needed a comfortable journey for his last time on the glove. He stopped and breathed in the cool, pure air of the high peak. Goyt was magical, so wild and free that the memory of his dad from last time he was here was an easy one to re-write. He looked at Midge. Epic. The perfect place to release a falcon.

"Come on, Trevor," called Elise. "Keep up!"

Trevor set off again. He glanced right, in the direction of Errwood. It was tantalisingly close. But that had to wait for another day, when they were alone. And this was Midge's time. Panting, he quickened his pace to catch Elise and Harry up. The hill path meandered its way through copses, over fallen trees and past clumps of nodding bracken. Midge was still... but alert beside him as they climbed higher. They left trees behind and views opened out beneath them; the valley dotted with swathes of water, heather, forest and field. And still the peak stretched out, up and away in front of them. After what felt like a never-ending climb they stopped by the sign for Shooter's Clough, out of breath, the wind whipping their hair.

The view was awesome now, but Trevor focused on Midge, taking in every detail. His pale yellow legs, talons gripping the glove, just a little harder than normal. His hooked beak, feathers bristling in the wind, his eyes sparkling like jewels. Jewels. With a start, he remembered.

Elise's voice trembled. "I think we're ready. The wind's—"

"Hang on," said Trevor. "Before he goes." He rummaged in his pocket with his free hand. "I have something for you."

He pressed the ring into Elise's right hand, and her eyes widened.

"Trevor! Where did you find it?"

"In the centre. A friend was… er, it was on the grass. I found it and shoved it in my pocket. You have to have it now, before I forget again."

Elise stared at him. "Thank you… so much. You've just made my day even better, if that was possible."

Her eyes shone as she pushed the ring on her finger. She glanced at Harry, a few paces away, who was checking the wind direction by throwing grass in the air, and leaned close to Trevor.

"I know there's more to all this. If, or when, you're ever ready, I'm here. You can trust me, OK?"

Trevor smiled and looked back at Midge.

"Go on then, Trevor. Take all his equipment off," called Harry. "Turn towards me, face the wind. Now's the time."

Trevor took off Midge's leash and jesses for the last time, trying to ignore the lump growing in his throat. Midge bobbed in his familiar way, up and down, scanning the peaks. Trevor could feel his grip through the glove, stronger, tense with excitement. He lifted his arm and held it wide. Strong gusts buffeted the falcon's body, an irresistible pressure against his feathers. Midge buzzed into one last rouse and stretched both wings wide. The wind pushed at Midge more insistently, impatient, urging to lift him.

Midge looked at Trevor. Then, in a heartbeat, he was gone. Flying towards the valley with rapid, powerful wing-beats, where the sun caught his feathers and made them glow. The little group watched as he adjusted wing and tail positions to match the changing wind currents, and he began to gain height, shrinking in the cloud-scudded sky. Midge changed course, turning sharply, heading back. As he flew overhead he gave a single call; high, long and pure as it carried in the wind.

"Friends forever!"

Trevor's heart swelled as he watched Midge fly onwards and upwards, circling the peaks, higher with every turn. Freedom beckoned, and as the peregrine cleared the summit of Shining Tor the path to the future stretched out before them both. An open road. A journey of trust, friendship and adventure.

THE END
(OF THE BEGINNING)

Author's Note

Thank you for reading *Spellboda*. I hope you enjoyed meeting Trevor and Midge as much as I loved letting them begin to believe in themselves, live their stories and fly free. They have so much more to discover, and other characters like Garnell and Bix are pretty desperate to meet you and join the adventures!

Although this first *Spellboda* book took several years to write, with lots of wonderful advice from people far more wise than I, and too many to thank individually, it's one I'm so grateful to share. Animal conservation is a passion of mine, and the plan was always to tell a story which could throw a spotlight here, and to help by pledging that donations from *Spellboda* will wing their way to a group of animal conservation charities, enabling them to do more good work in helping to save our planet and preserve it for generations to come.

For more information on how we're supporting

charities, on when Trevor and Midge will be returning, and for all sorts of news, updates and sneak peaks (but no spoilers!), you can visit my website www.jcclarkeauthor. com, or follow me @jcclarkewriting on Instagram, Twitter and Facebook.

This book is for Elf & Ed, who I love millions
…and for everyone who wants to fly and live life in colour
xxx

About the Author

Previously a falconer, consultant and writer-presenter of CITV's *Wild World,* Jo is now loving the writer's life and is also a script consultant and copywriter. She's been involved in falconry and conservation industries for over twenty years and is passionate about protecting wildlife. An alumna of the Curtis Brown Creative Writing for Children Course, Jo was shortlisted for Best Opening Chapter for *Spellboda* at the 2019 Jericho Writers Festival of Writing. She lives in Ashford, Kent, with her family – and a large number of animals!